The Caliph's Sister

Harun al-Rashid
and the Fall of the Persians

Novels of Islamic History in Translation Series

Written by Jurji Zaidan and published by the Zaidan Foundation.
(in historical chronological order)

The Conquest of Andalusia
translated with an Afterword and Study Guide by Roger Allen

The Battle of Poitiers
Charles Martel and 'Abd al-Rahman
translated with a Study Guide by William Granara

The Caliph's Sister
Harun al-Rashid and the Fall of the Persians
translated by Issa J. Boullata with a Study Guide

The Caliph's Heirs
Brothers at War: The Fall of Baghdad
translated with an Afterword and Study Guide by Michael Cooperson

Saladin and the Assassins
translated by Paul Starkey with a Study Guide

The Caliph's Sister

Harun al-Rashid and the Fall of the Persians

A romantic historical novel that takes place during the reign of the 'Abbasid caliph Harun al-Rashid. It describes the processions, lavish gatherings, lifestyles, and social mores in an extraordinary setting of pomp, splendor, and learning during the golden age of Islamic civilization. The novel depicts the fall of the Barmakids, the Persian administrators of the 'Abbasid Empire.

Jurji Zaidan

translated from the Arabic by
Issa J. Boullata

With an Introduction by the Zaidan Foundation and a Study Guide

The Zaidan Foundation
For Enhancing Intercultural Understanding, Inc.

7007 Longwood Drive
Bethesda, MD 20817
E-mail: george@zaidanfoundation.org
Website: www.zaidanfoundation.org

Tel: (301) 469-8131
Fax: (301) 469-8132

Table of Contents

The Caliph's Sister
Harun al-Rashid and the Fall of the Persians[1]

Introduction

About the Novel[2]

The events of this historical romantic novel take place in Baghdad shortly before the year 803 AD (187 AH) in the closing years of the reign of Harun al-Rashid, the fifth caliph of the 'Abbasid caliphate that stretched from 750 until 1258 AD (132 to 656 AH). His reign marked a period of notable cultural development. Harun was a generous patron of learning, poetry, and music, and his court was visited by the most eminent Muslims of the age. He is perhaps best known to the Western world as the caliph whose court is described in the *Arabian Nights*. In the Islamic world Harun al-Rashid's reign represented the peak of 'Abbasid power in a caliphate that is often seen as representing the golden age of Islamic civilization. And yet in this historical novel, Jurji Zaidan turns his pen to a dark side of al-Rashid's reign, set against the pomp, splendor, and learning of that age.

Zaidan's adventures usually unfold against a textured backdrop of history, culture, and politics, and *The Caliph's Sister* is no exception.

---

1 This introduction follows the historical events as recounted in the novel and as understood by Jurji Zaidan and historians of his times.

2 First published in 1906 in Arabic with the Arabic title of *Al-'Abbasa Ukht al-Rashid aw Nakbat al-Baramika*. The literal translation of the Arabic title is *Al-'Abbasa Sister of al Rashid* or *the Catastrophe that Befell the Barmakids*. The main title was translated in English to *The Caliph's Sister* and the subtitle now includes the name of the Caliph and was broadened to reflect that the catastrophe that affected the Barmakids – probably the most prominent of Persian families – encompassed a fall from favor of Persians generally until the end of the reign of al-Rashid's son, al-Amin.

As recounted by Zaidan, Harun al-Rashid was a popular ruler who relied on the Barmakid family to run the Islamic Empire. They were admirable viziers: wise administrators who filled the public treasury. It was through them that the glory of Harun-al-Rashid clanged from Morocco and Andalusia to the farthest bounds of China and Tartary. Chief among the Barmakids was Harun al-Rashid's best friend and vizier, Ja'far al-Barmaki—a central figure in the novel. When Ja'far was at the helm, he ran the state with a steady hand, but there were those among the caliph's inner circle who were unhappy that he had so much authority and so many possessions.

This was the situation until 803 AD (187 AH), when the Barmakids fell from power, beginning with Ja'far. Their disgrace and fall has been the subject of intense speculation. Many explanations have been put forward to explain Harun's ungrateful behavior toward men to whom he owed so much—the whole Barmakid family had served the 'Abbasids for three generations with competence and devotion. Harun never disclosed the reasons for their chastisement. When one of his sisters asked him for the reason, he is said to have replied, "If I thought my shirt knew, I would tear my shirt to pieces." Al-Rashid's secrecy fuels Zaidan's pen: relying on several clues provided by history, he is free to imagine the details of the circumstances that led to the fall of the Barmakids.

Romance and intrigue provide the central plot of the novel that is woven into the broader picture of the fall of the Barmakids. Harun held his sister 'Abbasa in great affection and loved to spend his evenings in her company. But his favorite companion was Ja'far. It was quite unsuitable for a man from outside the family to be admitted to the company of a young woman, which meant Harun could not socialize with both at the same time. He found a way to arrange things, however: he decided that 'Abbasa and Ja'far would marry in what the French call a *mariage blanc*. As he explained to Ja'far, "you see her only in my company, your body never approaches hers, and you have no conjugal relations with her. You may thus share our evenings of pleasure without risk." Ja'far accepted and swore solemnly in front of witnesses never to visit his young wife, stay alone with her, or even spend a minute under the same roof unless Harun was present.

But Ja'far was handsome, and 'Abbasa's beauty was second to none. The inevitable occurred. How and why no one is certain. There was a great political advantage for Ja'far to unite himself with the sister of the caliph. But did his mother, who was close to both her son and to 'Abbasa, prod them in that direction? Or was their deep love a sufficient reason to consummate the marriage, as Zaidan seems to imagine? No one knows for sure, and the novel does not speculate on what really happened. The only sure thing is that 'Abbasa became pregnant and gave birth to at least one child—perhaps two, as related in the novel. And when Harun learned of the relationship, that was the beginning of the end for the Barmakids.

The close friendship between Harun and Ja'far spawned jealousies among the caliph's entourage. Chief among these was the hostility that al-Fadl ibn al-Rabi' had toward Ja'far. The two men detested each other and did everything they could to destroy each other. Last but not least, Zubayda, Harun's favorite Hashemite wife, also did not like Ja'far. He had been a tutor to her son's rival, al-Ma'mun, the son of a Persian slave girl. It was known that Harun admired Ma'mun's gifts and was thinking of promoting him over al-Amin[3] in the order of succession. There is every reason to believe that Zubayda exercised her considerable influence against Ja'far. She comes across as shrewd, skillful, and willful.

Zaidan never explicitly speculates to what extent Harun al-Rashid's reaction was politically or emotionally motivated. The narrative and dialogue suggest a combination of those factors. Ja'far had been disloyal to Harun and had stained the family honor: his disobedience could not go unpunished. But Harun was shrewd and feared for his power and influence, even imagining that the Barmakids might usurp the 'Abbasid caliphate. Within this broad historical canvass, Zaidan's fast-paced narrative with its twists and turns is full of suspense. It covers only a few months of Harun al-Rashid's reign but one that fatefully changed the course of 'Abbasid history.

---

3 Following Harun's death there was a period of civil war between his two sons, al-Amin and al-Ma'mun. By the end of the ninth century, the 'Abbasids were unable to exercise real religious or political authority. The territories they controlled fell apart as independent states arose in regions previously under 'Abbasid rule. Although always honored to the end of the 'Abbasid caliphate as symbols of the unity of Sunni Islam, no claimant to the office has since achieved anything like the general recognition among the Muslims that prevailed until the reign of Harun al-Rashid.

Jurji Zaidan—The Historical Novelist

Jurji Zaidan (1861–1914) was a prolific writer who at the dawn of the twentieth century sought to inform and educate his Arab contemporaries about the modern world and the heritage of the Arabs. He is considered one of the most prominent intellectual leaders who laid the foundation for a pan-Arab secular national identity. Pioneering new forms of literature and style in Arabic, in 1892 he founded one of the first—and most successful—monthly journals, *al-Hilal,* a magazine that is still popular today in its 120th year. The *Dar al-Hilal* publishing house in Cairo is one of the largest publishing houses for periodicals in the Arab world. It is a fitting tribute to Zaidan's legacy that new studies reassessing his contributions and translations of many of his novels—this one among them—are being published nearly one hundred years after his death.

Zaidan was one of the pioneers in the composition of historical novels within the modern Arabic literary tradition and in their serialization in magazines. New editions of the entire series of novels are still being published almost every decade and are widely distributed throughout the Arab world—a testament to their lasting popularity. Zaidan's novels are not just for entertainment: national education was his primary goal. The twenty-two historical novels he wrote cover an extensive period of Arab history, from the rise of Islam in the seventh century until the decline of the Ottoman Empire in the nineteenth century. The stories depicted in these novels are grounded in the major historical events of various epochs. The particular manners, lifestyles, beliefs, and social mores of those periods, as well as political events, provided the context into which Zaidan weaved adventure and romance, deception and excitement. They were therefore as much "historical" as "novels," reminiscent of the historical novels of Alexandre Dumas in France and Sir Walter Scott in Britain, though Jurji Zaidan's novels more closely reflect actual historical events and developments.

Over the last hundred years, Zaidan's historical novels have been translated into many languages. Every novel has been translated at least once, and many have been translated into four or more languages. To our knowledge there are about one hundred translations of individual novels in more than ten different languages—most in Persian, Turkish/Ottoman, Javanese, Uighur (in China), Azeri, and Urdu, but several also in French, Spanish, German, and Russian. What is noticeable, however, is that not a single one had been translated into English until the recent publication of the first novel in this series, *The Conquest of Andalusia*.

The Zaidan Foundation has so far commissioned the English translation of five of Jurji Zaidan's historical novels, and more are being planned. The present novel, *The Caliph's Sister*, was first published in 1906. Since then there have been ten translations of the novel—four in Persian, two in Ottoman, and one each in French, Spanish, Russian, and Uighur. Other novels commissioned by the Foundation for translation include two novels set in Spain: the recently published *The Conquest of Andalusia* (*Fath-al Andalus*, 1903) as well as *The Battle of Poitiers—Charles Martel and 'Abd al-Rahman* (*Sharl wa 'Abd al-Rahman*, 1904). In addition to the present novel, one other novel is set in the 'Abbasid period: *The Caliph's Heirs—Brothers at War: The Fall of Baghdad* (*al-Amin wa'l-Ma'mun*, 1907). The events in that novel occur in the period immediately following the reign of Harun al-Rashid. The fifth novel, *Saladin and the Assassins* (*Salah al-Din al-Ayyubi*, 1913), takes place during the time of the Crusades.

The Zaidan Foundation

The Zaidan Foundation, Inc.,[4] was established in 2009, with the mission of enhancing understanding between cultures. To this end the Foundation's principal objective is the international dissemination of the secular and progressive view of the Arab and Islamic heritage. Its first program is the study and translation of the works of Jurji Zaidan. Our audience is the broader English-speaking world: the United States, England, and Canada to be sure, but also English-speaking Muslim populations with little or no knowledge of Arabic such as in Bangladesh, India, and Pakistan. To achieve its objectives, the Foundation supports, directly or through educational or other institutions, the translation and publication of historical, literary, and other works, in addition to research, scholarships, conferences, seminars, student exchanges, documentaries, films, and other activities.

---

4 More information about the Zaidan Foundation and its activities can be found on the Foundation's website at www.zaidanfoundation.org.

Acknowledgments and Thanks

The Zaidan Foundation was fortunate to have Professor Issa J. Boullata, PhD (London) undertake the translation of this novel. A noted scholar and teacher and an experienced translator of many Arab literary works, he is Emeritus Professor of Arabic Literature at the Institute of Islamic Studies of McGill University in Montreal. From 1975 until his retirement in 2004, he taught postgraduate courses at McGill University in the fields of Arabic literature, Qur'anic studies, modern Arab thought, and modern Islamic developments.

Many people have generously contributed their time and energy to the Zaidan Foundation by helping to craft our mission and goals, designing and advising on the implementation of our programs, and reviewing studies and translations. Foremost among these are Ambassador Hussein A. Hassouna (Ambassador of the Arab League to the United States), Ambassador Clovis F. Maksoud (Professor of International Relations and Director of the Center of the Global South at American University), as well as Edmond Asfour and Bassem Abdallah—all members of the Foundation's Advisory Council. Professor Thomas Philipp was instrumental in helping launch the Jurji Zaidan project several decades following our fortuitous meeting. Thanks are also due to Said Hitti, who read several manuscripts of the translated novels. Last but not least, my greatest debt is to my wife, Hada Zaidan, and to our son, George S. Zaidan, for their support of all aspects of this project. The original idea for the Jurji Zaidan program came from Hada, who had more than a marital interest in this project as her grandfather, Jabr Dumit, was one of Jurji Zaidan's closest friends. In addition to their general and unstinting support, both she and George Jr. helped design the program, made detailed reviews, and offered many suggestions regarding the products sponsored by the Foundation.

George C. Zaidan
President
The Zaidan Foundation

Washington DC
March 2012

Dramatis Personae

HARUN AL-RASHID	The 'Abbasid caliph
JA'FAR AL-BARMAKI	Al-Rashid's vizier
AL-'ABBASA	Al-Rashid's sister
ZUBAYDA	Al-Rashid's wife
ABU AL-'ATAHIYA	Al-Rashid's poet
AL-AMIN	Al-Rashid's son
'UTBA	Al-'Abbasa's maid
AL-FADL IBN AL-RABI'	Al-Amin's vizier
MASRUR AL-FERGHANI	The executioner

Chapter 1

The Historical Context

The capital of Islam during the reign of the Rightly Guided caliphs was Yathrib (Medina). When the caliphate passed into the hands of the Umayyads, they made Damascus their capital, for it was the seat of their partisans among the Arab tribes. It remained their capital until the 'Abbasids rose to power in 132 AH (750 AD) and made Kufa the capital of their state, at the borders of Persia where their political propaganda had started. Then they moved to al-Anbar on the Euphrates River, where Abu al-'Abbas al-Saffah, their first caliph, died and was succeeded by his brother, al-Mansur. The latter killed Abu Muslim al-Khurasani, leader of the 'Abbasid Shi'a soldiers, fearing he would aspire to the caliphate himself. Consequently, al-Mansur was afraid of Abu Muslim's followers, especially after the group called al-Rawandiyya rebelled and almost killed him. Had it not been for Ma'n ibn Za'ida, they would have succeeded. After quelling their rebellion, al-Mansur thought of guarding against another similar incident by building a stronghold to shelter him, his family, and government officials. So he built Baghdad in the form of a circle, and it came to be known as the City of al-Mansur. He built his palace in the center and named it the Palace of Gold. Around it he built the palaces of the princes, the state buildings, and their service departments, and in between them he established markets for trade. Around the city, he built three concentric walls: the first surrounded the central buildings with a space behind it for fortresses and the like; next to it was another strong wall, with a space behind it for traffic; then there was a third wall, behind which was a moat. He constructed four gates to the city and named each after the city to which it led. These were the gates of Basra, Kufa, Damascus, and Khurasan. He established four wide thoroughfares that led from the gates to the heart of the city.

Al-Mansur continued to reside at the Palace of Gold until conditions became settled and he felt secure. He then established for himself another palace on the banks of the Tigris River outside the city, and he named it the Palace of Eternity. These two palaces remained the seat of the 'Abbasid caliphs that came after al-Mansur until the reign of al-Rashid.

However, the City of al-Mansur was not large enough to accommodate the soldiers, craftsmen, merchants, and others, in addition to the general population of Muslims and others who flocked to it and built homes for themselves outside it. Al-Mansur decided to relieve this congestion, and so he built a palace and a mosque in the open country to the east of the city, in a place that was named al-Rusafa. He encouraged people to build in the area, next to the two edifices. Then it happened that his son, al-Mahdi, came back with his army from Khurasan. Al-Mansur let them camp in al-Rusafa and granted them tracts of land in order to build homes to reside in, so they did. The new city came to be known as al-Mahdi's Camp; then it grew to the south and north. The caliphs who came later continued the construction activities and built palaces to the east and west of the Tigris, including the Palace of Eternity and Zubayda's Palace on the western bank, and Ja'far al-Barmaki's Palace and al-Amin's Palace behind it on the eastern bank. Other neighborhoods rose near the City of al-Mansur on the west side, the most important of which were al-Karkh, where the Persian merchants and other foreigners resided, and the neighborhood of al-Harbiyya in the north, most of whose inhabitants were Arabs. The city came to be known as Baghdad.

During the reign of al-Rashid, Baghdad consisted of two parts—one eastern and the other western—connected by three bridges, the most important of which was the Baghdad Bridge connecting the City of al-Mansur with al-Rusafa. The neighborhoods were intersected by canals branching from the Tigris, on the banks of which rose palaces and gardens. Some of those canals were the following: Nahr 'Isa, Nahr Tabiq, Nahr al-Dajaj, Nahr al-Bazzazin, Nahr al-Sarat, and Nahr Ja'far.

The people of Baghdad in the reign of al-Rashid lived a life of plenty and opulence, for wealth poured into the 'Abbasid treasury in abundance and the caliph bestowed gifts and grants liberally and people flocked to the city seeking gainful work and a livelihood. Among them were Arabs, Persians, Byzantines, Turks, Kurds, Armenians, Georgians, Sindhis, Indians, Chinese, Abyssinians, and African blacks, and they were of different religions and various sects. They included artisans, merchants, slave traders, poets, singers, grammarians, and Hadith narrators;[5] among them were Muslims, Christians, and Jews under Muslim state protection, freemen, freed slaves who became clients, bondsmen, slave-boys, and slave-girls. They all hovered around the palace of the caliph or the mansions of the princes and viziers, selling them commodities or offering them flattering praise and all manner of sycophancy; these persons in high office gave them money with great munificence and were too proud to give small gifts of only hundreds of dirhams or so, instead believing that thousands or even hundreds of thousands of dirhams were in order.

No wonder, for in addition to their revenues from taxes and booties of war, money was flowing into their treasuries like a torrential stream, and they were sharing their riches with the people of the earth.

---

5 Scholars who knew by heart Prophet Muhammad's Hadith (that is, his sayings, actions, and traditions to be followed), as distinct from the Qur'an, which is believed to be God's speech revealed to the Prophet by the angel Gabriel and recited publicly by Muhammad. *Translator's Note.*

Chapter 2
Abu al-ʿAtahiya, the Poet

Abu al-ʿAtahiya was one of those who earned their living at the courts of the ʿAbbasid caliphs. Like most of the poets of his time, he was originally a *mawla* (a foreign client of an Arab tribe). At first, he used to make earthenware jars, carry them in a basket of palm fronds, and go about in Kufa to sell them. In the reign of al-Mahdi, son of al-Mansur, he went to Baghdad and soon rose there to become a companion of this caliph, who liked him and enjoyed his poetry, made him accompany him on hunting and recreation trips, and bestowed upon him many awards and gifts. Abu al-ʿAtahiya's role did not change in the caliphate of al-Hadi, son of al-Mahdi. After al-Hadi died a short time later, Abu al-ʿAtahiya vowed not to compose any more poetry.

It so happened that the new caliph, Harun al-Rashid, asked him to compose some poetry for him, but Abu al-ʿAtahiya declined, so al-Rashid was angry and commanded that he be imprisoned in a cell whose area was five by five spans of the hand. After a long time in prison, he wrote a few verses complaining of his situation and sent them to Ibrahim al-Mawsili, the famous singer, who sang them in the presence of al-Rashid. Whereupon, the caliph pardoned the poet and ordered that he be given fifty thousand dirhams. Furthermore, he drew Abu al-ʿAtahiya closer to himself, made him a great favorite of his who was hardly ever away from him except when he went on pilgrimage, and gave him an annual salary; this was apart from occasional gifts and in addition to the awards and presents the poet received from the officials of the state. Abu al-ʿAtahiya was famous for his greed and stinginess, so he went on receiving money and saving it and not spending anything, especially after he had given himself up to asceticism and vowed not to compose poetry. As a result, his earnings from poetry decreased, but he began to seize opportunities to earn money from other sources.

In about the year 178 AH (794 AD) during the caliphate of Harun al-Rashid, Abu al-'Atahiya used to attend the frequent social gatherings of Muhammad al-Amin, son of al-Rashid, in the hope of receiving some earnings or gifts from him; he was also one of those close to Zubayda, al-Amin's mother, and used to receive many gifts from her.

In those days, al-Amin was seventeen years old and had been inclined to revelry and amusement since an early age. His social gatherings were never without singers, profligate people, slave-girls, and slave-boys. Indeed, he was the first person to have an abundance of slave-boys and servants, and to select them skillfully and embellish them with make-up in imaginative and different ways. Likewise, many of the poets inclined to revelry and wanton behavior used to attend al-Amin's social gatherings, first among them being al-Hasan ibn Hani', famously known as Abu Nuwas.

Serious or shrewd people did not attend al-Amin's social gatherings unless they had an ulterior political motive that required approaching the caliph through al-Amin or his mother, Zubayda. To al-Rashid, Zubayda was the most beloved of his wives, and her word carried weight with him because she was his cousin, while most of his other wives were freed slave-girls, like the wives of most of the 'Abbasid caliphs who preceded him. That is why there was no caliph among them whose mother and father were both Hashemite[6]—the exception being al-Amin. And so those who wanted to curry favor with al-Rashid by any means ingratiated themselves with Zubayda by praising her son al-Amin, although they knew that he was not fit for the caliphate. At the same time, they were prejudiced against his brother al-Ma'mun because his mother was a Persian slave-girl, and they belittled his worth although they knew he was more refined than al-Amin in intellect and culture.

In this respect, al-Fadl ibn al-Rabi' was one who left no praise unspoken because his father had been a vizier to both al-Mansur and al-Mahdi, and he thought of himself as a candidate for the office. However, Harun al-Rashid drew Yahya ibn Khalid al-Barmaki close to himself, for Yahya was one of his first followers and supporters, and he appointed Ja'far, Yahya's son,

---

6 A Hashemite is a descendant of Hashem ibn 'Abd Manaf, great-grandfather of the Prophet Muhammad. *Translator's Note.*

to the vizierate. This annoyed al-Fadl ibn al-Rabi' and he was filled with envy, so he spared no effort in plotting revenge. He found no better way to ingratiate himself with Zubayda and her son, especially because Zubayda hated the Persians in general and the Barmakids in particular—and Ja'far ibn Yahya most of all because she knew he had persuaded al-Rashid to appoint al-Ma'mun, son of her slave-girl, as his heir apparent as a successor to her own son, al-Amin. Consequently, she brought closer to herself all those who supported her son al-Amin and who discredited al-Ma'mun. That is why al-Fadl used to attend al-Amin's amusing social gatherings, go along with him in his revelry, and flatter him.

It so happened that Abu al-'Atahiya attended a social gathering of al-Amin during which the latter expressed his wish to buy some white slave-girls who could sing so that he might add them to the female singers at his palace who, in those days, were mostly yellow[7] slave-girls. It was customary for people to own white slave-girls as concubines only, but since Ibrahim al-Mawsili, al-Rashid's singer, taught some of them to sing, their value rose.

Al-Fadl ibn al-Rabi' told al-Amin that the chief slave dealer had brought to market some beautiful white slave-girls and had put them up at the home of a Jewish slave trader in Baghdad named Phinehas and that their enchanting beauty had appealed to all people. Furthermore, he recommended that he buy some of them and ask Ibrahim al-Mawsili to teach them to sing. Al-Amin agreed, and al-Fadl took it upon himself to go to Phinehas's home the next day and select for him those among the white slave-girls who had the most beautiful faces and the most charming voices.

When Abu al-'Atahiya heard this, he felt he could make a big profit by colluding with Phinehas, for he knew that al-Amin did not care how much money he spent on the purchase. The sun had begun to set, so he thought he could hurry to Phinehas and tell him about al-Amin's decision, claiming that he—Abu al-'Atahiya—had been the one to recommend Phinehas to al-Amin and encouraging him to raise the price, on condition he would be rewarded for his efforts.

* * *

---

7 "Yellow" was used to denote the pallid complexion of slave-girls from the Byzantine Empire in particular. *Translator's Note.*

Abu al-ʿAtahiya left al-Amin's palace in the eastern part of Baghdad, heading for the home of Phinehas, the slave trader, in the western part of the city, next to the House of Slaves that al-Mansur had established as a residence for his slave-boys and slave-girls. Abu al-ʿAtahiya had a white complexion and black hair with a curly forelock. He usually wore clean and elegant clothes, had a handsome appearance, and was endowed with sound judgment. On that evening, he wore simple clothes, not his customary attire when attending the caliph's social gatherings or those of his son—that was a long time before he became an ascetic and abandoned the composition of verse. Perhaps it was his extreme stinginess that made him wear the clothes of a pauper that evening, with a simple cloak worn on top of them. On his head, he wore a turban like those of the common people, although he altered its shape and wrapped himself with his cloak in order to conceal his real identity.

When he reached the bank of the Tigris, he hesitated over whether to take a ferryboat to the bridge and then go on foot from there to the House of Slaves, or to walk all the way to the House of Slaves in order to avoid paying the fare on the ferryboat or the fee to ride an animal. As he hesitated at the riverbank, he saw a sailing boat speedily plowing through the water. He was delighted and decided to board it. Night had fallen and it was quiet in that area because it was far from the crowded streets of al-Karkh; all the buildings on the banks of the Tigris were high palaces with lush gardens belonging to the caliph, the princes, the viziers, and the like. He immediately shouted, asking the sailing boat to stop, and kept repeating his loud call until the captain heard him and shouted back that he could not stop. Abu al-ʿAtahiya continued to shout, entreating the man to take him on board. He then heard an uproar coming from the boat and saw the sailors quickly loosening the sail to reduce its speed; then he saw them bring the boat closer to where he stood. From their hurried movements and the fact that the night was moonless, he felt that they must have been going on an urgent mission and not on a river cruise as the people of Baghdad usually did.

"Who are you?" asked a man, who then appeared and stood at the edge of the boat.

"I am a stranger overtaken by the evening," Abu al-ʿAtahiya answered, "and I would like to go to the Harbiyya neighborhood but I don't know the way to get there."

When the man heard what Abu al-'Atahiya had said, he came down from his place on the edge of the boat and disappeared for a while inside, then came out and shouted, "Welcome, please come on board."

He brought the boat close to the riverbank and gave an order to some sailors, who placed a plank of wood between the boat and the riverbank. Abu al-'Atahiya boarded. He realized that the man who had talked to him was the captain, so he greeted him and sat on a bench next to the mast. He looked around but found no one on board but four sailors, who rowed in order to increase the boat's speed.

Turning to the stern of the boat, he saw in the dim light a man and a woman in Bedouin clothes sitting cross-legged with their heads bowed with sleepiness. Next to the man were rough sandals of the kind worn in Hijaz, and in front of them were two boys sleeping on the deck, with their heads on the woman's lap. They wore Bedouin clothes too, and the woman covered them with an embroidered silk shawl. Abu al-'Atahiya found that strange, and his curiosity was aroused.

The boat continued to glide through the water in the quiet atmosphere, and no sound was heard but that of its forward movement. They soon came to the built-up area of Baghdad, and the palaces were lit up on both banks. Then they heard the voices of the muezzins calling people to evening prayer. Abu al-'Atahiya seized this opportunity to converse with the captain.

"Do you have a carpet on which I can recite my evening prayer?" he asked.

The captain rose and brought him a carpet and spread it on the boat's floor at the stern, near the two strangers and their two boys. Abu al-'Atahiya stood up to start his prayer. He looked intently but discreetly at the faces of those sitting there, trying not to let them feel he was looking at them. He noticed that the man and the woman were older, and he thought they must be from Hijaz because of the desert roughness that marked their appearance. He then saw the two boys' faces in the dim light and surmised they were brothers, one of whom looked five years old and the other about four. He was surprised at their white complexion and the beauty of their eyes, which had long eyelashes that appeared as though they were blackened with kohl. He thought it unlikely that they were the sons of the two Bedouins. When he finished his prayer, his curiosity led him to approach the boat's captain.

"It seems to me that our companions tonight are strangers like me. What country are they from?" he asked.

"Why do you ask?" the captain said.

"Because strangers are like relatives to one another," Abu al-'Atahiya replied.

Forcing himself to smile, the captain said, "Don't be inquisitive. Did I ask you where you came from or where you were going?"

And he turned away and went to the edge of the boat; it had now passed the first bridge, which consisted of a few boats at anchor chained to one another, on which there were planks of wood for pedestrians and riding animals. The boat approached the City of al-Mansur and was close to the middle bridge, which was rarely opened. The captain said to Abu al-'Atahiya, "This is the end of our course. You can now go on your own way."

Abu al-'Atahiya was upset at the captain's rudeness and was about to tell him his name in order to gain his respect as one of the influential poets, but he decided to be silent and moved quickly to the edge of the boat, intending to disembark. He noticed he was close to the Palace of Eternity, where al-Rashid lived. The palace was lit with colored candles, and its lights shone from the windows onto the plants in the garden. Sweet scents were in the air: the smell of incense and perfume mixed with the fragrance of flowers and aromatic plants. Abu al-'Atahiya remembered the task he was coming for and the profit he expected. So he suppressed his inquisitiveness and said to the captain, "Are we landing at the palace of the Commander of the Faithful?"

"We'll let you off beyond it, next to the bridge," the man answered.

"That's fine," he said.

He then prepared himself to disembark. He adjusted his turban, tightened the waistband on his robe, and wrapped himself with the cloak. When the boat docked at the western bank, the sailors put down the gangplank for him and he disembarked, thanking the captain for his kind hospitality and thinking meanwhile of what he had seen on the boat. But his joy at the profit he was expecting made him soon forget everything else.

As soon as he landed on the bank, he walked hurriedly northward, crossed the Khurasan Gate road, and entered the street leading to the House of Slaves. He saw shops, most of which were closed, but the streets were crowded with pedestrians. He thought of renting a donkey to ride, but his stinginess got the better of him, so he continued on foot until he reached the house of Phinehas. It was a magnificent big building, and it looked like the palace of a prince or a vizier. No wonder: its owner was one of the wealthiest people in the city, having amassed his fortune from the sale of slaves to the caliphs, their children, the viziers, and other high-class people. Whenever a beautiful slave-girl or a handsome slave-boy was brought to him, he sent someone to the palace of the caliph or of one of the princes to lure him into buying the slave. Most of those intermediaries in those days were members of the retinue of the palace's owner, and many were poets and singers who frequented it. This was not the first time that Abu al-'Atahiya undertook such a task. When he came to the house of Phinehas, he noted that it was late and he feared that the man might have gone to bed, especially because Phinehas was not inclined to song and drink; all his interest was in trading, so he was accustomed to have his supper at sunset and then go to bed after supper.

However, Abu al-'Atahiya noticed that the house was unusually lit up, contrary to custom. He was pleased and thought it might portend good news. He advanced until he came to the house's outer gate, and there he noticed the indistinct shapes of people and heard some noises. Then he could discern two mounts and that two persons with two boys were dismounting from them. He was surprised to find that they were the strangers whom he had left on the boat. It occurred to him that the two boys might be slaves brought for sale, but then he regarded this as unlikely because the man was a Bedouin and his appearance did not suggest he was a slave trader.

Abu al-'Atahiya hid himself in a corner. He saw the man carry one of the two boys on his shoulder after dismounting and watched him approach the door and knock on it with vehemence. The man stood and waited as the woman stood behind him carrying the other boy. Abu al-'Atahiya heard her say to him, "Do you think they are waiting for us?"

"There is no doubt about that," the man answered. "Don't you see the lights of the palace are lit up? Our mistress must be waiting for us on tenterhooks because we are late!"

From their dialect, Abu al-'Atahiya surmised that they were not from Mecca or Medina. He thought they were most likely from Baghdad's population of Arabized foreigners. His curiosity to find out the truth increased. Soon afterward, he saw the window in the door open, and a woman's head appeared. She was about forty years of age and in her hand she held a lantern that shone on her face and made her features fully clear. Abu al-'Atahiya saw that she had a brilliant face, black eyes, curved eyebrows, pleasant lips, and simply braided hair. At first he thought she was one of the white slave-girls, but no sooner had he scrutinized her face than his heart throbbed, for her face resembled that of a woman he had loved more than a dozen years earlier, before circumstances had separated them. As he was thinking of that, he heard her say to the stranger knocking on the door, "Thank God, you have finally arrived. Why are you late, Riyash?"

"We have been delayed against our will," Riyash answered. "Ask Barra about the hindrances we met on the way. We had gone first to our master, may God keep him strong, and he kept us at his place until evening. After that, we came here directly. Is our mistress here, 'Utba?"

When Abu al-'Atahiya heard the woman's name, he was certain she was the slave-girl he had known and loved at al-Mahdi's palace. He had composed love poems about her but had not dared propose to her. At the spring festival of Nayruz, he had resorted to an artful trick: as a gift he gave al-Mahdi a clay vessel in which he had placed a perfumed robe on whose hems he had written verses of poetry alluding to her and asking for her hand. The verses were:

My soul is enamored of something in the world, which

God and the ruling al-Mahdi can satisfy.

I lose hope of attaining it, and then what gives me hope of

Possessing it is your scorn of the world and everything in it.

Al-Mahdi understood the poet's intention and would have given 'Utba to him, but she objected. "O Commander of the Faithful," she said, "how can you hand me over to a man who sells jars and earns his living by composing verse?" So the caliph kept her and filled the poet's clay vessel with money as a reward for him, but prohibited him from composing love poetry about her. Abu al-'Atahiya reluctantly ceased doing so. When al-Mahdi died, his slave-girls were dispersed, and Abu al-'Atahiya did not know 'Utba's fate until he saw her that night. The memory of his old love for her was revived.

* * *

'Utba turned away from the window and ordered the doorman to open the door. Riyash entered carrying one of the two boys on his shoulder. The boy with his head on his arms lay on the man's head and was sleeping; likewise, the other boy was sleeping on the shoulder of the woman. Holding up the lantern, 'Utba led them to the courtyard and they disappeared from Abu al-'Atahiya's sight. He then saw the two mules being driven away in the alley by the muleteer. He remained standing in place thinking about what he had seen, having forgotten the transaction he had come for. His task now was to uncover their secret, especially after he had heard them wondering about their mistress. "Who could that mistress be?" he thought. "Perhaps there is a secret here and I can gain some money by uncovering it." He decided to delay his entrance for a moment lest the people in the house suspect that he knew something about the newcomers. He waited until he heard the door squeak as it was being closed, and then he heard it being locked. He went to it and knocked and heard a man ask, "Who is it?"

He knocked again and the window of the door was opened and a man appeared. His name was Hayyan, a peasant from the rural areas whom Phinehas had made his doorman. He knew Abu al-'Atahiya and was surprised to see him at that late hour of the night, but he opened the door and welcomed him. Abu al-'Atahiya entered and, feigning ignorance, asked, "Is your master at home, Hayyan?"

"He went to sleep. Do you wish to see him?" Hayyan spoke in a peasant dialect, mispronouncing certain letters of Classical Arabic.

Walking in the courtyard, Abu al-'Atahiya said, "I would not have visited you at this hour had I not seen the house shining with lights contrary to custom, for I did not know that Master Phinehas stayed up after supper. I was surprised and wanted to know the reason—perhaps it was a wedding ceremony or a celebration for a newcomer?" He was jesting with the doorman and hoping he would give away some information.

"There is nothing to be disturbed about," the doorman replied in his dialectal Arabic, "but I don't know the reason for the party." Changing the subject of the conversation, he added, "Do you want to see my master now?"

"Yes. Where is he?" Abu al-'Atahiya asked.

"I'll go and call him," Hayyan said.

He moved quickly, entering a corridor from which he went up a flight of stairs. Abu al-'Atahiya followed him not wanting to remain outdoors in the courtyard lest something should prevent him from going upstairs. The corridor and the stairs were all illuminated with candles, but he did not see any servants or slave-girls on his way and did not hear any noise. He knew that the people there wanted to keep certain things hidden. Hayyan entered the room in which Abu al-'Atahiya usually met with Phinehas. It was dark, so Hayyan brought a candelabra with several lit candles and invited Abu al-'Atahiya to sit down while he went to call his master. Abu al-'Atahiya stayed behind waiting for Phinehas and thinking of a stratagem that would allow him to stay there that night. He wanted to know where in the palace those guests were. When he heard the laughter of a boy, he knew that they were in a nearby room, to which he knew the way.

Hayyan returned and said, "My master has gone to bed. Shall I awaken him?"

"Don't disturb him, let him sleep," Abu al-'Atahiya said with an auspicious feeling, "I will see him in the morning."

Saying this, he yawned and stretched his limbs, pretending to be drowsy.

The doorman asked, "Do you want to sleep or shall I bring you food first?"

"I need no food," he said, "but I am very tired, for I have been traveling from a faraway place and I got tired from riding. When I approached your palace and saw its lights shining, I was surprised, and I came to spend an hour with Master Phinehas. So I sent the muleteer and his riding animal away. I don't know whether I will find another riding animal near this place if I were to leave."

Hayyan said, "If you have to leave, there are many riding animals in the stable. But I don't think there is any need for you to be in a hurry. Rest with us tonight, and if you would like to sleep, I will take you to a room with a bed."

"But I can't sleep with the lights shining in the house," Abu al-'Atahiya said.

"We have begun extinguishing the lights," Hayyan said, "and very soon, you will see the palace dark."

"If that is so," Abu al-'Atahiya said, "then I shall sleep here rather than leave now and come back tomorrow, for I am bringing a deal for Master Phinehas in which there is a lot of gain, God willing."

The doorman was now more desirous to keep him, knowing that his master's greed always surpassed his ever-increasing wealth. Phinehas was interested in making money and did not care by what means he achieved his end. For this purpose, he often condoned certain matters that a freeman would not. He believed that people were wrong to let considerations of "honor" or "dignity" affect their ability to reach a deal. They would sacrifice their lives or lose their wealth to live up to meaningless words—and thus lose an opportunity to earn money. Honor or dignity would not feed them if they were hungry, or warm them if they were cold, or give them drink if they were thirsty. As for money, it was the scepter that made its holder a king to whom heads bowed. Those were the principles of Master Phinehas, and Abu al-'Atahiya knew them and often sought his help in projects that would profit them both.

When the doorman realized that inviting Abu al-'Atahiya to be a guest would please his master, he insisted on having him stay the night and led him out of the room. Abu al-'Atahiya followed him, looking right and left in the hope of finding the room which had the guests whose identity he wished to discover. Hayyan then stopped at a door, opened it, and invited him to enter. Abu al-'Atahiya saw a mattress on a rather good carpet, and he said, "This is a clean mattress, thank you." He pretended to be sleepy, so Hayyan left him and went away. After the lights had been extinguished and everyone had gone to sleep, silence reigned over the place. He took off his turban and his cloak and went in search of the people whose secret he wanted to discover. He groped for the wall as his knees trembled and walked until he came close to the room from which he had heard voices earlier on.

When he reached the door of the room, he heard people whispering as though they were being careful not to be heard. He stood at the door and peeped through the keyhole and saw a woman with angelic features wearing royal clothes and sitting on a bedstead in the foremost part of the room. On her lap were the two boys, whom she embraced and repeatedly kissed while her eyes glistened with tears. Her face showed expressions of joy mixed with sorrow. Abu al-'Atahiya did not know whether she was weeping out of joy or out of sorrow, but he kept looking at her face. He guessed she was thirty-five-years old; he had never seen as beautiful and dignified a face as hers, in spite of the many beautiful slave-girls he had seen at the houses of the caliphs and princes and at the house of Ja'far al-Barmaki or of other Barmakids. He noticed a great difference between the beauty of those others he had known and the beauty of this woman, which was awe-inspiring and dignified. The source of this awe shone through her wide-open eyes that radiated brilliant beams. They did not produce the languid glance of a coquette, but rather a sharp look that made the person looked at feel they penetrated his chest, pierced his heart, and uncovered its hidden secrets. She did not have a white complexion, although in those days people prided themselves on having such a complexion; rather she was of a tawny color tinged with a glowing red. She had a mouth that was expressive without the need for words and was as indicative of her feelings as a mirror was of its image. On her forehead, Abu al-'Atahiya saw a headband studded with gems, and it surprised him for he had never seen the likes of it before. The first person ever to wear such a headband was 'Aliyya bint al-Mahdi, sister of al-Rashid. Her forehead was excessively wide and impaired her beauty, so she invented the fashion of headbands in order to conceal that defect. It was one of the most beautiful inventions.

She had combed her hair in a topknot known as a Sukayna topknot, named after Sukayna bint al-Husayn, who was the first to wear her hair that way. At the front of the topknot, Abu al-'Atahiya saw a forelock bejeweled with a diamond in the shape of a bird whose eyes were made of emeralds and whose wings had stones of red ruby interspaced with diamonds in an amazing arrangement. The way it glittered in the light made Abu al-'Atahiya think the room was lit by the topknot and not by the candles. The woman's head was covered with a jujube-colored silk veil embroidered with gold thread. Around her neck, she wore a necklace of jewels, and in her ears she had earrings, each of which had a single pearl the size of a pigeon's egg.

Her gown, made of the most expensive fabrics, was extremely simple; its color was sky blue and its hems were finely embroidered. Abu al-'Atahiya was amazed on seeing the lady and thought to himself, "There is no doubt that this heavenly nymph is a member of Caliph al-Rashid's family, and she must have a purpose which, if I come to know it, will let me fleece them."

He looked around the room and saw the man and the woman still in their Hijaz clothing sitting on the floor in utter awe. The man was a mature person with gray hair, and when Abu al-'Atahiya looked intently at his face, he did not see any Bedouin features so he knew that he was disguised in that clothing for a purpose. When he looked at the woman's face in the light, it became clear to him that she was a slave-girl who had grown older. His friend 'Utba attracted his attention. She sat in front of the bedstead trying kindly to soothe her mistress' pain. He contemplated 'Utba and saw that her face was still beautiful; she had changed a little by having put on some weight that made her skin smoother. On that night, her head was uncovered and her hair was plaited in more than a dozen braids with coins or jewelry hanging from the end of each. She had a valuable necklace around her neck and bracelets and bangles around her wrists, and she wore a lovely red robe, adorned with designs that looked like green branches.

Abu al-'Atahiya was amazed at the scenes and was so emotionally affected that his knees trembled. He was getting tired of bending because he could not see through the keyhole in the door unless he bent down. But he endured and listened to the conversation. The first words he could hear when he had reached the door were the words of his friend 'Utba, which he recognized by her twang.

"Take it easy, my lady," she said. "Why do you cry?"

In a voice suffocated by weeping, the lady raised her head to 'Utba while embracing the two boys and said, "My heart tells me, 'Utba, that this is the last time I will see them."

"God forbid, my lady," 'Utba quickly responded. "I hope you will see them often each year, as you have been doing up till today. Riyash here, may God keep him, will spare no effort to bring them to us whenever you command... It is hoped that you will regain your freedom, God willing, and that they will be with you all the time."

The lady sighed and said, "Ah! You hope for the impossible, O 'Utba. Our opponent is an unjust man, a tyrant who has absolute power. He wallows in his pleasures and enjoys all that he desires. He no longer cares whether another person dies of thirst, perishes of hunger, or expires of a broken heart. He is a man with no pity and no mercy. All he is interested in is his pleasures..."

Saying this, she took from her sleeve a silk handkerchief embroidered with gold thread and wiped her tears with it.

"This is how all men are, my lady," 'Utba said. "They have dominion and are in command. They prefer themselves to women, allow themselves what they deny women, and enjoy what they forbid women. A man marries several women, has concubines, and owns slave-girls; yet he prevents a woman from marrying the man who loves her and whom she loves. But..."

Interrupting the slave-girl, the lady said, "There is no man who has done what my brother has done, and there is no woman who has been afflicted with my affliction... He introduced me to a man whom he made me love, and with whom he agreed by contract that I should marry. Then he forbade us this contract's fruits, which God has permitted to his lowest creatures. Meanwhile he struts in his palace, surrounded by hundreds of white, brown, and black slave-girls."

At this point, she choked on her tears. The two boys were on her lap and the elder looked at her face with some perplexity as she spoke. When he saw her weeping, he started weeping, and when his brother saw him weeping, he started weeping too; then 'Utba wept and the sound of sobbing and wailing filled the room.

18

'Utba then took heart and began trying to ease the pain of her mistress, saying, "You know well, my lady, that your brother, the Commander of the Faithful, may God guard him, has forbidden you to marry the vizier because he is not your equal; for you are a caliph's daughter and another caliph's sister, and your lineage goes back to Prophet Muhammad's uncle, while the vizier is a Persian client like the rest of the clients of foreign origin. How would you marry him when someone like you could marry a Hashemite? The Commander of the Faithful loves you. He has forbidden you to marry him only because he honors your high station."

"Woe to you, 'Utba," she answered. "Are you still duped by this bunk? If my brother really considers marriage to clients or slaves to be a lowering of the station of the caliphate, why then does he marry slave-girls and sire children from them whom he appoints as heirs apparent? Or is a slave-girl higher in rank than a client? And note that he has many slave-girls whom he owns in his palaces. Why does he not limit himself to his cousin Zubayda for a wife, whom he appears to love and respect? The fact is that he has obeyed his lusty desires and found no one to oppose him. So he plunged himself into pleasures and luxury, and he found me to be weak, so he treated me despotically. He brought me together with a young man, whom not one of my cousins from the House of Hashim surpasses; he married me to him, and then forbade me to contact him, so that we came to consider closeness together to be treason and we feared that anyone would come to know our secret, as though we were fornicators, God forbid... But who can say that to my brother and escape death?"

Chapter 3

Al-'Abbasa, the New Bride

From the conversation, Abu al-'Atahiya learned that the lady was al-'Abbasa, sister of al-Rashid. He knew that al-Rashid had contracted to marry her to his vizier, Ja'far ibn Yahya al-Barmaki, so that it would be lawful for the latter to see her. That was because Ja'far was al-Rashid's favorite companion, and he longed for his company; he also liked his sister al-'Abbasa, whom he wanted to see as often. So he arranged a *mariage blanc*[8] between Ja'far and his sister—a legal marriage that would not be consummated. It would then be permissible for Ja'far to see her in their council, without fearing the consequences.[9]

Abu al-'Atahiya also learned from what he saw and heard that Ja'far had secretly consummated the marriage with al-'Abbasa and that the two boys were the fruit of that marriage—and he learned that al-'Abbasa was afraid that her brother al-Rashid would know this and have her executed. Abu al-'Atahiya was exceedingly happy because of this discovery, for he hoped to gain much money from it; the enemies of Ja'far would buy such information for thousands of dinars, especially al-Fadl ibn al-Rabi'.

Tears welled up in Abu al-'Atahiya's eyes, not in sympathy for al-'Abbasa, but because he had been staring for so long through the keyhole. He felt he was about to sneeze and feared this would expose him, so he rubbed the tip of his nose until the sensation of imminent sneezing disappeared, and then he resumed his stealthy spying. He heard 'Utba

---

8 A French term for a legal marriage with no conjugal relations. *Translator's Note.*

9 As al-Rashid is said to have explained to Ja'far, "You are to see her only in my company, your body may never approach hers, and you are to have no conjugal relations with her. You may thus share our evenings of pleasure without risk." *Translator's Note.*

soothing al-ʿAbbasa's pain and saying, "Stop crying now! You have endured the hardship of coming and taken the risk of being here in order to see your sons, so kiss them and enjoy their presence, and let destiny ordain as God wishes."

Al-ʿAbbasa obeyed her; the two boys sat on her lap looking at her in astonishment at what they were seeing. When she saw them looking at her with tears in their eyes, she could not help smiling as tears flowed from her eyes, and she embraced the elder and kept kissing his cheeks, his eyes, his forehead, his head, his neck, and his chest. She lovingly inhaled his scent while he was laughing heartily, thinking she was playing with him. How could he know what was going on in her mind or what she was feeling, for he knew nothing of the world's pleasures but eating and drinking, playing in the sand and with blocks, and had experienced nothing of the vicissitudes of time. For him, the world's most coveted object was his mother's breast and, after being weaned, his interest was his stomach and his desire was a wheel he could turn or a ball he could play with; his entertainment was a collection of stones he could build a house with or some clay he could fashion into a statue. He would see a dead person and think he was only sleeping; he would see a snake and think it was only a rope. He would not fear abandonment, he would not be worried about being poor, and he would not know the misfortunes of time. He might perhaps love a cat playing in front of him more than he might love his parents, because he would love only what his hands could reach. If he could think, he would compare his attachment to a bird he had for a few days before it flew away with the attachment of a mother to her son who was the apple of her eye and a part of her soul. But children cannot be blamed if they do not realize how much their parents love them, for this is a mystery unknown to all but parents. And however highly developed the emotions of young men may become, and however much they may socialize with families and see the tender love of mothers, they will not understand the reality of that tender love until they have their own children. Only then will they taste the bittersweetness of bringing up children: sometimes playing with a son whose face beams with good health and whose cute speech is rendered additionally sweet with a lisp, and sometimes staying up at night to keep watch over a baby suffering from pain but unable to locate it because of an inability to talk or a fear of ingesting a bitter medicine. Meanwhile, both parents observe his movements and count his breaths, unable to do anything, with broken hearts and deep anguish, especially the mother who is usually closer to her child at a young age. When he walks, her heart walks with him; when he laughs, she rejoices with him; and when he talks, she is all ears for anything he may request that pleases him—even if obtaining it may cause her misery. Her love for him increases the more she suffers in bringing him up, and her tenderness grows with the growth of her misery in helping him. How can anybody but the parents understand this or know a mother's tenderness? Even married couples who have not been blessed with having children cannot understand a mother's love for her child, except by imagination. But imagination cannot be compared with reality.

Al-'Abbasa began to inhale the scent of her sons while weeping, her heart wavering between hope and despair. The two boys laughed, with a clear natural innocence on their faces and purity of heart and good intentions evident in every one of their movements. Image-makers such as poets are right when they compare children to angels, for they are the epitome of purity, saintliness, and candor; they don't conceal their emotions and don't suppress their inner feelings and thus their natural instincts are transparent, the strongest being love of self. A child loves himself and likes all that he finds to be beneficial to him. He is jealous but does not suppress his jealousy; rather he expresses it and is not shy in showing it. That is why when one of the two brothers saw his mother play with his sibling and kiss him, he threw himself on her chest as though competing for her love. Al-'Abbasa kissed him and turned to 'Utba, her eyes expressing what she said. "How lovely these two boys are and how lovely their names are, al-Hasan and al-Husain! Will God allow me to live with them, even in a simple hut or a tent in the desert?"

"God has the power to do everything," 'Utba quickly responded. Then she added, "Don't you think that it is time for you to go back to your palace? Dawn is close, and we are afraid that someone may become aware of us, and then what we have feared will befall us."

"It is difficult for me to leave, 'Utba," al-'Abbasa said. "But I think I must... Where are the coins I brought? Give them to Riyash."

'Utba took out a purse and handed it to him. He took it, thanked al-'Abbasa, and stood up. He kissed her hand and so did Barra, and al-'Abbasa said to them, "I don't need to impress on you the necessity of taking good care of al-Hasan and al-Husain, for they are my very heart and soul."

When al-Hasan, the elder boy, knew his mother was about to leave and saw her stand up, he threw himself on her, held her by the hand, and leaned his cheek on her palm.

"Come with us, Mama," he said, choking. "And tell my father to come with us too."

Al-'Abbasa looked at the boy as he gazed at her with teary eyes, his lips quivering and making him unable to speak. He tried to pronounce the words but was afraid he would weep and be unable to speak and so he choked. On hearing the boy utter his sentence, and on seeing him in that condition, al-'Abbasa's heart was moved. From the moment she saw her sons, she dreaded the time of separation. She tried to control herself and show some hardiness, though she was dismayed at being forced to suppress her emotions. So when she realized her condition and heard al-Hasan mention his father and demand that she bring him, her emotions got the better of her, and she felt the pain of separation overwhelming her and the burden of fear weighing down on her. Suddenly, she could not help sitting down as she hugged the boy tightly and said, "You are right, my dear son!" And she burst into tears and then lost consciousness.

'Utba was standing by, observing the movements of her mistress and sharing her emotions, intending to soothe her. When she saw her sit down suddenly, she was afraid she would swoon because she had seen her become unconscious in that manner more than once before. So when she heard her screaming and crying, she knew she would lose consciousness. She took out one of the candles from the candelabra, hurried to the door, and opened it in order to call a servant to bring her some water to sprinkle on her mistress. Abu al-'Atahiya was still standing there looking through the keyhole of the door, so when 'Utba opened the door hurriedly and unexpectedly, with the candle in her hand, he was taken aback and at a loss what to do. He felt his blood was about to freeze in his veins, and he stood there like a statue, staring with fixed eyes as though he was seeing nothing. As for 'Utba, she thought at first he was one of the house servants, so she shouted at him, "Bring some water." Then she noticed his clothes and realized that he was not one of the servants; she was astonished to see him standing there. As for him, he was not immobile for longer than a moment. As he became alert he took to his heels. She remembered that she had known him and soon became aware that he was Abu al-'Atahiya, but she could not fathom what brought him here. However, her concern for her unconscious mistress overwhelmed her, so she ran to the servants' room and shouted at them, waking them so one of them brought her water. She returned to her mistress and sprinkled the water on her, and her mistress came to. 'Utba then began to soothe her, but her mind was preoccupied with Abu al-'Atahiya. She had noticed his confusion at seeing her and realized that he was surreptitiously listening and watching, and may have heard part of their conversation. She knew that he could not be trusted to keep a secret and that, by his coming to know about those two boys, al-'Abbasa was in danger. She continued to speak with her mistress and soothe her, while anxiety and confusion were clearly visible on her face. She hesitated whether to tell al-'Abbasa about the matter or not. In the end, she preferred to keep it secret in order not to add to her mistress's fears and sorrows. She decided to devise a plan that would prevent Abu al-'Atahiya from divulging this secret. Having so decided released her from her anxiety, and she resumed soothing al-'Abbasa and calming her down. Then she ordered Riyash to take the boys away with Barra. He obeyed her, stood up, and carried the two boys on his shoulders, meanwhile playing with them and jesting, for they had been accustomed to his amusing playfulness. 'Utba remained by al-'Abbasa, talking to her as she sighed, still recovering from the effects of unconsciousness. When Riyash and Barra left, 'Utba ordered the servant who had brought her the water to summon Hayyan. So he left and came back accompanied by Hayyan, who had been suddenly awakened and was still groggy. 'Utba said to him, "My mistress wants you to send someone with these two people and rent riding animals to take them to the Tigris."

He left, and she followed him. She called him to one side and spoke to him confidentially, conveying her mistress's thanks to him. Then she gave him a money bag as a gift from her mistress and another as a gift to his own master, Master Phinehas.

Hayyan thanked her for her generosity and her gift. But she interrupted him and asked, "Has Abu al-'Atahiya been here for a long time?" She mentioned his name purposely so that Hayyan might know that she was certain he was there.

"He came to us only tonight," he said.

"Tell me the truth," she insisted.

"I have told you the truth," he emphasized. "He came here tonight for some business with Master Phinehas, who had already gone to bed at the time. So I invited him to stay with us tonight, and he did." He said this without hesitation or fear, so 'Utba was sure he was telling the truth. She then said, "I would like to ask you for a favor that will not cause you any trouble. Will you do it?"

"I am at your service," he assured her.

She said, "I would like you to keep this poet at your place and not let him leave before I return tomorrow morning."

Astonished at her request, he said, "I am afraid my master will not accept to keep him."

"Tell him," she replied, "that the Commander of the Faithful wants to hold him back for a matter of interest to him."

On hearing the mention of the Commander of the Faithful, his heart throbbed agitatedly, for he did not know anything about al-'Abbasa but that she was a woman from Baghdad's upper crust who had rented the room that night for a private matter.

"I will tell my master," he quickly said.

"Beware of taking my words lightly," she cautioned.

"At your service," he said.

"So, prepare the mules for us to return," she said, and hurried to her mistress. She found her waiting and wondering what was taking her so long. She told her that she had ordered Hayyan to prepare the mules, and her mistress believed her. Then they both went out and left.

As for Hayyan, he began to think about what he had just heard from 'Utba with regard to keeping Abu al-'Atahiya longer, and he could not think of any reasonable excuse to do so. Her mention of the Commander of the Faithful frightened him, so he decided to inform his master in the morning about what he had heard from her, in order to relieve himself of any responsibility in this matter. Most of the night had passed, so he went to bed.

As for Abu al-'Atahiya, he ran away from 'Utba, having been surprised and scared to the point his blood was about to freeze in his veins. But he thought she did not recognize him. He reached his bed, his knees trembling, and he lay there after closing the door. He remained silent, expecting to hear a noise or the sound of footsteps or any movement that would indicate what was happening. For some time he suppressed the sound of his breathing in an exaggerated effort to listen for any faint noise, while the darkness thickened and 'Utba's specter stood before his eyes. He began to think of possible consequences and was afraid and overwhelmed by a feeling of circumspection.

The closed window of the room in which he was staying looked out on an alley that led to the door of the house. He soon heard the clatter of bridles and the uproar of stablemen. He got up and looked through a crack in the window and saw Riyash and Barra mounted and the two boys with them. He waited to see what was happening to al-'Abbasa and her maid; he heard the movement of the stablemen preparing their mounts, and then he saw them going out on two mules, al-'Abbasa's mule being brought out by a groom with his hand on its rump. Al-'Abbasa wore a cloak and a turban-like covering on her head. So he was sure that they were leaving, and his heart was at ease. He returned to his bed, thinking of the purpose of his visit to Phinehas. He decided to meet him early in the morning and broach that subject with him; then he would go to the palace of the prince or that of al-Fadl ibn al-Rabi' and come back with whomever they would entrust to select the slave-girls.

* * *

As he thought about the day's events, Abu al-'Atahiya had difficulty falling asleep. He had not slept for long when he heard a noise in the alley, mingled with the clatter of bridles and the neighing of horses. He was scared and jumped out of bed and opened the window. He saw that morning had dawned. He looked out and saw several men on horses whose saddles and silk covers indicated to him they were from al-Amin's stable. His heart throbbed as he scrutinized the riders and saw al-Fadl ibn al-Rabi' surrounded by the retinue of al-Amin. In their company, there was a group of servants, and he heard al-Fadl saying, "I see that the people here are still sleeping."

One of the horsemen answered him, "What if I wake them up? Master Phinehas prefers money to sleep."

Al-Fadl laughed and said, "Unless he thinks we are coming to take his money or his life..."

One of the servants came forward and knocked on the door, and the horsemen began dismounting, the first being al-Fadl. He was tall and slender; he had a beard with light hair and a brown complexion tinged with yellow. He was still in the prime of youth, and his predominant disposition was what is called a bilious or choleric temperament, which helped him disguise his feelings, pretend to his enemies to be a friend, and take steps to defame them. People of this temperament are most capable of suppressing emotions, impersonating whomever they wish, and concealing what their consciences harbor. Consequently, they can patiently endure being wronged and then seize the opportunity to achieve their aims. Anger does not make them lose judiciousness, as it does people of the sanguine or nervous temperament, who, when angered, exhibit signs of anger in their eyes and on their foreheads; that is why one rarely finds among them persons who are self-possessed and able to face adversities with patience.

When Abu al-'Atahiya saw al-Fadl, he thought, *There must be a reason that urged him to come here, and al-Amin must have made him do so because of his yearning for the promised slave-girls, his interest in revelry and luxurious living, and his desire for singing.* Abu al-'Atahiya was afraid that al-Fadl's coming at that early hour might prevent him from the profit he was expecting, as he had not yet spoken to Phinehas. He moved away from the window and headed for Phinehas's room. He saw that the people in the house were in a tizzy, Hayyan leading them hurriedly in the corridor to receive the visitors, having been informed by the doorman of their arrival. He did not notice Abu al-'Atahiya, who kept walking to Master Phinehas's room. He found the door locked, so he called out, "Is Master Phinehas still asleep?"

He heard footsteps inside the room. The door was opened and Master Phinehas appeared wearing his nightgown. His hair was disheveled and his beard and side ringlets were in disarray. His beard was slightly gray and a little too long, and it was divided into two parts at the bottom. His nose was big and narrow, and its length concealed the fact that it was eagle-shaped. He had been awakened suddenly, so when he got up his nightgown was open at the top and the lower part of his neck and the upper part of his chest were visible, disclosing some wrinkles permeated with curly hair, which made him look as if he were a vagabond.

As soon as his sight fell on Abu al-'Atahiya, he shouted, "What is the matter with you?"

Abu al-'Atahiya entered the room. Closing the door behind him, he said, "I came to you last night for some business, but you had gone to sleep. So I waited for you until now, and when you overslept I decided to awaken you. I hope I have not disturbed you."

"Not at all," said Phinehas, adjusting his nightgown and smoothing his beard and mustache. "Tell me, what is the matter?"

"Don't be afraid," Abu al-'Atahiya said. "It is a profitable matter. I have suggested to our lord, the heir apparent, to acquire some slave-girls he would buy from you; and you know the influence of poets with caliphs and men of the state. Since I have come to let you know the news, I hope you will not let my effort go in vain."

"I understand," Phinehas interrupted. "Rest assured. When his messenger comes, I will add your share to the price. God bless you, you are an earnestly concerned and loving man. And if you like, I will make your share a beautiful slave-girl."

"I am in no need of slave-girls," Abu al-'Atahiya said.

Phinehas laughed and, as he began looking for his robe and outer garment, he said, "Fine. I understand a hint. Now, you understand: you will be paid only after the sale occurs."

"The sale will occur immediately," Abu al-'Atahiya reassured him, "for al-Amin has sent al-Fadl ibn al-Rabi' to your house, and I think they have let him in the House of Slaves just now. But beware of letting anyone know what went on between us."

Phinehas put his hand on Abu al-'Atahiya's mouth and said, "My goodness! How slow-witted you are! I thought you were intelligent." Then he continued to comb his hair and improve his appearance. He combed his beard, twisted the edges of his mustache, tied a waistband over his robe, put on his outer garment, and then went out, with Abu al-'Atahiya on his heels. At that moment, Hayyan came in a hurry toward them and, when he caught sight of Abu al-'Atahiya, he was startled and remembered 'Utba's request; he wanted to stop his master in order to inform him about the visitors and tell him what 'Utba asked for. But before he could say a word, Phinehas said, "I understand. I am on my way to them. Where are they?" He thought Hayyan was coming to inform him about the arrival of al-Fadl. Hayyan did not dare tell him in the presence of Abu al-'Atahiya what he had originally intended to say. So he said, "Our lord, al-Fadl ibn al-Rabi' came to us, so we let him in, and he is now in the House of Slaves waiting for you." He postponed telling his master about Utba's request to a later occasion.

As for Abu al-'Atahiya, he looked at Hayyan and smiled, not knowing what he was concealing in his heart. Hayyan greeted him politely and walked behind him.

* * *

Master Phinehas walked, trailing his long outer garment, and then left the corridor of his house and turned to a door next to a large gate, which was the entrance of the House of Slaves. He came to a large courtyard surrounded by many rooms, perhaps more than thirty in number. The courtyard was crowded with al-Fadl's servants, looking in the direction of the rooms as though they were seeing something strange. Next to the door inside the courtyard, there was a room whose floor was covered with carpets, and there were cushions arranged alongside walls that were decorated with colorful paintings. Al-Fadl had entered the room with some of his entourage and waited there for Master Phinehas. When the latter arrived and saw al-Fadl sitting cross-legged in the foremost place of the room, with his elbows on his knees, he rushed to him and bent down to kiss his hand and invoke blessings on him. Al-Fadl laughed, gave him his hand, and said, "We think we have disturbed you with this visit."

"Certainly not, my lord," Phinehas said, "Your visit is a great honor."

Gesturing for him to sit down, al-Fadl said, "Our lord, the heir apparent, has asked us to bring him some beautiful slave-girls who know how to sing. So we came to visit you to see the House of Slaves and to take pleasure in viewing the slave-girls and slave-boys it has. We were told it contains all kinds of fascinating delights."

"By taking the trouble to visit," Phinehas said politely and with a measure of submissiveness, "you have rendered me an honor I don't deserve. You were in no need of doing that—all you needed to do was beckon, and we would have moved the whole House of Slaves to our lord, may God preserve him. But it is our good fortune that you took the trouble to come. If you would like to see the slaves in this house, you will notice that it has what others don't, for I did not spare any effort to acquire the most beautiful white, yellow, red, and black slave-girls and slave-boys. They are of various builds, languages, and ages; some are born in Iraq or Hijaz, some are imported from the far lands of the Turks and the Byzantines and from Tabaristan, Khurasan, Sind, and the Maghrib. Among them you will find male and female Slavs, male and female Byzantines, male and female Turks, male and female Persians, male and female Armenians, male and female Sindhis, and male and female Berbers…"

"Do you have any singing slave-girls?" al-Fadl asked.

"Of course…," he answered, "and they learned singing from the singer of our lord, the Commander of the Faithful himself. They have memorized delightful poems, and they are perfect players of musical instruments. Among them you will find players of the lute and the long-necked mandolin, as well as players of the tambourine and the ancient Arab lute."

Al-Fadl laughed and said, "It is as if you are describing the very slave-girls of the Commander of the Faithful. Anyway, perhaps the singers you have referred to are yellow and black slave-girls, but our lord wants only singers who are white slave-girls."

"I have all that our lord asks for," Phinehas assured him.

"But as far as I know," al-Fadl said, "the people of Baghdad have not taught white slave-girls to sing for, as you certainly know, men have taken them only as concubines. I know no one who taught singing to white slave-girls except Ibrahim al-Mawsili, the singer of the Commander of the Faithful."

"Did I not tell my lord he would find I have all that he asks for?" said Phinehas.

Al-Fadl prepared himself to rise, so Master Phinehas and the rest of the entourage got up. Phinehas walked in front of them until they were out of the room and in the courtyard. The servants hastened to the sides, opening the way for al-Fadl, and he walked with Phinehas in the lead and the men of the entourage behind al-Fadl. When they crossed the courtyard, they went to the first room on the right. Its door was ajar, so Phinehas pushed it open with his hand, and al-Fadl saw a group of white little girls there, the oldest of whom was no more than ten years of age. Their bodies were bare except for rags that covered their pudenda, and the coarseness of desert living was clearly visible on them, with their hair hanging down naturally and not having been touched by a comb. He saw the beauty of nomadic life evident in their shining faces whose whiteness imbued with a red color denoted good health, to say nothing of the beauty of their eyes. Among them were blondes with blue eyes, black-haired girls with black eyes, and others in between. As for the girls, they were scared when the door was opened, but when they saw al-Fadl and his men, they bolted as gazelles would from hunters and fear was all over their faces. However, the room was too small for them to escape anywhere, so they hid behind one another staring blankly. Some of them started to cry and ask for help in a language that none of the men standing there understood. Al-Fadl was astonished at that strange scene and looked at Phinehas, who hastened to say, "Don't be surprised, my lord, at the primitive desert life you see in those girls. Most of the beautiful slave-girls, songstresses, and musicians were at first like these ones; in fact, I have brought you to this room to show you the conditions of the slave-girls when they arrive here, so that you may know how much we suffer in educating them until one of them emerges with superior qualities and can be sold for one thousand or ten thousand or twenty thousand dinars."

Al-Fadl said, "It is truly hard work. Were Farida, Minna, Dinar, Umm al-Khal, and other charming slave-girls as crude as these?"

"Yes," Phinehas answered, "most of them were imported when they were in this condition."

"And where do you bring them from?" al-Fadl asked.

"The slave traders go far into the countries of the Turks, the Slavs, and the Byzantines, enduring difficulties and facing dangers in order to obtain them."

"And how are they obtained?"

"Some are obtained in raids and some are bought from parents or relatives at a low price by intermediaries who sell them to us at the highest prices."

Al-Fadl asked, "Is it permissible to deprive them of their kin and let them be carried away so young in this fashion?'

Phinehas smiled and said, "Being enslaved is one of the most important causes of their happiness, for they move from the coarse life of the desert and its rugged existence to the city and its luxuries. They may achieve an opulence of living that the daughters of princes may not achieve, especially those that have beautiful faces and melodious voices. But very few of them do achieve distinction—perhaps one in fifty or eighty. When we find one who has intelligence and a pleasant voice, we teach her singing and make her memorize poems. As for the rest of them, we teach them to do house chores and the like according to their abilities. In the rooms you will pass by, you will see various kinds and classes of slave-girls."

Al-Fadl was amazed at what he had heard and wanted to be satisfied with what he had seen, but Phinehas went ahead of him to the next room and opened it. He showed him little girls with black skin, curly hair, and flat noses. Al-Fadl knew that they were black girls and noticed that they were closer to a wild and squalid desert state than the girls in the first room. Phinehas noticed that al-Fadl was inclined to move away from there, so he walked in front of him, saying, "These young black girls are brought to us by slave traders from the far reaches of the Sudan as captives and as kidnapped girls whom they have obtained without paying any price for them, and we buy them at a very low price. Most of them learn to be servants, and we mostly make them serve white slave-girls."

Before the group reached the third room, Phinehas said, "In this room, there are Berber girls who are brought to us by slave traders from the African desert. Most of the slave-girls of this kind are sent to Baghdad in lieu of the tax, as my lord surely knows. In the next room, there are yellow slave-girls from Sind; in the one after it, there are red slave-girls from the land of the Byzantines; and in the other rooms are classes of slave-girls such as concubines, hairdressers, nursemaids, cooks, bakers, and women of similar services. And in some of these rooms are classes of white and black male slaves who have been trained to be house workers such as cooks, bakers, valets, and grooms. Among them are some who mastered les belles-lettres, memorized poetry, and are scholars of the Arabic language and some who are singers, boon companions, jesters, and the like. They are white and black, and of various ages."

* * *

Al-Fadl deemed that viewing everything would take too long, so he said, "Show us samples of the strangest of what you have, and spare us the details, for we don't have sufficient time to see all those who are in these rooms."

"Would you like me to show you small, white and black slave-boys?" Phinehas asked. "They are similar to what you have seen."

"Show us young slave-women," al-Fadl said.

Phinehas walked past several rooms before reaching one whose door he opened. In it there were white girls whose ages ranged between fifteen and twenty years. They appeared to be naive and wore simple robes. Their hair was flowing or plaited. They wore earrings and necklaces of colored beads. They possessed women's beauty and shyness. When they saw al-Fadl and his men, they were overcome by shyness and overwhelmed by fear. Al-Fadl caught sight of one of them in whose eyes he saw enchanting looks and in whose body he observed elegance. Her innocence increased her beauty and her attraction. She made a good impression on him, so he called to her in Arabic, but she did not understand what he wanted. She realized he was calling her, so she shied away and hid behind her neighbor; then she turned her face away and covered it with her arm. Al-Fadl liked that coyness of hers, so he said, "Where is Abu al-'Atahiya or Abu Nuwas to describe this scene for us with poetry?"

Phinehas remembered Abu al-'Atahiya and turned around expecting to see him next to him but did not find him. He was about to mention his name, but remembered his reticence, so he said, "My lord is right. This slave-girl is from Tabaristan, and I bought her with a group of other slave-girls of her kind, but none of them is as beautiful as she is… But what will you think when you will see the non-Arab slave-girls raised in Basra and Kufa? They have pleasant speech, svelte bodies, slender waists, curly temple locks, and eyelids darkened with kohl. Beautifully dressed and embellished, they are white and tall, brown and red-lipped, and yellow with fat buttocks. Among them are ones with such large posteriors that if you were to pour a jar of water on them as they are standing, the backs of their thighs would remain dry—just as is told of 'A'isha bint Talha who, when she wanted to get up, had to have two persons to help her."

Al-Fadl laughed at Phinehas's expertise in describing women in spite of his old age, and he said to him, "I see that you are skillful in describing beautiful women, Master Phinehas!"

His hand on his beard, Phinehas immediately answered, "How do you think I spent the days that have turned my beard white, my lord?"

Al-Fadl said, "Take us to the non-Arab slave-girls."

Phinehas crossed the courtyard to the other side, and al-Fadl and his men followed him. He said, "I think you have become tired of standing. Let us go to the slave-girls who are singers and have memorized poems and who can play the lute and other musical instruments."

He led them to a room and opened the door, giving al-Fadl the right of way to enter first. The latter looked in and saw a room whose floor was covered with carpets and cushions. On one side of it sat three white slave-girls exuding the scent of musk. One of them was wearing a red gown under a wrap dyed with safflower and had a brocaded headband on her head. She had two side locks hanging down, with a red ruby attached to the edge of each, and had let down her pitch-black hair. She had scented herself with aloes and wore a fragrant perfume. She was in front of her two companions, because she was more beautiful. Her companions wore similar clothes, but she surpassed them in beauty and excelled with her elegant figure and her black eyes that looked as though they had been darkened with kohl. Her complexion was white and as clear as crystal. Around her neck, she wore a necklace of carnelian. She sat between her two companions on a cushion.

When Phinehas opened the door, he said to her, "Get up, Qaranfula, and kiss the hand of our lord, al-Fadl ibn al-Rabi'." She knew this name and its relation to the court of the caliph, so she started to get up, but it took her too long to do so because of her heavy hips. It was as a poet once said:

Because of her weight, her getting up is difficult
When she rises, but her sitting down is easy.

When she rose, she walked with a sway, her pants brushing her feet. When she was close to al-Fadl ibn al-Rabi', she smiled amiably at him as she greeted him with a measure of kindness and tenderness, and she bent down to kiss his hand, but he prevented her and turned to Phinehas with a look of appreciation.

Phinehas said, "Speak with her, my lord, for she is eloquent."

Al-Fadl greeted her, and she answered eloquently. He realized from her manner of speaking that she was from Basra, but she differed from the people of Basra by the color of her face and the rest of her features. He turned to Phinehas and wondered, "Is she perhaps one of the people of Basra?'

"No," said Phinehas, "but she grew up in Basra. She is originally from Georgia. I bought her as a little girl, like those you saw in the first room, and I noticed her intelligence and beauty, so I sent her to an agent of mine in Basra who taught her the Arabic language and the Qur'an and made her memorize Arabic poetry. When she returned to me, I liked her speech and her beautiful voice. I knew that the men of the state desired to follow the example of the Commander of the Faithful by teaching singing to white slave-girls. So I asked al-Mawsili to teach her, but he declined until I offered him a large sum of money. I then sent her to him every morning to learn from him one song after another until she perfected this art; she became a rarity among Baghdad's slave-girls and had no one to match her, even in the court of the caliph."

As Phinehas was talking, al-Fadl was contemplating the beauty of the slave-girl. As she brought down a lute hanging on the wall, her sleeve was pulled away, revealing her hand and showing her tender wrist with its bracelets and bangles, and displaying her palms with their dyed skin. He also saw her earrings glittering in her ears.

"You said she has memorized poetry and knows Arabic, did you?" asked al-Fadl.

"Ask her what you wish," said Phinehas, "and listen to her speech or look at her headband and read what she embroidered on it."

Al-Fadl came closer and looked at the headband. He saw a verse of Arabic poetry embroidered on it in letters of gold thread, saying:

A beautiful dye is not an embellishment to my palm,
My beautiful palm is an embellishment to every dye.

He liked that, and he turned to Phinehas and said, "How beautiful these headbands are! And how wonderful their inventor is!"

"I think you are referring to our lady 'Aliyya, sister of al-Rashid," Phinehas said. "She has truly found in them a great source of beauty for lovely women."

Al-Fadl asked, "Do you know why these headbands have come to be used?"

"No, my lord," Phinehas replied.

"I will tell you the reason," said al-Fadl. "'Aliyya's forehead was too wide and her beauty was thus impaired. She wanted to conceal this defect, so she used headbands studded with gems to hide her forehead. Doing so, she created something which, by God, is the most beautiful invention of women that I have seen."

Phinehas was convinced that al-Fadl would buy this slave-girl regardless of the price, so he wanted to interest him in buying the other two. He gestured to one of them, and she understood what he meant. She withdrew into a corner of the room and looked into a mirror hanging on the wall so that no one could see her face. Al-Fadl was preoccupied with observing the first slave-girl, who was amusing herself strumming the lute. When Phinehas knew that the second slave-girl had done what he had suggested to her, he turned to al-Fadl and said, "And look at the face of this one." Beckoning to her, he said, "Come closer, Sawsana." So she came forward with a swinging gait, her purple gown shimmering as it undulated.

Al-Fadl examined her face closely and saw that she had written *Al-Fadl ibn al-Rabi'* on her face with musk. He was charmed with that and desired to buy this slave-girl too.

The third slave-girl guessed his intent and was afraid of being left behind. She believed that going with al-Fadl would be a great success that would exceed her highest hopes. So she stepped aside with an apple in her hand that she coyly handled, and then she returned to al-Fadl and offered him the apple. He took it and found a verse of Arabic poetry written on it with ambergris and musk, saying:

I say, as the riders' turbans were inclined

And staying up at night made them sleepy:

Al-Fadl realized that she was referring to what the composer of this verse, Abu Dhuhl al-Jumahi, said after it:

Along with my clothing and my camel,

I wish I were a hired slave to your people this month.

If it is fate that has given you a gift

And deprived us, then fate is not fair.

It was as if she was insinuating that she desired to go with her two companions. Al-Fadl appreciated her intelligence and decided to buy all three of the slave-girls. He had intended to hear their singing, but realized now that he was late. He was not personally inclined to amusement and revelry, but nonetheless complied with al-Amin's wishes for political reasons. So he decided to leave immediately.

* * *

Al-Fadl left the room, and his men followed him. Phinehas was in front saying, "If my lord wishes, I will show him other kinds of slave-girls: white, brown, red, and black; but he has seen the best that I have." He said this to increase al-Fadl's desire for those he had chosen. He walked on and led them to a reception room, where they sat down. Phinehas ordered that drinks be served on a table, but al-Fadl apologized and declined, because he thought there was not enough time for that. Turning to him, he said, "Sell me these three slave-girls."

Phinehas stood up respectfully and said, "In dealing with the heir apparent, there is no condition or bargaining. All the slave-girls are his. We are all his slaves indeed, whether he pays us any money or not."

Al-Fadl did not fall for the ruse of Phinehas and said, "We are all servants of the heir apparent, but buying and selling is still lawful."

"I am ashamed of mentioning a price," Phinehas said. "Impose the price you like."

"That is for you to say," al-Fadl replied. "Therefore, ask the price you want."

"Someone like you knows the value of things," Phinehas said, "and our lord, the heir apparent, is generous. If he likes anything, he will not care how much he pays for it. We shall accept from him what our lord, the Commander of the Faithful, paid."

He said this and smiled as though mixing serious talk and jesting.

"And how much did the Commander of the Faithful pay?" asked al-Fadl.

"One hundred thousand dinars for one slave-girl," said Phinehas, "and she was no better than Qaranfula or Sawsana." And he laughed.

Al-Fadl split his sides with laughter, and then said, "Don't you know what the result of that generosity was? He paid so much only at the beginning of his caliphate, but when he later ordered his vizier Yahya ibn Khalid to pay that kind of money, the latter apologized and declined, and the Commander of the Faithful became angry with him. Then Yahya wanted to show him how much of a burden the amount was for the treasury, so he brought its equivalent in dirhams, amounting to one million and five hundred thousand dirhams, and he placed the money in the corridor through which the caliph would pass. When the caliph saw it, he found it exorbitant and knew that he had been extravagant."

Phinehas said, "If our lord, the heir apparent, does not wish to pay as much as his father, he may wish to pay as much as his father's vizier did."

Al-Fadl knew that Phinehas was referring to his enemy, Ja'far al-Barmaki, and was reminded of the rivalry between them. But he ignored the remark, and his face betrayed no emotion. He asked, "How much did he pay?"

Phinehas said, "Did he not pay four hundred thousand dinars for a slave-girl? Will it be seemly for the heir apparent to buy a slave-girl for less than that? Anyway, I will send the slave-girls to the palace of the heir apparent, and whatever he pays will be acceptable."

Al-Fadl resented this haggling, and it was hard for him to make al-Amin appear less generous than his enemy, when people in those days tried to win political loyalties by generosity. Phinehas knew about the rivalry and of the secrets of those in politics. He said what he said, knowing that al-Fadl would not bargain with him, in order to preserve the dignity of his lord, al-Amin, and in order to raise his own standing among statesmen by not letting them find anything in his behavior that would demote him in their eyes. As a result, Phinehas was successful. Al-Fadl wanted to show al-Amin's generosity, so he said, "If these slave-girls of yours are of the same class as the slave-girl whom the caliph bought, it will be right for you to ask this price. At any rate, I am going to set the price of the slave-girls at one hundred thousand dinars."

Phinehas pretended he was not too demanding and said, "Everything that our lord offers is a sign of his generosity, for we and our possessions are indebted to his favors."

Al-Fadl did not fail to see through Phinehas' flattery, but he went along with it and said, "May God bless you. Send the slave-girls to the palace of our lord, accompanied by your agent, who will then receive the money."

"I will send them immediately," said Phinehas. "Receiving the money is not an urgent issue."

Thereupon, al-Fadl got ready to stand up, but those accompanying him preceded him in rising. One of them rushed to the servants in the courtyard and gestured to them to prepare the mounts quickly. Al-Fadl occupied himself with responding to Phinehas's words of courtesy and praise while he was covering his face with the cloth tail of his turban, in order to conceal his identity from the public and the purpose for which he had come.

Chapter 4

The Arrest of Abu al-'Atahiya

Al-Fadl had hardly left the house when he heard some uproar and saw a group of men fighting. They were wearing cloaks that covered their clothes and looked as though they were in disguise. But he recognized them as soldiers of the state because they were wearing tall headgear that was propped on the inside by sticks. The first ruler to make soldiers wear this attire was Abu Ja'far al-Mansur. Al-Fadl was surprised to see them disguised with cloaks worn over their clothes. Before long, he heard someone say aloud, "I am one of the men of al-Fadl ibn al-Rabi'. Leave me alone."

When al-Fadl heard his own name mentioned, he stepped forward. The men with the tall headgear had dispersed and were attempting to use ropes to tie a man up as he tried to escape. As soon as he caught sight of the man, al-Fadl recognized him as Abu al-'Atahiya, and he was surprised to see him embroiled in this way. He looked right and left, and saw a partly-disguised woman in one corner of the alley ordering the soldiers to tie the man up; when she saw al-Fadl, she tried to cloak herself further in order not to be recognized. The soldiers were still trying to bind Abu al-'Atahiya tightly, and he threatened them by saying he was one of the men of al-Fadl. They replied, "We have nothing to do with al-Fadl. You have to come with us and report to the caliph."

When al-Fadl noticed that Abu al-'Atahiya was silently pleading for his help and expecting to be supported, he shouted at the men, "Leave the man alone. Who ordered you to take him?" They did not heed his words and answered as they bound him, "He is being sought by the Commander of the Faithful."

Al-Fadl said, "And who believes that the Commander of the Faithful ordered the man to be taken, and why are you involved in all of this?"

The leader of the men stepped forward and looked at al-Fadl. He concluded from seeing his clothes that he was one of the elite of Baghdad, but he wondered at the reason for his disguise. The leader explained, "I am one of the soldiers of the Commander of the Faithful, and he has ordered us to arrest this man."

Al-Fadl said, "I don't see that you are soldiers, for you are not wearing any of the badges of the state."

The man smiled as he took off his cloak and turned his back to al-Fadl to let him read what was embroidered on his robe between his shoulders. Al-Fadl read, "And God will surely protect you against them, for He is all-hearing and all-knowing." The leader then pointed to his sword hanging from his belt.

Al-Fadl laughed and said, "These are old clothes that date back to the days of al-Mansur, for he was the one who ordered his men to have this statement written on their clothes and to hang swords from their belts. You may have bought these clothes in order to arrogate to yourselves the task of soldiers. Otherwise, where is the name of al-Rashid, the Commander of the Faithful?"

The man stretched out his arm, and al-Fadl read the name of al-Rashid embroidered in gold thread at the shoulder: "Harun ibn al-Mahdi, Commander of the Faithful." The leader of the men then turned away from al-Fadl, shaking his head disdainfully, and went to his men, who were still struggling with Abu al-'Atahiya. He urged them to bind him quickly and tightly. Al-Fadl's men were standing by, waiting for his command to save Abu al-'Atahiya; they did not want to do so until he ordered them to, because they feared he wanted to remain unrecognized.

When he noticed the disdainful attitude of the leader, al-Fadl said to him in a quiet but threatening tone, "But he is telling you that he is one of the men of al-Fadl ibn al-Rabi'."

"And who vouches for the truth of what he says?" the leader said. "And even if he is truthful, we have been ordered to arrest him," he added without turning to al-Fadl.

Al-Fadl shouted at him, "I too tell you that he is one of the men of al-Fadl, so leave him alone."

When the leader heard him speak like someone with authority, he turned to him and scrutinized his veiled face; then he turned to the woman standing there and saw her slinking away from the crowd, so he knew that she wanted to escape. He realized that the man speaking to him was a powerful and feared man, but he did not care and returned to his men and shouted at them, "Bind him."

Phinehas was standing beside al-Fadl at first, and he was displeased about the fact that Abu al-'Atahiya was being arrested in his home. He did not understand the reason and was about to step forward to save him with the help of his own servants. But then he remembered that Abu al-'Atahiya intended to share the price of the slave-girls with him and thought that his arrest would provide an excuse for him to get out of this commitment. Hayyan then came to him and, whispering, told him what had happened the day before—that the slave-girl had asked him to keep Abu al-'Atahiya until she returned and that her mistress was a member of the family of the Commander of the Faithful. Phinehas was reassured because he assumed that this arrest was a consequence of what Hayyan had told him and decided to remain silent. He entered his home and pretended to busy himself with something.

When al-Fadl heard the threatening shout of the men's leader, he stepped forward and said firmly to him, "No. You ought not to bind him until we know his offense. Otherwise, you will bear the responsibility of this deed before the Commander of the Faithful."

The leader turned to al-Fadl and asked, "And who are you to threaten me with the Commander of the Faithful? Mind your own business, and go away!"

When al-Fadl's men heard the disdainful words of the leader, they were about to pounce on him and tell him the truth. But they left that to al-Fadl himself and continued to wait for his order. As for al-Fadl, he remained calm and only gestured to his men to save Abu al-'Atahiya. They attacked and there was a noisy scuffle. The soldiers were about to unsheathe their swords, but al-Fadl shouted at them, "You don't need swords. Release the man, and if you are asked about him, say, 'Al-Fadl ibn al-Rabiʿ took him.' If the Commander of the Faithful or any other person needs him for any purpose, let him ask me for him."

When they heard what he said, they were taken aback and stopped. The leader came to al-Fadl and said to him, "The man is wanted by the Commander of the Faithful. How can we release him after we had arrested him? What will we answer if we are asked about him?"

Being about to unveil his face, he said, "Tell the one who wants him that the man is with al-Fadl ibn al-Rabiʿ. Or tell him that he is with the heir apparent."

The men's leader was no longer in doubt that he was facing al-Fadl. He looked at the men around him and heard one of them whispering to him, "You are talking to an important vizier. This man is al-Fadl himself."

The leader approached him and said, "Why did our lord not tell us right from the beginning who he was? But here we are, and we obey his command." He then beckoned to his men, and they untied Abu al-ʿAtahiya and stood aside, whereupon, Abu al-ʿAtahiya joined al-Fadl's men. His turban had fallen off his head, revealing his disheveled hair and his ugly appearance. When al-Fadl's men brought him to their master, Abu al-ʿAtahiya fell down on his knees and tried to kiss the edge of al-Fadl's robe, but al-Fadl lifted him and said, "What has caused you to fall in this disastrous predicament, when you are known to be an ascetic poet?" And he laughed, thinking that the cause of his arrest was a matter that did not match his ascetic reputation.

Abu al-ʿAtahiya said, "I will tell you the reason, and it will interest you."

Al-Fadl gestured to him to walk with them and ordered his men to get on their horses, and they all went to the palace of al-Amin.

* * *

The leader and his men returned to the palace of al-ʿAbbasa, who had sent them to arrest Abu al-ʿAtahiya on ʿUtba's advice. Meanwhile, what had happened was that when al-ʿAbbasa and ʿUtba returned to the palace toward the end of the night, as we said earlier, ʿUtba remained uneasy about what she had learned concerning Abu al-ʿAtahiya. She was almost sure that he had discovered her mistress' secret. When they reached the palace, al-ʿAbbasa went to her room to sleep. ʿUtba, however, was worried and could not refrain herself from going early to her mistress' room. She told her what she had observed and advised her that Abu al-ʿAtahiya should be promptly arrested lest he divulge her secret. Al-ʿAbbasa was alarmed at the news and was apprehensive. She could think of no solution but to have Abu al-ʿAtahiya arrested in order to keep his story hidden until she could plan her next steps. So she ordered ʿUtba to send a troop of soldiers from those in service at her palace to arrest him by order of the caliph. ʿUtba went with them, and when they reached Phinehas's house, she found that al-Fadl had arrived before her and had entered the House of Slaves. Abu al-ʿAtahiya was determined to leave stealthily so that al-Fadl would not be aware of his presence and find out about his collusion with Phinehas. It did not occur to him that he was wanted, but Hayyan felt that this was the case, so he occupied him with conversation until his master would return from the House of Slaves so that he could tell him what ʿUtba had advised. When Abu al-ʿAtahiya felt that al-Fadl was about to arrive, he hastened to leave. But the soldiers and their leader had arrived, and Hayyan told them to arrest him. They approached him intending to arrest him, but Abu al-ʿAtayiha saw ʿUtba there and immediately understood their purpose, so he began to hold them up until al-Fadl arrived and saved him.

The leader returned to al-ʿAbbasa's palace and told ʿUtba about Abu al-ʿAtahiya's rescue by al-Fadl, and she informed her mistress. Al-ʿAbbasa was greatly disturbed and was sure her secret would soon reach al-Fadl, so she began to lament her bad fortune. She had a private moment with ʿUtba and consulted with her about the matter, and ʿUtba said, "We have no other choice, my mistress, than to seek the help of my lord, the vizier."

"But how can we tell him when he is with my brother in the field, playing polo today?" For that day was scheduled for such games in the field close to the Palace of Eternity.

"We must," she said. "And if you like, I will take it upon myself to convey the news to him."

"Do as you see fit, for I am out of my wits," al-ʿAbbasa said.

"Shall I ask him to come to you here?" she asked.

"Do what you think is right," al-ʿAbbasa said, "for I am afraid our secret will be revealed before we can organize a plan of action to prevent this."

"Leave it to me, God willing," she said.

She started to leave, but al-'Abbasa called her and said, "Take this card to him." She wrote on the card a note that said, "Rush to me at the first moment you can in order to save us from the claws of the enemies."

She gave her the card, and 'Utba concealed it under her robe and went immediately to her room. She disguised herself with the apparel of a messenger coming from Khurasan, wrapped her face with a travel veil, mounted a horse, and hurried to the field, which was near al-'Abbasa's palace.

She reached the field as the sun was crossing the noon meridian. The field was crowded with government officials on their horses and was enclosed by a fence of double ropes tied to poles that cordoned off the place. Soldiers stationed around the rope fence prevented people from entering. 'Utba on horseback stopped and looked at the players in the field in order to locate Ja'far. In one corner of the field, she saw a large pavilion from which al-Rashid emerged on his horse. He was wearing a light turban made specifically for the game, and he was carrying a polo mallet in his hand. The government officials on horseback were ready to play, and each had his polo mallet in his hand. They stood in two opposing lines, in one of which was al-Rashid. She then saw al-Rashid galloping on his horse, polo mallet in hand, and hitting the ball on the ground with his mallet and sending it up in the air. The other players, competing with one another, rushed to meet the ball with their polo mallets and goaded their horses in its direction. Among them was the vizier Ja'far on a black horse. He was wearing a blazer with a wide silk belt around the waist and a cap on his head with a light turban. 'Utba noticed that no one but Ja'far dared approach the caliph in the game. The other players, that is, the government officials, galloped in the field along with the caliph, keeping pace with him. But they did not dare go ahead of him lest any of them should get the better of him, for courtesy required that the caliph should be the winner. Only Ja'far competed with al-Rashid for the ball and played with him; al-Rashid treated him amicably, laughed when Ja'far made an error, and shouted at him in jest. Meanwhile, Ja'far pretended to be unable to defeat him.

The caliph's polo mallet was made of bamboo wrapped with gold braces, and its head was of pure gold. Ja'far's polo mallet was made of bamboo too, but without the gold covering. The polo ball was made of silk floss stuffed in a spherical bag of strong silk, tied with encircling rings of pliable string. A horseman would hit the ball on the ground with the lower edge of his curved mallet and it would go flying in the air, and the other horsemen would urge their horses to follow its movement, their eyes fixed on it and their mallets ready in their hands. The excited horses would be drenched with sweat from being goaded, and the froth from their mouths would mix with the sweat on their necks and chests. But they would not show any exhaustion because they were trained and prepared for a day such as this. Al-Rashid was fond of this game, and his officials sought to gain his favor by mastering it and playing with him.

* * *

Ja'far had spent the past night very worried after he had seen his two sons brought to him by Riyash before being taken to the house of Phinehas. Ja'far had kissed them, smelled their scent, and played with them for a while. He was deeply moved, and his fatherly tenderness toward the two boys was stirred, much as their mother's motherly tenderness was that night. To him, they were as far away as the two bright stars of Ursa Minor, for the caliph's conditions required that they be kept away from the lap of their parents under penalty of death.

Ja'far had spent that night imagining al-'Abbasa embracing her two sons, and he thought about her emotional attachment mixed with the fear of separation and other anxieties. He was greatly disturbed and could not sleep. He had an appointment in the morning to play polo with al-Rashid. So he went in a procession accompanied by his retinue. He exhibited delight even though he knew he was surrounded by envious and slanderous persons. His mind, however, was at rest because he was sure that al-Rashid held him in high esteem and was therefore not afraid of enviers and slanderers. It did not occur to him that al-Rashid might be thinking otherwise under the influence of backbiters. They had tried to incite the caliph's anger against him by alluding to the increasing authority of the Barmakids, their ownership of estates and palaces, and their possession of wealth, the like of which al-Rashid himself did not have. All this in addition to Ja'far's tyrannical hold on matters of state. However, al-Rashid led them to believe that he was not interested in listening to them as they heard him lavish praise on his vizier. He even gave Ja'far a free hand in running the affairs of the common people and the elite, and he permitted him to enter into his presence without prior permission. Furthermore, he handed control of the treasury over to him and gave his father Yahya a free hand in overseeing his houses and palaces and in handling matters of his harem, to the extent that the father was able to lock the gates of the palace and take the keys with him. As was mentioned earlier, al-Rashid wanted very much to enjoy the company of both Ja'far and his sister al-Abbasa at his gatherings and had therefore arranged for them to marry in a legal contract that would not be consummated—a condition that Ja'far had accepted.

However, Ja'far considered his marriage to al-'Abbasa to be not only a legal contract but also a real marriage. He had pretended to acquiesce to al-Rashids' conditions only because he feared his anger. It never crossed his mind that living with al-'Abbasa as man and wife would ever be revealed to anyone. It was as if his success had deluded him and had blinded him to the enviers who surrounded him. His excuse might be that they flattered him and pretended to respect him and to hold him in high esteem. Even though he did notice this, he was so intoxicated with the apparent love of al-Rashid for him and the respect in which he was held, as well as his appreciation of the honors bestowed on him and the constant referral of important matters of state to him, that he deluded himself into feeling safe in consummating his marriage to al-Abbasa.

Chapter 5

Al-'Abbasa's Meeting with Ja'far al-Barmaki

'Utba continued to scrutinize the players until she found Ja'far: he was quite far from her, with men and ropes in between. So she stood there, thinking of how she could deliver the card without anyone noticing. Her eyes fell on one of Ja'far's servants who used to come often to al-'Abbasa's palace on errands and in whom she had confidence. She picked a moment when his friends were not paying attention, and she gestured to him and called, "Hamdan!" and he came to her alone. Hamdan was one of the oldest slave-boys of Ja'far and had grown up in the home of Yahya, Jaf'ar's father, since he was a child. Ja'far himself had grown up in Hamdan's arms as a child. Hamdan was now fifty years old, but he was still nimble and active. He was a Persian from Khurasan and was a favorite of Ja'far; he could enter into his presence whenever he wanted, and Ja'far treated him like a member of the family. When Hamdan heard 'Utba call him by name, he recognized her and realized she was in disguise for an important purpose.

"What brings you here?" he asked.

"I have brought a message for the vizier," she said. "How can I have it delivered to him?"

"They will soon finish playing," he said, "and the vizier will return to his tent to rest. It will then be easy to approach him. Give me the message, and I will deliver it."

'Utba was pleased and gave him the card. He hid it in his pocket and said, "You can now go in peace. I will deliver it to him immediately."

'Utba returned to her mistress and found her waiting for her impatiently. She told her what had happened, and they both sat down waiting on tenterhooks for Ja'far's return.

Al-'Abbasa's palace was located on the bank of the Tigris between Zubayda's palace, called the Abode of Repose, and al-Rashid's house, called the Palace of Eternity. Al-'Abbasa's palace had a balcony overlooking the Tigris and another overlooking the road leading to the polo field, which was the road by which 'Utba had come back. Al-'Abbasa sat on the latter balcony, and she looked out from behind a curtain but saw no one on the road. She waited an excruciatingly long time, her eyes fixed on the horizon. She saw an obscure figure of a man and for a moment thought he was her sweetheart and husband, the vizier of her brother. But he was not. The sun was about to set, the shadows of the minarets were becoming longer on the roofs of Baghdad's palaces. As the sun disappeared, the muezzins called for sunset prayer.

Al-'Abbasa was disturbed by the muezzins' call, although she usually liked to hear it. She was disturbed now because it told her that the day had come to an end and darkness had fallen over the horizon. 'Utba was standing next to her and was no less anxious than her mistress. When she heard the call of the muezzins, she noticed the uneasiness of her mistress so she said, "I think circumstances forced him to be late."

"Why?" al-'Abbasa asked.

"So that he may come to you in secret and unnoticed by the Commander of the Faithful or by others," 'Utba surmised.

"And when was it that my brother has ever noticed his going and coming?" she asked. "He is not accusing him of anything; besides, the keys to the palaces are all in his father's hands... I am afraid there is some disturbing cause for his delay. Since that jar-seller of a poet got to know our secret, I have begun to fear for my life..." She choked on a lump in her throat.

'Utba said, "Don't ever be worried by this thought, my mistress. I am not sure that Abu al-'Atahiya has come to know our secret. I only accused him, and I wanted to have him arrested as a precaution. But suppose he knew it, would he dare mention it to the Commander of the Faithful?"

When al-'Abbasa imagined that possibility, she shuddered at the thought in fear of her brother's anger; for she knew that when angered, he attacked fiercely and there was no way of stopping him. She also knew that no one dared mention anything of the sort to him, but she said, "I am not so much afraid that Abu al-'Atahiya will tell my brother as I am that he might disclose it to one of Ja'far's enviers, and they would then use it as a means to undermine him. And yet, I fear no one as much as I fear that woman."

'Utba understood that her mistress was referring to Zubayda, her brother's wife; for she knew of the rivalry between the two women, a rivalry that usually exists between a wife and her sister-in-law. This rivalry was especially bitter because al-Rashid used to lavish his love on his sister, al-'Abbasa, and could not bear being far from her. On the other hand, his wife, Zubayda, boasted to the other womenfolk of the caliph of her honorable Hashemite lineage as a granddaughter of al-Mansur and a paternal cousin of al-Rashid. Al-Rashid loved her too, respected her, and never rejected a request of hers, but she was not content with that and was jealous of his sister, al-'Abbasa. Perhaps the high esteem in which al-Rashid held his sister intensified his wife's jealousy, especially after she had learned of the relationship of al-'Abbasa and Ja'far.

All this was not unknown to 'Utba, and she was rather more knowledgeable of it than her mistress for, as the saying goes, "News reaches one's ears and stops there." This was especially so in an age when people curried favor with those in high office by flattery and by efforts to satisfy them and avoided telling them what they did not want to hear. A person might have, for example, committed a crime and thought he was successful in concealing it from others when in fact people were gossiping about it in their gatherings. He thought they were unaware of it, but no one dared tell him the truth. So when 'Utba heard al-'Abbasa admit her fear of Zubayda, she said, "I don't see any reason for what you now fear."

Al-'Abbasa asked, "And how is it that you don't see any reason when you know what Zubayda feels toward me, deep in her heart? And if she were to know of this secret, her antagonism would become much greater!"

'Utba said, smiling, "Do you think Zubayda does not know?"

"Does she?" al-'Abbasa asked in alarm. "Who told her?"

'Utba replied, "You are a wise and rational woman, and someone like you is not deceived by appearances. How can it occur to you that it will remain unknown to the people, when my lord, the vizier, enters this palace when he likes without any hindrance...?"

Al-'Abbasa said, interrupting her, "Do the people of the palace know that too?"

'Utba was now afraid how all this would affect her mistress. She said, "No. But I think Zubayda must have known from the reports she receives from her spies and followers. But that does not mean that she will divulge it to her husband. For she knows that no one dares mention anything of the sort to the Commander of the Faithful—if not in fear of him, then in fear of my lord, the vizier, for he is a very powerful man of the state and can do or undo anything. Who dares harm him?"

Darkness shrouded the balcony where they both sat, while the rest of the palace was shining with lights and candles, its people unaware of the condition of their mistress and her inner feelings. None of the palace slave-girls, eunuchs, or the others had the privilege of sitting with her or knowing what was in her heart. Only 'Utba did, because she had been al-'Abbasa's companion since childhood at the palace of her father, al-Mahdi, and therefore al-'Abbasa trusted her.

She talked to 'Utba that evening, with her eyes constantly fixed on the horizon, even though it was dark. But her eyes often turned unwillingly to the beaming lights in the Palace of Eternity on her right and to those of the Abode of Repose on her left. Each palace harbored a watchful observer that she feared. When she felt Ja'far was overly late, she became very anxious. She stood up and said, "Let us go to the balcony overlooking the Tigris, perhaps he is coming that way..."

All of a sudden, they both heard the sound of footsteps in the corridor leading to the balcony. When al-'Abbasa heard that sound, her heart fluttered, for it resembled the sound of Ja'far's footsteps, and she said, "I think he has come." 'Utba walked in front of her and said, "Go to your far room, mistress, and I will bring him to you. No observer can spy on you in that room."

Al-'Abbasa complied and went to the room. 'Utba headed for the corridor, which had lit candles all along its walls. She saw Ja'far entering, wearing the official 'Abbasid black attire: the black outer garment and tall headgear. She approached him and kissed his hand, but before she could say a word, he asked, "Where is your mistress?"

"In her room," she said. "She has been awaiting you for several hours."

He walked on and 'Utba followed to the door of the room. She helped him take off his shoes and then retreated into a far corner as she usually did.

Ja'far was thirty-seven years old at that time. He had a cheerful and handsome face, a joyful appearance, and eyes that shone with intelligence. He was of medium height; he had chestnut-colored hair and a light beard and mustache; his hair was only lightly peppered with grey. He had cocked his headgear slightly backward; his white forehead was visible and his face showed signs of concern. Whoever has delicate sensibility and strong emotions will show his feelings on his face; he cannot suppress them. Nor can he bear injustice. This is the nature of his temperament. Some people have a sharp temper, and they become angry quickly; others are very patient, and they are tolerant. In between these two extremes, there are many degrees of dispositions. Ja'far wore his heart on his sleeve; this was contrary to al-Fadl ibn al-Rabi' who was inscrutable.

* * *

Al-'Abbasa was standing in her room, shaking as a result of extreme contradictory emotions of love, fear, rebuke, and hope. Although her room was large with its embellishments—its candelabra, its pictures hanging on the walls, and its carpets spread on the floor—she felt trapped in a little box. Waiting for Ja'far at that moment felt longer than waiting for him most of that day. Then she heard his footsteps at the door and heard 'Utba take off his shoes, put them on the shelf made for that purpose, and then withdraw.

As he entered, al-'Abbasa approached him, wearing a simple gown she usually wore when they met. Her hair was braided in one plait that she gathered on top of her head with a gem-studded pin. Over her gown, she wore a silk shawl embellished with verses of poetry embroidered on its edges in gold thread. Her anxiety had left a frown on her facial features that only increased her awe-inspiring appearance and beauty. On seeing

Ja'far she smiled and forgot the words of complaint she had rehearsed. The apprehensions she had imagined dissipated, and she felt the sheer delight she had become accustomed to whenever she met her lover. This is the case of true love, for it always overcomes all the causes of misery. A person in love forgets all difficulties when meeting the beloved and is thus distracted from all else. Love is a source of real happiness, and misery only makes it stronger—very much like gold, which only becomes more resplendent and pure when exposed to fire.

In spite of al-'Abbasa's love for Ja'far and her wholehearted dedication to his happiness and comfort, he could not forget that her lineage, as was clear to all people of that age, was considered to be more honorable than his. For she was a Hashemite Arab, the daughter of a caliph, and the sister of another caliph, while he was a Persian and a foreigner who, despite the status and power he had achieved, was still considered a mere *mawla,* or a foreign member of an Arab tribe. Since the beginning of Islam and until this time, no person among the non-Arabs, whatever power or high rank he had achieved, could aspire to any position similar to the one which Ja'far had reached—not even kings and potentates. The first who dared do so was the Seljuk Sultan Tughrul Bey, who wanted to marry the daughter of the 'Abbasid caliph, al-Qa'im Bi'amr-illah; the caliph was upset by his request and only consented to the marriage under duress in the year 454 AH (1062 AD), when the 'Abbasid caliphs were in a period of decline. But conditions were not so during the reign of al-Rashid, which was the golden age of the 'Abbasids. With this in mind, Ja'far's fear of having his relationship with al-'Abbasa revealed is understandable, as well as his apprehension of al-Rashid's knowledge that this marriage had been consummated. Al-Rashid considered the fictitious marriage he granted Ja'far as a subterfuge for him to see al-'Abbasa with Ja'far in public a great favor he had granted his vizier, his friend, and the person who was completely in charge of all matters of state. But for Ja'far, the power of love swept all caution and reason to the wind!

When the two lovers met, they forgot why they had come together, for as the poet nicknamed the Madman of Layla said:

O Layla, how many an important thing of mine
Do I forget as soon I come to you at night!

Then al-'Abbasa remembered the danger that threatened her, so she began the conversation. She flirtatiously began to rebuke Ja'far, which is the way lovers begin a conversation as a pretext to move to reciprocal complaints. In this manner they clear their hearts, increase their mutual attraction, and kindle the fires of passion. She said, "Why has it not pleased Ja'far to respond to al-'Abbasa's request until now?"

Looking at her as the infatuated man he was, he answered, "Al-'Abbasa's request is one that cannot be rejected, but conditions required that I delay my coming in fear of the prying eyes of spying observers. I have finally come by boat on the Tigris, and asked my slave-boy to bring my horse here so that I may ride it back."

She then knew why she did not see him from the balcony when he arrived.

She sat on an embroidered silk cushion holding his hand and asked him to sit down next to her. He felt the coolness of her hand and her shivers. He sat on another cushion close to her, careful not to look away from her, and waited for her next words. She said in a trembling voice, "How long should we tolerate these precautions, Ja'far? Is it not high time that we lived or died?"

He thought she was alluding to the fear they had as to what al-Rashid might do. He sighed and said, "Destiny has ordained that we should both suffer, because it has placed a curtain of honorable lineage between you and me: it made you one of the honored descendants of the tribe of Hashem, Prophet Muhammad's folks, and made me a *mawla,* one of the non-Arab clients."

She said with a reproachful look, "It is an illusory curtain. You are indeed more exalted in spirit than those honorable descendants, and you are higher in my esteem than all the tribe of Hashem. But..." And she fell silent.

He said, "You have asked me to come in a hurry. Has anything new happened?"

Having overcome her worries and confused feelings after seeing him, she said, as her fears returned, with tears in her eyes, "Yes... We should either die or live, for I can no longer bear the fears we are suffering."

He was taken aback and said, "Of the things that we have feared so far, what has really happened? As for death, I will readily die for the sake of your comfort and happiness."

She said in a trembling voice, "Our affair has been revealed, and my brother will soon know our secret." And she choked.

He was alarmed and said, "What secret? Who discovered it? How and when?"

She said, "Our secret was revealed yesterday when I was at the home of Phinehas with our two sons, while I was kissing them and being happy to be with them."

"And who discovered it?" he asked. "Who dared?"

"Abu al-'Atahiya, may he be cursed."

"Abu al-'Atahiya?" Ja'far shouted in alarm. "He must be killed immediately."

"I too wanted to have him killed," al-'Abbasa said, "and I sent a troop of soldiers to arrest him this morning at that house, but he was able to escape."

"How did he manage to escape from the soldiers?" he asked. "May they perish!"

She replied, "The one who saved him was your vicious enemy."

"Which one of them?" he asked. "They are many."

"True, they are many," she said. "But I mean the one who is most envious of you and the one among them who tries most to harm and slander you. Don't you know who he is?"

"I think you mean al-Fadl ibn al-Rabi'," he said.

"Indeed, I do," she said, and burst out weeping.

Ja'far's anger flared up on seeing her weep. He was infuriated and said, "Al-Fadl ibn al-Rabi'—what a despicable scoundrel, may God disgrace him! Did he not fear my power? Was he not afraid of my sword? How did he dare commit this insolence?"

She said, "He dared because he is a close favorite of Muhammad al-Amin, the son of Zubayda whose influence over the caliph you know well. He happened to be at the House of Slaves to buy some singing slave-girls for that dissolute boy, Muhammad. As he was leaving, he saw our soldiers about to arrest Abu al-'Atahiya, who then asked for his help. My maid 'Utba saw Abu al-'Atahiya signal to him with eyes promising to reveal a secret of great importance. So he asked his men to intervene and saved him. He threatened our men, so they left Abu al-'Atahiya and came back to tell me the story. I was very angry and did not know what to do. My trustworthy maid suggested that I should let you know immediately, so she went to have my note delivered to you while you were playing polo. She gave it to your servant Hamdan, who passed it on to you. I waited for you for hours that seemed as long as eternity, until you finally appeared. This is my story, what do you make of it? I feel that I am not safe here for even an hour, and it seems to me that the very stones of Baghdad and the water of the Tigris know my secret. And I feel as though my own servants and my slave-girls are soldiers about to arrest me. If the danger had been a threat only to me, my affliction would have been easy to bear. But I am afraid of my brother's anger and violence and the harm he can do to you." Saying this, she cried and took out her handkerchief to wipe off her tears.

Ja'far listened, his eyes staring at her, his heart racing, and his beard shaking with anger. When she stopped talking, his emotions were boiling and he was burning with anger. He suddenly stood up and said, "Don't be afraid, my love. They will not touch a hair of yours, or they will all be put to death."

She held the edge of his black garment and made him sit down, saying, "Don't let anger overcome you, for the matter needs reflection and clear vision. Your opponent is the caliph himself, the Commander of the Faithful, and he has the support of the Hashemite tribe and the rest of the Arabs, their parties, and their soldiers. And remember, you have enviers who expect you to make a false step, and they will use it as a pretext to harm you. I am afraid you will expose yourself to ruin if you face this situation unprepared."

* * *

Ja'far smiled, but his lips were taut and his eyes smoldered. He said, "Don't think that your lover speaks haphazardly. I have a solution prepared for every eventuality. Not one of those honorable people of the tribe of Hashem and the other statesmen whom you referred to is siding with al-Rashid, for I have lavished gifts on them and they are in the palm of my hand because of what they owe me. I have not given them extravagantly without a purpose, and I have not been overly generous to them without an aim. I considered this to be a price to be paid for any problems such as the ones we now face or even worse ones. As for the soldiers, I must say that the Persian generals are all resentful of your brother because of his excessive persecution of the followers of ʿAli.[10] In Khurasan, I have thousands who take orders from me, and they are all hostile to the ʿAbbasids since the time when your grandfather, Abu Jaʿfar al-Mansur, killed Abu Muslim al-Khurasani, his general and the one who established the ʿAbbasid state for him. Excuse me for speaking out to you so frankly about all of this; I have never told anyone else about these matters. And don't be angry on hearing what you have just heard about your grandfather and brother, for I was only pressed to do so by the fear that you expressed."

When she heard his words, she was awed by his boldness, and she bowed her head. But she said nothing, so he asked, "Are you afraid of what you have just heard? If you object to my opposition to your brother, the caliph, say so."

She raised her head and looking at him straight in the eyes said, "I am not ashamed of speaking my mind, after having heard you speak yours. You should know that no one in the world concerns me more than you. Every enemy of yours is my enemy too, and I don't exclude anyone. But I am afraid you are embarking on an action that is too dangerous and that need not be so. You should know, my love, that I have no desire in this world but to be beside you, with our two sons, the fruit of our love. It matters little to me if I am with you in a palace or in a hut, for I am disgusted with palaces and all that is in them and around them. Find a way to escape from this city, and let us go to a place where we have no fear of anyone or anything. Let us forget about the vizierate, the caliphate, and power—for these worldly concerns are all loathsome. After all, no matter how long a human being lives and however vast his power is, nothing remains of him in the end except the span of one's outspread arms of earth where he will be buried." She then began to weep, holding her handkerchief to her eyes.

---

10 Al-Rashid suspected that the followers of ʿAli were preparing to depose him and proclaim their leader as caliph to replace him.

When he heard her words and saw her crying, he almost cried with her—but managed to hold himself together in a show of endurance. He was affected by what she had said about their two sons. He bowed his head and pushed back his headgear from his forehead as he thought of what his haste in rashly showing hostility might drag him into. He returned to his sober self and realized that her approach was much safer. So he said to her as he removed her hands from her eyes, "Don't cry, my love. I will do what you want. You are right, unhurried action is worthier of judicious, resolute people. I have an idea that I think you will agree with."

She smiled, the tears still lingering in her eyes, and she looked at him inquisitively. He smiled and said, "It is not likely that the news will reach your brother, as you fear; for there is not a single statesman, be it al-Fadl or others, who will dare mention you to your brother or even hint to him about our secret. Trust me—I am the best judge of people in these matters. We have nothing to fear in this regard for a long time, and in the meantime we will plan to escape from Baghdad and go to a safe place."

She looked up and asked, "And how will we do that?"

"I told you," he continued, "that Khurasan is on my side, and its people are at my beck and call. When I am there, neither your brother nor anybody else can threaten me; this is to say nothing of the Shi'a groups, the followers of 'Ali, who will fight on my side to the last breath. Isn't that so?"

"Yes, indeed," she said.

"For a long time," he said, "I have been trying to rid myself of the vizierate and obtain the governorship of Khurasan instead. Your brother has promised it to me, and if I ask for it tomorrow, he will give it to me."

"Is that true?" al-'Abbasa asked. "I am afraid that there is some deceit in his promise, for he cannot be trusted to keep a promise like this one."

Ja'far said, "He did promise it to me and assured me of his promise several times. My enviers and slanderers will also help. Their calumnies should send me far from the caliph's court so they can increase their influence in my absence. Just a word from me is enough to realize this wish."

Her face brightened revealing her joy, and she said, "Do, by all means, hasten to realize it, for I see no better scheme for us. If you go to Khurasan, I will follow you in no time, and we will have our sons brought to us. We will then live in happiness, and I am sure al-Rashid will not bother us there because he will fear for the stability of his rule."

He said, "Be at ease, the matter will be quickly dealt with."

She said, "I feel that my anxiety is beginning to dissipate, for I believe, as you said, that they will not dare mention the news of the two boys to my brother because they know his zeal in protecting the honor of his womenfolk. I am certain that he will kill anyone who knows our secret."

He said, "You are, therefore, in agreement with my plan."

She said, "Yes, it is an excellent one." Then she added, gnashing her teeth, "Oh, may this wish be realized and may our sons be with us and you be my husband in public, as you are in reality even if my brother refuses to acknowledge it and enviers hate it!"

Preparing to stand up, he said, "How I would love to stay here and not be separated from you, my dear! But I must leave, because I have come stealthily in accordance with our decision to keep our relationship concealed. I must leave quickly in order not to give informers an opportunity to slander us."

She held him by the hand and made him sit down, saying, "No. Don't go, for I..." And then she choked.

He said, "I see that your fears have come back. Don't be afraid, for we shall meet soon, God willing!"

She said, "We shall, indeed, for we have not committed any offense, and our marriage is lawful. It is only my brother who is tyrannically stubborn and has forbidden us from what God has permitted. Was he not the one who asked you to marry me?"

"Yes, indeed," he said, shaking his head in disdain. "But he does not think others have a right to enjoy themselves like he does."

He got up and she did likewise. He held her hand to bid her farewell, but he could not get himself to say good-bye. So he stood for a while looking at her, and she looked at him, their eyes understanding what words could not express. He then adjusted his headgear with his other hand and walked away, and she walked by his side. He said, "Be at ease until my messenger brings you good news."

Feeling unable to let his hand go, she replied, "Go, my master, with the Lord's protection. May God help you to achieve your goal."

He backed away, gave her a reproving look, and said, "Don't say 'my master' to me. I am your *mawla,* and you are my mistress, according to their law and tradition. Who am I compared with the sister of the Commander of the Faithful?"

When he said that, she pulled her hand away from his, looked askance at him, and said in a coquettish reproof, "Let us not talk about their law and tradition, for you are my master in God's law and the tradition of the just."

He laughed and quickly took back her hand, saying, "May God be with you until we meet again, and I hope that after that we will never separate again. For now, I think I should refrain from visiting you until I have arranged a plan for us to meet in a safe place."

She said, "It will be difficult for me not to see you, but I shall tolerate that in the hope that you will achieve what you have set out to do."

Then she clapped to call 'Utba, in her customary way, and 'Utba came quickly. She said to her, "Escort your master until he leaves the palace discreetly."

With a gesture of obedience, 'Utba walked in front of him in the corridor whose candles were now extinguished. He followed until he left the palace and reached a place where his horse and his servant Hamdan were waiting. He mounted his horse and went home.

Al-'Abbasa was alone, but she remained standing and listening to Ja'far's footsteps until she could hear them no longer. Then her apprehensions returned, and she felt a need for 'Utba. When she came back, 'Utba recounted some of her conversation with Ja'far, who told her of his plan; al-'Abbasa was comforted and went to bed.

* * *

Meanwhile, al-Fadl ibn al-Rabi' returned home from the House of Slaves with his retinue and Abu al-'Atahiya. The latter was angry at 'Utba and her mistress. If 'Utba had not intended to harm him in that fashion, some remorse might have arisen in his heart and he might have considered keeping al-'Abbasa's secret, despite what he hoped to gain by divulging it. He might have had pity on the two boys, or he might have felt awkward toward al-'Abbasa or have been afraid of Ja'far or al-Rashid. Or he might perhaps have postponed revealing the secret for a while until he found an opportunity to offer it to al-Fadl or somebody else. But 'Utba's intention to harm him absolved him of any remorse and encouraged him to reveal the secret. The presence of al-Fadl ibn al-Rabi' gave him the perfect opportunity to do so

Al-Fadl's *cortège* proceeded toward the palace of al-Amin and had to cross the Baghdad Bridge. After leaving the street of the House of Slaves, they passed by the polo field on its north side, and they saw dignitaries of the state coming to the festivities of the polo game. They went behind the stable on the road leading to the bridge. The sun was at its zenith, and the bridge was crowded. The bridge consisted of boats next to each other and bound together by ropes or iron chains; over them were planks of wood on which people and animals crossed the bridge. Al-Fadl knew that the bridge had guards who secretly observed all those crossing it, for it was common in those days for people to spy on one another.

Before leaving the House of Slaves, he had covered his face and so had his followers. They crossed the bridge and went north to al-Rusafa. From there, they turned southeast to al-Mukharrim and stayed close to the river bank most of the way until they reached the palace. Al-Fadl went early to the House of Slaves to accomplish the task he had undertaken and return to al-Amin before noon so as not to miss the happy hour of morning drinking with him; he would thus fulfill his promise to have him hear the white slave-girls sing on that same day. He was keen on pleasing him and remaining close to him by doing all that made him happy because he knew that al-Amin was the heir apparent to al-Rashid and that there was no way to harm the Barmakids except through him. For al-Amin hated the Persians, and the Barmakids in particular—and

Ja'far ibn Yahya most of all because he had helped have his brother al-Ma'mun designated as his successor, notwithstanding the fact that al-Ma'mun's mother was a slave-girl while al-Amin's own mother, Zubayda, was a Hashemite.[11]

---

11 Al-Rashid had designated first al-Amin and then al-Ma'mun as successive heirs to him and made both swear at the Ka'ba to abide by his wishes. *Translator's Note.*

Chapter 6

Ja'far Ibn al-Hadi

Al-Fadl thought that he deserved precedence over the Barmakids in running the affairs of the state and politics, in facilitating the collection of taxes, and in pleasing al-Rashid. But when al-Rashid entrusted Ja'far al-Barmaki with the reins of the state and gave him a free hand, al-Fadl resorted to ruses in order to undermine the Barmakids. He was a shrewd and patient man, so when he saw that al-Amin hated the Persians, he sided with him and drew himself closer to him by all possible means. He did not have to go himself to the House of Slaves, but by doing so wanted to prove to al-Amin that he was loyal to him and had dedicated himself to his service with heart and soul.

However, having been preoccupied with viewing the various kinds of slave-girls and distracted by Abu al-'Atahiya's problem and arrest, he was delayed a little and he reached al-Amin's palace after midday. Yet he thought he should know Abu al-'Atahiya's secret before being in the presence of al-Amin, although it was not in his nature to hastily seek information. He was one of those people with a choleric or bilious temperament, who are patient with matters and are not anxious about appointments or hasty in seeking knowledge of a secret. On the other hand, people with a sanguine or nervous temperament when promised a secret or a piece of news remain anxious and troubled until they discover it. That is why persons of the latter temperament do not do well in politics or at embarking on difficult projects that require effort, control of feelings, long waiting periods, and delays.

Yes, al-Fadl ibn al-Rabi' was not one who is hasty in seeking knowledge for its own sake, but instead only seeking it to help him achieve his aims. When he approached al-Amin's palace, he ordered his men to go with their horses to their assigned places. He and Abu al-'Atahiya dismounted and walked along a wide passageway shaded by trees on both sides and ending in a large courtyard. In the front of the courtyard was the gate of the palace or, rather, the gate of the garden in which the palace stood on the side facing the Tigris. It had its own surrounding wall. When building palaces in those days, it was customary to make their outer walls strong and high, like the walls of a fortress. On the higher parts of the walls, there often were parapets for archers to shoot arrows or battlements where ballista stones could be hurled because of the expectation of political disturbances and the struggles for power. The gate of the garden was large and strong; it was closed and locked; only with much effort was it possible to open it. Guards constantly stood guard at the closed gate. When someone came, they opened it for him; if he was on horseback, he dismounted outside the gate and left his horse with the groom, or sent it to the stable next to the wall which had stalls for the animals. The palace of the heir apparent had many such places, for there were many people currying favor with him. They frequented him to gain influence when he became caliph and assumed the reins of power.

Al-Fadl and Abu al-'Atahiya withdrew to a secluded place on the side of the road. As the latter began to relay al-'Abbasa's story, the former listened in amazement almost doubting the truth of what he was hearing. But after listening to the whole story, he soon thought it was most likely true. He bowed his head for some time, and then he looked at Abu al-'Atahiya and wanted to be sure there was no mistaking what he had heard. He said, "Take care! I hope you have not invented this story, for I don't believe it. Perhaps you have been deceived into thinking it really happened. Our mistress al-'Abbasa is one of the farthest people from such a suspicion. Beware of mentioning it to anyone lest you find yourself in the worst situation your deeds have ever caused you."

Abu al-'Atahiya understood al-Fadl's purpose in questioning the truth of his story, and he played along, saying, "I too believe our mistress is far above this, but I have told you what I saw. I would not have revealed this to you had you not saved me. Yet, I don't know whether my eyes deceived me, for they often deceive a person who can see and he falls into a pit in which a blind man would not fall!" Saying this, he shrugged his shoulders and then bowed his head as if to say, "What is all this to me? It is none of my business, is it?"

Al-Fadl knew of Abu al-'Atahiya's love for money and did not doubt that he had told him the story in the hope of some gain. So he wanted to please him, for he might need him in the future. He took out a small bag of money from his pocket and gave it to him, saying, "You are a poet, and poets are accustomed to receive a gift whenever they speak, even if it is not poetry. Take this little prize, and you will receive many others from our master, al-Amin. He will be happy about our success in buying white slave-girls for him. I will tell him that you helped us in obtaining them." Saying this, he guffawed in a fake manner and placed his hand on Abu al-'Atahiya's shoulder saying, "God bless you!" And he walked on.

Abu al-'Atahiya felt that al-Fadl wanted to go alone, so he said good-bye to him and kissed his hand. Al-Fadl said, "Beware of going to a place that the vizier knows, for they will arrest you and harm you. It is safer for you to stay in this palace with some of my men or go to my house and reside there. At any rate, don't wander very far from me." Abu al-'Atahiya bowed his head and left.

As for al-Fadl, he removed the cover from his face, for he was now safe, and walked to the garden's courtyard. He saw the gate wide open and the guards talking to a group of strangers who were from Basra, judging by their appearance. They were mostly servants or grooms, and some of them were tethering horses or arranging their harness. Looking inside the garden, he knew they were the attendants of Ja'far ibn Musa al-Hadi, whom he saw walking with al-Amin in the garden. As soon as al-Fadl approached the gate, the guards recognized him and hurried to open the way for him and be of service to him.

Al-Hadi had assumed the caliphate before his brother, al-Rashid, but he did not remain in power long for the following reasons. Their father, al-Mahdi, had designated his two sons, Musa al-Hadi and Harun al-Rashid, to be his heirs apparent on condition that al-Hadi would assume the caliphate first and then al-Rashid after him. When al-Mahdi died in 169 AH, he was succeeded by al-Hadi, who thought of deposing his brother, al-Rashid, and designating his son, Ja'far, as heir apparent so that the rule would remain in his own progeny. He consulted his private counselors and they agreed with him, so al-Rashid was deposed and Ja'far was declared heir apparent. Al-Rashid could not resist because he had no supporters to help him, the statesmen having all sided with the caliph except Yahya ibn Khalid al-Barmaki. The latter came to al-Rashid, heartened him, and assured him he would help him become caliph, disregarding the risk to his life if his desire to keep al-Rashid as heir apparent and depose Ja'far ibn al-Hadi had become known. But al-Hadi learned of this, imprisoned Yahya, and threatened to kill him. Yahya was able with his judiciousness and strong arguments to persuade al-Hadi to keep his brother, al-Rashid, as heir apparent until Ja'far would come of age, at which time al-Hadi would depose al-Rashid and designate Ja'far as heir apparent. A short time after al-Hadi accepted this compromise, he fell sick and died suddenly, having ruled only one year and three months. It was rumored in those days that his mother, al-Khayzuran, had hastened his death. She had become furious when he prevented her from managing the affairs of state; moreover she was earnestly concerned for his brother, al-Rashid. Upon the death of al-Hadi, Yahya al-Barmaki went by night straight to al-Rashid and announced to him the good news of his rise to the position of caliph and acknowledged him as such. Al-Rashid was grateful for this support, which resulted in Yahya having great influence with the caliph. Al-Rashid never acted on any important matter without first consulting him; he also appointed Yahya's son, Ja'far, as a vizier with great authority to act on all matters of state.

Ja'far ibn al-Hadi was a boy at the time of his father's death and had no choice but to keep quiet. But, in his heart, he bore a grudge against Yahya and his sons because he believed al-Rashid colluded with Yahya and al-Khayzuran to kill his father and usurp the caliphate from him. He suppressed these feelings for years, during which time he resided in Basra, where al-Rashid had given him a large estate and assigned him a big salary like the other Hashemites.

In those times, politics dictated that a person in power should be generous to others in order to pacify any ill will they may harbor. Whoever reached the position of caliph knew that he was being envied— and mostly by his own relatives. If he was wise, he provided them liberally with income and acted generously toward them; furthermore, he distracted them with all kinds of luxury and revelry to prevent them from aspiring to the caliphate and rising against him. That is why during the rule of al-Rashid and his successors, the Hashemites were among those who indulged most in luxury and revelry; they had no occupation other than to select singers, enjoy eating and drinking in gardens, and own various kinds of slave-girls as singers, concubines, and servants. Most often, they resided in their palaces in Basra, and they came to Baghdad only to receive their salaries or to buy slave-girls, necessities, and the like. For the most part, the caliph would send them their salaries while they resided in their palaces.

Like other Hashemites, Ja'far ibn al-Hadi received his salary as he resided in his palace in Basra, but luxury and revelry did not attenuate the grudge he bore in his heart against his uncle, al-Rashid, and Yahya al-Barmaki and his sons. The fact that Ja'far al-Barmaki was given a free hand in the affairs of the state increased his jealousy and resentment. However, he still hoped that the caliphate would revert to him at the death of al-Rashid, but when he learned that the latter had given his own sons, al-Amin and al-Ma'mun, the right to succeed him, he realized this was not to be and that he needed to avenge himself and act. He looked for ways of revenge and for persons to help him, until he came across al-Fadl ibn al-Rabi'. They discovered their mutual hatred for Ja'far al-Barmaki and their general dissatisfaction with the ruling group, so they began to support each other in working to overthrow the current government. Ja'far ibn al-Hadi's first aim was to remove Ja'far al-Barmaki from the vizierate in order to facilitate the removal of al-Ma'mun as heir apparent, which this vizier had helped him attain. Only al-Amin would then remain as an obstacle between him and the caliphate: his removal would then be easier because of his extreme weakness. To achieve his aim, Ja'far ibn al-Hadi would use similar means as those of al-Rashid in keeping his own caliphate—namely, showering the Hashemites with luxury and opulence and providing slave-girls and amusements to distract them from seeking the caliphate.

When he saw al-Amin indulging in luxury and revelry, he encouraged him instead of restraining him, urging him to indulge in them more—even if that would lead him to occasionally appear dissolute and shameless himself. Al-Amin was unaware of this and oblivious to the danger of plots and designs being woven around him by self-interested parties. When Ja'far ibn al-Hadi arrived in Baghdad a few days earlier, al-Amin welcomed him and gave him a private palace near his own to reside in with his retinue, and they spent most days together in amusement and carousal, from morning till evening. And it was Ja'far ibn al-Hadi who suggested to al-Amin's that he buy white singing slave-girls and urged al-Fadl ibn al-Rabi' to set out at dawn to purchase them and bring them back before the happy hour of the morning drinking elapsed so that they might all enjoy hearing their beautiful voices as early as possible.

Al-Amin was concerned when al-Fadl was delayed, so he went to a balcony overlooking the Tigris and sat there, his eyes constantly looking out for al-Fadl, who might be returning by boat. When noontime passed and al-Fadl had not returned, al-Amin tired of waiting, and so he went out to the garden with his cousin, Ja'far ibn al-Hadi. They both looked in delight at the cages that were as large as houses, some of which contained various kinds of colored birds brought from India and central Africa; then they looked at other cages made of iron and housing different kinds of animals such as lions, elephants, and tigers. When they finished and al-Fadl had not yet returned, al-Amin ordered the man responsible for the rams to bring them out for a butting match. He then went to sit in a gazebo shaded by a high trellis in the middle of the garden. As he was about to enter it with his cousin, a servant came to inform him that al-Fadl had arrived, so he ordered that he be led to the trellis, thinking that the slave-girls were with him.

Al-Fadl entered the garden and saw the prince and his cousin walking toward the trellis. The garden was divided into planting beds, and it had intersecting paths on which colored gravel was strewn. Various kinds of beautiful trees grew along the paths, some native to Baghdad and others imported from India, Khurasan, and Turkestan. In addition, there were many kinds of aromatic plants with colorful flowers. All was coordinated in the best manner, for the gardener took care of the plants and trees with a clipper, making some look like animals, others like a peacock or other beautiful bird, and still others fashioned in the shape of whales or wild beasts. Whoever entered the garden and saw these trees and plants imagined they were crouching lions or moving birds.

Between these planting beds, there were basins fed by invisible streams. They contained beautifully colored fish of various shapes and sizes, and the gardener fed them bread crumbs and leftover food from the excess of the princes' kitchens—those were days of bounty and prosperity. The pathways of the garden were decorated with figures of living creatures and inanimate objects made with colorful, gravel-like mosaics; these were shaped into flowers, birds, lions, elephants, and other animals or objects.

These artistic figures were undertaken by Persian, Byzantine, or Indian craftsmen who were experts in agriculture and skillful in artistic arrays and layouts.

The fragrant flowers in the garden did not compare with the sweet scent of perfume, especially musk, exuding from the clothes of al-Amin, the heir apparent. It was customary for people at amusement parties to take off their official clothes and to put on clothing of red, yellow, or green colors, called "clothes of boon companionship." They usually consisted of a fine, diaphanous cape and a wrap so well polished and smooth that it almost stood firm. Instead of a turban or a tall headgear on one's head, one wore a diadem of flowers and aromatic plants beautifully woven by the gardener to resemble a tiara, and on one's feet, one wore light sandals from Sind. Al-Amin's companion, Ja'far ibn al-Hadi, was wearing similar clothing, but his wrap was green, and on his head he wore a cap encircled by a small headband of expensive embroidery. He had combed his hair in the fashion of Baghdad's young men of those days, that is, he let it down on his forehead to the level of his eyebrows, then turned it around his ears and let it hang down his temples.

Al-Amin and his cousin sat under the trellis waiting for the rams, but he was more anxious to see al-Fadl because he expected the slave-girls to be with him. When he heard his footsteps on the gravel near the trellis, he asked aloud, "What news have you for us, O Fadl?"

"Nothing but good news, my lord," he answered.

"And where is the singing slave-girl or the other slave-girls?" al-Amin asked.

"They will be here soon," al-Fadl answered.

When al-Amin realized that al-Fadl had noticed the clothes he was wearing, he asked, "How do you like this diadem and these clothes?"

"You look like an angel in the form of a man," al-Fadl replied.

At that time, al-Amin was seventeen years old. His cheeks had begun to show the fluff of his growing beard, and his youthful face was full of life. He was handsome, tall, and of white complexion; he had small eyes, an aquiline nose, and lank hair falling down on the sides of his face. He was strong-bodied and muscular and could face a lion with no fear. He possessed valor, bravery, eloquence, refinement, as well as the gift of amiable and light-hearted chatter. When one met him, one was awed by him and loved him. But he had bad judgment and was extravagant and frivolous. His main interest was amusement and revelry and owning slave-girls and slave-boys. Perhaps he was led to these excesses by those with ill intentions who wanted to undermine his suitability to rule and by those who desired to please him only to seek his generous gifts. As for Ja'far ibn al-Hadi, he was slender-bodied, handsome-looking, and short of stature, and he had a light beard and sharp eyes. He was older than al-Amin and of better judgment, but he encouraged al-Amin's revelry and amusement for his own purposes.

* * *

When al-Fadl entered the trellis, al-Amin said to him, "Take off this robe and put on the clothes of boon companionship. Your lateness should not deprive us of the joy and pleasure we had planned, and although the time for the morning drinking hour has passed, let us spend the rest of the day enjoying music and conviviality."

He then clapped and a handsome Turkish slave-boy whose beard had not yet grown came to him. He wore a loose red garment with a wide silk belt on his waist, embroidered with gold thread. He had a long braid hanging down his back. On his head, he wore a pyramid-shaped hat embroidered with gold thread; it was cocked to one side, and on its top was a silver crescent that was too heavy for it to remain straight up, so the top bent a little. The slave-boy looked more like a girl than a boy because of his delicate features. If one heard him speak, one would think he was a girl because his voice was high pitched, for he was a eunuch. In al-Amin's palace, there were many like him whom he had brought from the far lands of the Turks and the Circassians and whom he had divided into groups to serve him and to wait on his convivial gatherings.

The slave-boy stood politely, and al-Amin asked him, "I wonder, what poets are standing at our gate?"

The slave-boy replied, "Abu Nuwas al-Hasan ibn Hani', as well as Abu al-'Atahiya and..."

Interrupting him, al-Amin said, "Forget Abu al-'Atahiya, for he is one of the ascetics. His asceticism will not serve us in our gathering. As for al-Hasan ibn Hani', he is the right man for it, and he is a charming poet." Saying this, he laughed and turned to the slave-boy, saying, "Send away all the poets but admit Ibn Hani'. And tell the barman to prepare for us a fabulous party full of amusements."

Al-Fadl said, "Abu al-'Atahiya is not a bad poet, my lord. He is a charming poet, and don't believe what they say about his asceticism."

Shouting to the slave-boy, al-Amin said, "And Abu al-'Atahiya too."

The slave-boy bowed his head in a gesture of obedience and left.

Chapter 7

At al-Amin's Gathering

When al-Amin grew tired of waiting for the rams, he asked one of his slave-boys, "Where is the man responsible for the rams? I would like my cousin to see two rams butting one another, the likes of which he will see neither in Baghdad or Basra, nor in all of Iraq."

The slave-boy said, "They have been ready for butting for an hour, but he has not brought them here because he was afraid they would tear out the floor mosaics under the trellis with their hooves during their butting. Besides, the rams don't have all their strength when fighting on gravel. If my lord wishes, he can move to where the rams are now standing just behind this trellis."

"Fine," al-Amin said as he stood up and walked. Ibn al-Hadi and al-Fadl followed him, winking at one another with regard to the childish games preoccupying the heir apparent of the Muslims as though each one of them was thinking, *How can a caliphate continue to remain strong if this is its heir apparent? How can someone in his condition be able to rule a kingdom stretching from the Indian Ocean to the shores of the Ocean of Darkness (the Atlantic Ocean), a kingdom which harbors many kinds of human beings of different dispositions, various customs, and ethnically antagonistic races that have not lived together in any single kingdom—to say nothing of the competing political parties and the ambitious designs of its influential people?*

However, they both followed al-Amin in his smooth, colorful garments and his headgear full of flowers and aromatic plants. They reached a round spot in the garden, in the middle of which was a man with a long and wide beard, who was wearing a merchant's headgear. He appeared to be an Indian. He had two white rams in front of him on which he had painted images and forms in various colors on their bodies and had hung a necklace of carnelian on their necks. He had stained the horns of one ram green and the horns of the other red.

When al-Amin arrived, the man stood up and came forward to kiss his hand, but al-Amin prevented him and asked, "Which one of them is my ram?"

Pointing to the ram with the red horns, the man said, "This one, my lord."

Looking at al-Fadl, al-Amin said, "The other is then your ram. Let them butt one another and the winner will have another necklace to be hung on its neck, on condition that the necklace should be bought by the owner of the losing ram."

Al-Fadl could do nothing but show his gratefulness for this honor, and he said, "I hope that my lord's ram will win. If my ram wins, it will embarrass me."

Al-Amin convulsed with laughter, saying, "And I ask God that your ram will not win, not because it is yours but..." and he continued laughing.

Al-Fadl did not understand what al-Amin meant. He turned to Ja'far Ibn al-Hadi and saw him smiling, so he asked him with an inquiring look. Ibn al-Hadi explained in a low voice, "Because its name is Barmak!"

Al-Fadl then realized that al-Amin thought it was a good omen for him that his own ram would defeat the one called Barmak, for this would be like a victory over Ja'far al-Barmaki. He also realized that the other ram was not named Ja'far because al-Amin's cousin was named Ja'far too.

The two rams began to butt one another. Their shepherd knew al-Amin's desire to have his own ram win, so he did his best to ensure al-Amin's ram was the winner. Al-Amin laughed and was happy, and he ordered that the man responsible for the rams be given an award. Then the slave-boy came and said, "The man responsible for the cocks is coming. Will my lord grant permission to see a cockfight?" Al-Amin said, "Send him away. The butting of rams that we have just seen is sufficient for now, for the happy hour of drinking with our companions has come." Saying this, he walked toward the palace on the gravel-strewn garden path.

Al-Amin's palace stood on the left bank of the Tigris. It had windows, skylights, and balconies overlooking the river. It had a large hall in the

76

middle, which was more like a raised platform paved with colored marble and shaded by a ceiling with colorful gilded pictures made by Persian painters or images created by a blend of Persian and Byzantine arts. The roof stood on marble columns inlaid with gold. If it were not for the high external palace wall, it would have been possible for someone sitting in this place to see the boats going up and down the Tigris. In the external wall, there was a door from which one could go down to the river bank on a jetty, where fireboats[12] and other vessels were anchored. Al-Amin was fond of possessing navigational craft of various kinds and shapes. Fireboats were made for him in the shape of a lion, an elephant, a falcon, a snake, and a mare, and he spent much money in having them made.

On the garden side, the palace had a large gate that once was its original gate, from which visitors entered. It was in the shape of a semicircle in the middle of the wall, and visitors entered it by going up a few steps. Outside the gate, there were marble seats on each side of it parallel to the wall. On top of the gate, there was an inscription in beautiful Kufic letters that said, "Muhammad al-Amin, son of Harun al-Rashid." The palace was surrounded by a high external wall according to the custom in those days.

As al-Amin walked in the garden, the servants and eunuchs scattered about and in front of him, hurriedly telling others of his coming. When he reached the palace, the doormen stood up to express their respect, but he did not pay them any attention. He ascended the stairs and entered through the door, followed by al-Fadl and Ja'far. They passed through a corridor leading to a round courtyard, at the front edge of which was a door leading to another corridor that led to the Women's House, which was an independent palace, some of whose halls were connected with the raised platform described above. On the right side of the round courtyard, there was a door leading to many rooms, in which servants, helpers, slaves, and the like resided. On the left side of the courtyard, there was another door leading to the guesthouse consisting of many rooms, kitchens, and tables, all looking like a small town.

---

12 Fireboats were ships with the capability to throw fire on enemy ships at sea or in large rivers. Fireboats also came to denote light-going ships. (See E. W. Lane, *Arabic-English Lexicon*. Cambridge, England: The Islamic Texts Society, 1984. Vol. I, p. 552, under the word *hJarra>qa* .) *Translator's Note.*

* * *

Upon reaching the palace's courtyard, the head of the black eunuchs rushed to al-Amin and walked in front of him until they reached an embroidered silk curtain, hanging from the top of the door leading to the Women's House. He pulled it to the side, and al-Amin entered the corridor and invited al-Fadl and Ja'far to follow him. The sound of their footsteps could not be heard because they walked on thick, furry carpets made in Tabaristan. When they reached the second corridor, they came to a garden with flowers and aromatic plants. In the rear stood the Women's House, which had a flight of stairs consisting of six steps of red marble. On its door, there was an expensive, sky-blue silk curtain on which were written in brocade the following verses of Hatem al-Ta'i:

> *I am not one to lead my camel by its long halter*
> *To drink from the water basin before other mounts,*
> *Nor am I one to close the leather bag of its saddle*
> *And set out lightly, leaving my friend behind.*
> *If you are the owner of a young she-camel,*
> *Don't let your friend walk behind it on foot.*
> *Make it kneel down, and let him ride behind you. If it can carry you both,*
> *Fine; but if punishment is due, punish (yourself by walking).*

The head of the eunuchs walked in front of them; when they came to the door, he moved the curtain to the side. Al-Amin and his two companions entered a large hall that looked like a reception hall; on its opposite sides were two doors: one of them led to the women's bedrooms and the other to private sitting rooms, each of which had furnishings of a different color. Al-Amin was not interested in going there but wanted to go out to the raised platform behind the house. When al-Fadl and Ibn al-Hadi entered the hall, they heard lutes being irregularly played as if their musicians were tuning them, so they waited to see what al-Amin would do.

The hall was covered with embroidered silk, and on its wall were images of Persian and Byzantine kings on their horses, interspersed with images of land and sea animals, many of which were inlaid with gold or ivory on ebony boards hanging on the walls from golden nails. On the inside of the hall's doors, there were curtains hanging from large silver nails. On the floor, there was a single carpet whose surface area was probably twenty by twenty cubits[13], and around it next to the walls were circular embroidered silk cushions stuffed with ostrich feathers. In the corners of the hall stood large candlesticks with candles to light up the hall.

When al-Amin arrived in the hall and heard the sounds of lutes in the background, he sat on a sofa of ebony inlaid with ivory, and he gestured to his two companions to sit down. He then motioned to the head of the eunuchs, and the latter bowed his head and left. Meanwhile, al-Fadl was anxious, not knowing whether Qaranfula and her two companions had arrived, and Ibn al-Hadi was looking at al-Amin, trying to conceal secrets which if revealed would surprise everyone and cause agitation. But he was a patient man and was able to control his emotions.

They soon began to hear the lutes playing in unison. One of the hall's doors was opened, and a bevy of slave-girls came out carrying lutes in their hands. They entered the hall, ten of them at a time, playing their lutes beautifully and singing together. When the first ten finished, they went out through the other door, and ten others came in, and so on until ten groups of them had completed the show. Nothing of all this surprised al-Fadl or Ja'far because they had seen similar shows in the homes of the Barmakids and the house of al-Rashid. What really surprised them was the show that came after the slave-girls': it consisted of bevies of slave-boys and eunuchs wearing dazzling and expensive clothes, which no one in the history of Islam before al-Amin had ever presented. He went beyond all bounds in owning eunuchs, and he sought them in distant countries; he spent generously in order to procure them—and even more after he became caliph. He called them al-Jaradiyya (the Locust Group), and he allocated a special fund to them. He also created another group made up of black slave-boys and called them al-Ghurabiyya (the Raven Group), allocating funds to them as well. People reproached him for that, and poets composed poems about all of this. However, during the period when he was heir apparent, he was still at the beginning of his interest in such bizarre forms of amusement. The slave-boys entered the hall in successive groups, their

---

13 A cubit measured about 19 inches. The carpet would therefore measure more than 30 by 30 feet.

hair flowing in single or dual braids; they had tambourines or lutes in their hands, which they played while singing. Al-Amin enjoyed every sound and song, and he laughed but did not ask for a drink because he intended to have his morning drink in the hall with the raised platform.

When they had all filed through, al-Amin gestured to the head eunuch once more and then to his two companions, so they all stood up. The head eunuch opened a door in the front of the hall, and they went through it, descending a few steps, and walked down a corridor with doors on both sides leading to many rooms and halls. At the end of the corridor, they reached the raised platform and felt as if they had gone out of a tent into the open country. Large as the place was, it was furnished with cushions and carpets. There were high mattresses on a sofa of ebony inlaid with gold that were only accessible by stepping on a stool. Next to it there were many chairs, as well as cushions on the carpets, arranged around the pillars and along the walls. In the middle of the raised platform, there was a beautifully crafted skin rug covered with a silk sheet on which stood a large but low round table that was only as high as the span of one's hand. Crystal and silver pitchers with drinks and wines were placed on it, as well as cups of various shapes and colors, bowls of fruits, plates of cold meats, and flower vases; the place was redolent of fragrant scents.

Al-Amin rose to his sofa and gestured to his cousin to sit down. He then turned to al-Fadl and said, "Why are you still in your usual clothes? Take them off and put on the attire of drinking companionship." Then he shouted, "Boy, bring the attire of drinking companionship."

So al-Fadl was brought a safflower-dyed robe, and al-Amin insisted on making him wear a crown of flowers like his. He clapped and the head eunuch entered, and he said to him, "Bring us the singing women. Have any new slave-girls been brought to us?"

"No, my lord," the head eunuch said, "but we have singing women who cannot be surpassed by any others in all of Baghdad, even by those in the house of the Commander of the Faithful. Shall I bring them forth?"

"First, bring the maids with the fans," al-Amin said. "Then select for us the best women singers so that we may divert ourselves with them before the others come."

"I hear and obey," the head eunuch said and went out.

A short time later, a slave-girl came in, charming and alluring. She appeared to be of Georgian origin, to judge by her facial features. She entered the platform area, bolting like a gazelle escaping from a hunter's net. She wore a transparent Alexandrian gown that let all her underclothing shimmer through; over it, she had a tunic with an open front like a slip-on garment. Her white complexion was bright and dazzlingly radiant. She let her hair flow in a forelock on her brow, and she wore a headband on which the following distich verse was embroidered in gold thread:

Why was it that my arrows did not hit you when I shot,
Yet you hit me when you shot me, O marksman?

Her ear locks curled on her temples, and her eyebrows arching over her eyes conveyed magical enchantment. Her nose was like a reed of pearl, and her mouth like a wound dripping with blood. In her hand, she held a broad fan made of ostrich feathers covered with brocaded silk on which the following verses were embroidered in gold thread:

With me, life is pleasant in the summer;
And with me, rejoicing is delightful.
Anyone who holds me dispels the annoying heat
When it becomes intensely sweltering—
Liberality and generosity are a light
That shines from the face of God's al-Amin.

She held the fan with her fingers stained with henna, and she wore bracelets and bangles that when she moved her hand to fan made a whispering sound. On her bosom, she had a golden crescent studded with jewels, and the following verse was engraved on it:

I slipped away from the coterie of the paradise houris,
And I was created as a temptation to those who see me.

Ja'far and al-Fadl were enchanted on seeing her but also awed, knowing she was al-Amin's maid who had come to fan him. Moving on tiptoe, she walked and swayed till she was close to al-Amin. Al-Fadl made place for her, and she climbed onto a bench next to al-Amin's sofa and began to fan him. In her other hand, she had a handkerchief with which she wiped away the sweat on his forehead.

Then another slave-girl entered who appeared to be Greek, to judge from her features. She wore a loose outer garment dyed with a rose-red color. Her plaited hair flowed on her back like bunches of grapes. On her head she wore a bejeweled crown and around her neck an expensive necklace from which a bejeweled cross was suspended. On the crown, the following verses composed by Abu Nuwas were engraved:

> O bowman, who does not know what he has done,
>
> Your arrow has hit—save my mind.
>
> You have let it run in my body and through my soul,
>
> And so my spirit is weary and my heart is occupied.

Around her waist, she had a sash on which she hung a fan, and on the fan the following distich verse was written:

> Do you love to live without becoming crazy?
>
> Then stop observing (the beauty of) eyes.

When she entered, al-Amin gestured to her, so she stood beside his cousin Ja'far and began to fan him.

Then a third slave-girl entered, whose attire differed from that of her two friends. She had combed her hair into a topknot known as a Sukayna topknot, ascribed to Sukayna bint al-Husayn, who in Medina more than a century earlier was the first to wear this hairdo. The slave-girl did not wear a headband, but the following verses were written on her forehead:

> O crescent that appears from the palaces:
>
> My sight has fasted and prayed to your eyes.
>
> I don't know whether my night is long or not;
>
> And how would someone know, lying awake and suffering?

She wore a tunic of white velvet, on the right side of which was embroidered:

Your eyes have written a letter in my heart,
Sealed with eagerness and passionate love,

and on the left side of which was embroidered:

My eyes have been an affliction to my heart,
My eyes are an ill-omened misfortune to my heart.

When she entered, al-Fadl knew that she would stand beside him to fan him. She walked with her eyes on al-Amin; when he gestured to her to go to al-Fadl, she went, stood beside him, and began to fan him.

A group of slave-boys then entered carrying drinks. They wore a variety of clothes: some had red or yellow or green robes and others had red-and-yellow robes or robes of several colors. All were in the prime of youth and extremely handsome. Most of them did not know Arabic. When those who did know it spoke, they jabbered with thick accents because some of them were Slavs and others were Georgians, Turks, or Greeks; all were recent residents of Baghdad. Most of them were eunuchs, and the head eunuch had embellished them skillfully using diverse arts just as the head of the slave-girls had done in embellishing the maids mentioned above.

One of the slave-boys wore an outer garment with full-length sleeves, on the right shoulder of which was written:

His face is a full moon on a tender branch,
And his chest is a source of fragrance,

and on the left shoulder of which was written:

His cheek's surface has been copied
From the face of the shining moon.

Some slave-boys stood with the drinks, a pitcher in one hand and a cup in the other. Some of the cups were of colored crystal and others of pure gold with lettered engravings, most of them praising and describing wine, such as the following verses by Abu Nuwas:

Drink on seeing an elegant, beautiful scene

And mix my saliva with that of the sweetheart.

Undo the sash of the buxom girl tenderly

And take gentle care of her slender waist.

And say to him who blames for dalliance:

"Away with you, and open the way!"

Al-Amin and his two friends sat waiting for the women singers, and suddenly they began to hear pleasant singing and lutes playing a lovely tune. A female singer then appeared. She had a yellow complexion and was not beautiful at all. She walked as she played bewitchingly and sang in a melodious voice although, by tradition, white slave-girls were not taught to sing. She was followed by four slave-girls carrying lutes and dancing to the rhythm of their instruments. When al-Amin heard the singing, he shouted, "Bring me the man responsible for the drinks." The chief cupbearer came and began to direct the cupbearers. He sent a slave-boy to al-Amin carrying a cup of wine. Al-Amin drank it and ordered two similar ones for al-Fadl and Ja'far. They took the cups and pretended to drink in an attempt to please al-Amin. The slave-girls sat on a set of cushions prepared for them on one side of the raised platform. After cups had been served all around and al-Amin was transported with joy, he said, "Where is al-Hasan ibn Hani'? Where is Abu Nuwas?"

The head eunuch said, "In the guesthouse, my lord."

"Bring Abu Nawas to me," al-Amin ordered.

"I hear and obey," the head eunuch said as he started to leave.

But al-Amin called him back and said, "Now beware, don't let him enter into my presence without the attire of a drinking companion."

The head eunuch gestured in obedience and left.

Very soon afterward, he returned and said, "Abu Nuwas is at the door."

"Let him enter," al-Amin said with joyous excitement.

Abu Nuwas entered. Although he was past forty years old, his features were still attractive. The features of someone from al-Ahwaz dominated his appearance because his mother was from that Persian city.

He had let his beard grow, and it was light and flecked with gray. His eyes were blue and twinkled with intelligence and a sense of humor. Instead of a tall headgear or a turban, he wore a red cap. His attire of drinking companionship was bright yellow.

As he approached, al-Amin said to him, "Welcome to our poet. This gathering cannot be pleasant without a poet, for poets are the ornaments of singing gatherings."

Abu Nuwas bowed and remained standing. Al-Amin gestured to him to sit next to the singing slave-girls and gestured to one of the slave-boys to offer him a cushion, on which Abu Nuwas sat.

Al-Fadl remembered Abu al-'Atahiya and that this would be an opportune moment to mention the newly-purchased slave-girls. When he had left him, he had secretly told him something, and he was afraid that Abu al-'Atahiya had forgotten it. So he began to think of him as he pretended to be preoccupied with the amusements he was experiencing, yet still showing respectful reverence for the gathering of the heir apparent. Meanwhile, deep down, he was thinking of what his companion Ja'far ibn al-Hadi had urged him to do.

Ja'far seized the opportunity of al-Amin's preoccupation with the singing and asked al-Fadl about the slave-girls he had bought and when they would arrive. Al-Fadl answered with a gesture, joining all his fingers together as if to say, "They will arrive in a short while." He then turned to Abu Nuwas and said to him, "Recite some verses that the slave-girls can sing and bring joy to the heir apparent."

When al-Amin heard what al-Fadl requested, he said as the wine had gone to his head. "He will not say anything before he drinks a quart of wine." He gestured to the cupbearer, and the latter filled a beaker with a quart of wine and offered it to Abu Nuwas, who drank it all in one go and returned it to the cupbearer, gesturing with his head as though saying, "Give me more!"

Al-Amin was overjoyed, for he liked to drink. He laughed boisterously as he ate an apple, and said while still chewing, "Make us merry, O son of the Ahwazi woman."

Abu Nuwas answered saucily, "Does my lord want to be overjoyed by praise or by defamation?"

Al-Fadl ibn al-Rabi' quickly remarked, "Will you not cease jesting? How can the prince be asked such a question? And would anyone be overjoyed by defamation? The prince has asked you to teach these women singers verses they will sing so that he may be overjoyed."

Abu Nuwas looked askance at al-Fadl. Then he said saucily, "And what do you know about what makes the prince overjoyed? Do you want to be a drinking companion as a profession in addition to being a vizier? I am here talking to my master, and he understands what I mean!"

Al-Fadl was surprised at Abu Nuwas's brazenness and wanted to respond, but he heard al-Amin say, "I understood what he meant." And then he heard him add, "Make us overjoyed by defamation, so that al-Fadl may see that defamation may make one overjoyed as no praise can. Recite a verse or two of this kind to the slave-girl."

All those present listened with surprise visible on their faces. Their eyes followed Abu Nuwas as he brought his head close to the slave-girl holding the lute and whispered a few verses to her. She arranged her hold on the lute while everyone was silent, even al-Amin, and then she began singing:

> I wonder at Harun, the Imam, and what
>
> He likes in you and what he hopes for, O son of the she-wolf.
>
> I see Ja'far becoming more stingy and slender
>
> The more the Compassionate God increases his wealth.
>
> If anything but stinginess comes out of Ja'far,
>
> People will think it is nothing but his stupidity.

The slave-girl sang beautifully, and al-Amin shouted with joy on hearing every verse. Al-Fadl understood the gist of it, right from the first verse, for he realized that Abu Nuwas was alluding to Ja'far ibn Yahya al-Barmaki, his enemy. His joy was therefore greater than al-Amin's, and Ja'far ibn al-Hadi felt even greater joy than either of them and shouted to Abu Nuwas, "Hurrah! Well said!" He had a necklace of jewels that he was fondling with his fingers, and he was about to throw it to the poet, but he remembered that he was in the presence of the heir apparent and that protocol required that he not precede him in rewarding the poet. So he turned to al-Amin and asked his permission to do that and it was granted. He then threw the necklace to Abu Nuwas, and it fell in his lap. Abu Nuwas picked it up and looked at al-Amin as though asking his advice. Al-Amin laughed and said, "I see that you are looking for a place to put the necklace. Put it here." He pointed to the slave-girl standing next to al-Fadl, and he added, "And she is yours, too, but only after this gathering comes to an end. If you give us more, we will reward you more as well."

Abu Nuwas stood up to express his thanks, but al-Amin motioned for him to sit down and continue doing what he had started to do. The heir apparent then beckoned to the cupbearer, who then offered another round of drinks, changing the kinds of wine he offered from apple wine to date wine to grape wine. The wines sparkled in the cups with yellow, red, brassy and golden-chestnut colors. Al-Amin then gestured to the man responsible for drinks, and the man ordered one of the eunuchs to offer Abu Nuwas a cup for himself. He was a plump slave-boy with frizzled curly hair that he had arranged on his brow in a fascinating way. Overwhelmed by the wine, Abu Nuwas looked at the boy and then at al-Amin, who quickly said, "Describe him and he is yours." Abu Nuwas took the cup from the boy's hand and said:

> An effeminate boy with a gentle disposition carries it,
>
> Who monopolizes the onlooker's eyes and allures him.
>
> His eyes exude an (intoxicating) malady in his sockets,
>
> Which may haply be of use in the vehemence of (sexual) malady.
>
> I will drink (a glass of) pure wine from his eyes,
>
> And another with my drinking companions.

When al-Amin heard Abu Nuwas's verses, he shouted, "Woe to you! That's enough. He is yours."

When al-Fadl saw that wine had gone to al-Amin's head, he wanted to seize the opportunity, so he said, "Has my lord forgotten the white songstresses?"

"How can I forget them?" he said. "Have they arrived?"

He looked at the house superintendent to ask, and the latter said, "Yes, my lord. They arrived an hour ago."

"Bring them to me now," al-Amin ordered.

The superintendent left, but he soon returned in a hurry, alarmed and followed by a short man wearing the skin of a monkey. On the man's head was a pyramid-shaped headgear with jingles on its top, and he was snickering like a monkey. He jumped toward the center of the raised platform and began to dance. Al-Amin burst out laughing, flinging himself backward, and everyone joined in and added to the uproar.

Al-Amin said, "Isn't this Abu al-Husayn, the shameless clown?"

"Yes indeed, my lord," said the superintendent. "It is he himself, may God disgrace him! He has taken my mind away."

"Leave him," al-Amin said, "and go bring the slave-girls."

Those present laughed until the superintendent returned with Qaranfula, the songstress, who had a lute in her hand on which she was playing beautifully. She had put kohl on her eyelids and had adorned herself attractively, letting her hair flow down on her shoulders. Two other slave-girls entered after her, each with a lute in her hand, and one of them stood in front of al-Amin, playing a tune that had not been heard earlier. Al-Amin beckoned to her to sit down, so she did and sang:

> He was not born by a handmaid
> Offered in the market for sale;
> Nor was he ever punished, nor did
> He betray anyone or incur disgrace.

Meanwhile, al-Fadl was observing the reaction of al-Amin, and he saw him kick the ground with his feet in joy, and then he heard him shout, "True, true. May God disgrace you!"

Al-Fadl was not surprised at that but rather expected such a reaction from al-Amin because al-Fadl himself was the one who had suggested to Abu al-'Atahiya to teach al-Amin those verses—this in order to arouse his hatred for his brother al-Ma'mun by alluding to the fact that al-Ma'mun's mother was a slave-girl and that his father, al-Rashid, had punished al-Ma'mun because he had once found him with a slave-girl.

Chapter 8

Isma'il Ibn Yahya

The gathering continued with joyful entertainment, laughter, and drinking until late afternoon. Al-Amin then heard the barking of the guard dogs that he had placed on the bank of the Tigris behind the raised platform hall. He ordered one of his slave-boys to investigate and find out why the dogs were barking. The slave-boy left from a secret door leading to the riverbank and returned quickly, saying, "I see a boat coming close to the riverbank, and I think it is the fireboat of Isma'il ibn Yahya al-Hashimi."

When they heard the name, they were awestruck and shivered in their boots, especially Ja'far ibn al-Hadi, who turned pale and looked baffled. Al-Amin gestured to the songstresses, and as they fell silent chaos turned into confusion. When they heard the boat's captain order the sailors to undo the sail and come close to the bank, everyone was silent. Al-Amin was dumbfounded; as his intoxication dissipated he realized the condition he was in. So he took the flower crown off his head, intending to conceal his wanton behavior and disgraceful conduct. Everyone else imitated him, but how could they conceal their wanton behavior when the cups were still in their hands, the pitchers were full of wine, the table was set, and they were wearing the attire of drinking companions and exhibiting its attendant dissoluteness and amusement?

Al-Amin put on a determined performance, stood up, and shouted at his slave-boy to ask those on the fireboat to identify the owner. The slave-boy went out, then he returned and said, "Isma'il ibn Yahya asks permission to be admitted."

Al-Amin said, "Let him in. He is quite welcome."

Those present noticed al-Amin's desire to conceal their wanton behavior. So they sent out the shameless jester, ordered the slave-girls to be silent, and sat down motionless waiting for the arrival of Isma'il. The slave-boy soon returned followed by a venerable old man who had a handsome face and a high forehead and who was tall and broad-shouldered. He wore a black outer garment and tall headgear with a silk turban, the official attire of the 'Abbasids.

Isma'il ibn Yahya was one of the most revered Hashemites, the caliph's kindred. He was known for wisdom and resoluteness, and his old age made his demeanor all the more dignified. He had a long beard and his hair was gray, but he did not dye it because he disdained worldly ostentation. For he was a judicious and enlightened man who saw matters as they were and who appreciated people according to their virtues and talents rather than their lineages and appearances. Although he was a Hashemite and one of the caliph's paternal uncles, he did not consider him in any way superior to others except as concerned his piety and good deeds. He was fully aware of the inner workings of the state and was cognizant of the statesman's preoccupations. He liked al-Rashid not because he was a Hashemite, nor did he dislike Ja'far al-Barmaki because he was Persian; rather he looked at matters in a detached manner, his first concern being the strength of the 'Abbasid state and its protection from flaws and causes of failure. He did not care who would be the one who kept it strong and secure.

He looked at the plots and counterplots—hatched by al-Rashid and his vizier, or by al-Amin and his brother, al-Ma'mun, or by members of the competing parties—as would an insightful and critical wise man who viewed people's passions with the detachment of his wisdom and philosophy. He would do his best to eliminate the mischief that people of worldly aspirations and personal interests harbored. He was not so much concerned with whether the caliphate would come down to him as he was with its well-being, the strengthening of its foundations, and its survival. More than anyone else, he was knowledgeable about the strengths and weaknesses of al-Rashid and his vizier. He had the audacity to speak without restraint to both of them and to be effective, especially with al-Rashid, who revered him, respected him, and exalted his position because he was sure of his magnanimity, his fairness, and his good intentions in addition to his intelligence and levelheaded opinions.

It is natural that anyone of such qualities would be feared and respected by the people and even by monarchs; for, however arrogant and proud they may be, they do not scorn a man who gives sincere advice and discusses all matters with impartiality, sagacity, and the utmost care. Their respect is all the greater when, in addition to these qualities, they know of his honorable lineage, his high-mindedness, and his old age.

It was no wonder then that Isma'il was held in high esteem by al-Rashid and the men of his state, for he was known for his earnest devotion to the state and its security. However, he never offered any advice or counsel unless he knew that it would be effective and that it was possible to express it freely. If he sensed fickleness or hypocrisy on the part of those to be advised or counseled, he distanced himself and avoided involvement. That was why he did not like al-Amin, and he did not think advising him was of any use. So he used to keep his distance and avoided attending his gatherings.

He came to al-Amin's palace that day because he had observed Ja'far ibn al-Hadi and knew of the grudge he bore against al-Rashid and the Barmakids. Isma'il and Ja'far resided in Basra, like most of the retired Hashemites who lived on the caliph's stipends, monetary gifts, and estates. But Isma'il was not one of those who liked amusement and revelry. He was rather virtuous and solemn, and he disliked the luxury and revelry he observed among the Hashemites. He knew they would not appreciate his advice, and so he ceased to give it to them, except for Ja'far ibn al-Hadi, whom he had sponsored since his childhood when his father had died. That is why Ja'far grew up without an inclination toward amusements and intoxicating drinks. Nevertheless, he befriended al-Amin and prodded him to indulge in luxury and amusement with an ulterior motive in mind that was not unknown to Isma'il. He was afraid that Ja'far ibn al-Hadi would implement his scheme, which Isma'il felt was not in the interest of the state but rather was detrimental to it. He often advised him to desist from his scheme, and Ja'far would promise to do so but would then break his promise.

When Isma'il had learned in Basra a few days earlier that Ja'far had gone to Baghdad, he thought at first that he had gone there to divert himself or receive his stipend. But when Ja'far was late in returning, Isma'il feared the consequences of the delay so he followed him, pretending that he was coming for another purpose, a private matter of his own. When he reached Baghdad and inquired about Ja'far, he learned that he was staying at al-Amin's palace and that he had not left it. Isma'il felt it was necessary for him to meet him there. He had a boat, moored on the Tigris that he used for travel to Baghdad, so he boarded it that day and headed for al-Amin's palace.

When Isma'il entered al-Amin's gathering, all those present were awed, even al-Amin himself despite his drunken state. Al-Amin stood up to meet and welcome him, but Ja'far ibn al-Hadi stood on the side at a loss about what to do. Only al-Fadl ibn al-Rabi' remained composed and self-possessed—because of what we had mentioned earlier about his natural disposition, let alone his shrewdness. He approached Isma'il and pretended he wanted to kiss his hand, saying, "Welcome, my lord." Then he offered him a chair.

The venerable old man looked around at the slave-girls, the slave-boys, the lutes, the pitchers of wine, the cups, and the other paraphernalia of joy and merry-making. He knew that if he sat with them, he would disturb their day's pleasure, so he pretended that he did not intend to pay a visit at that hour but that he had only heard the voice of Ja'far ibn al-Hadi there. He said this while ignoring him.

Ja'far's face betrayed his dread but he came forward politely, trying to remain calm, knowing that Isma'il would not want to sit down. He said, "I intended to leave this morning, but the heir apparent held me back to attend this gathering in order to let me listen to the white slave-girls, and he asked me to wear the attire of a drinking companion. If my lord would like me to serve him, I would."

Isma'il pretended to be happy to see him and said, "Never mind, my son. I am eager to see you. So if you would like to leave, do come with me to the boat and leave the people in their gathering, for my staying here is of no use to them." Saying this, he turned on his heels and walked away. Ja'far asked permission to change his attire before following him to the boat.

Isma'il walked out as the people in the gathering were still hushed in awe of him. Al-Amin was relieved at his departure. Ja'far ibn al-Hadi hurried to his room, changed into his headgear and black attire, and went down to the boat. He found Isma'il walking on board with his headgear pushed back and an expression of concern visible on his forehead and in his eyes. When he approached him, he bent down to kiss his hand, but Isma'il withdrew it and said, "What is this gathering, Ja'far? I am surprised that someone like you would participate in such a thing!"

Ja'far backed away and did not reply. Isma'il then ordered the boat's captain to take them to a mooring far away from the palace. He then took Ja'far's hand and walked with him to a seat in the boat's stern overlooking the water. He seated Ja'far beside him and said, "I have never known you to keep this boy's company. Since when have amusement and immorality appealed to you?"

Ja'far said, "Do you notice any effect of drinking on me? By God, I have not tasted any wine."

"I am not saying that you are drunk," Isma'il said, "but I have known you to be a wise and serious man. I thought that if you ever saw al-Amin in such a situation, you would rebuke him and scold him. I did not expect that you would sit with him and go along with him in order to please him!"

Ja'far sighed and turned his eyes away toward the stern of the boat, looking at the sailors as they probed the depth of the water with poles in order to move the boat to a safe haven. When Ja'far still did not speak Isma'il realized what he was thinking and said, "It seems to me that you still have a low opinion of these people. It is as if you still harbor ambitions..."

Ibn al-Hadi could not help interrupting and blurted out, "I don't have ambitions, sir. I only seek my right!"

"What right do you mean?" Isma'il asked.

Lowering his voice as he looked around lest anyone should hear him, he said, "I mean that these *mawali,* these non-Arab clients, have robbed me of my right after they killed my father and usurped the caliphate from me. You know very well that I deserve it more than anyone else."

Isma'il pretended to attach little importance to what he had heard and said, "I am not arguing with you concerning the right you claim. But I don't see any connection between what you seek and what you do. What is the relation between your seeking the caliphate and sitting in this gathering? You have often put me off by saying something like this. Tell me: what is your right, and from whom do you seek it?"

With his frowning eyebrows showing clear anger, Ja'far said, "Do you permit me to speak freely and express what is in my heart? I stand in awe of you and fear speaking to you about this."

"Speak, and don't be afraid," said Isma'il. "If I see that what you say is right, I will help you achieve it. If not, I will say so and keep your secret."

Ja'far said, "You know that my father, al-Hadi, may God have mercy on him, assumed the caliphate by the will of my grandfather, al-Mahdi. You also know that he willed me to be his successor as caliph."

"I think," Isma'il said, "that you wish to execute his will. But don't you know that he exceeded his authority? For al-Mahdi willed the succession to the caliphate to your father, al-Hadi, and *then* to your uncle al-Rashid after him. When your father became caliph, he wanted to deprive al-Rashid of the right of succession to the caliphate and to nominate you as future caliph instead. Do you consider this to be a right?"

Ja'far said, "I don't deny that my father violated the will of al-Mahdi. But when he was confronted about his action, he returned the right of succession to the caliphate to al-Rashid on condition that it would be mine after his death. Don't you remember that?"

"Yes, I do," Isma'il said.

Ja'far continued, "Why then, after that, did they attack my father and kill him? He was caliph for only one year and some months."

"Kill him?" Isma'il said in surprise. "How so? I don't know that he was murdered. Rather he died of a sickness. But if you say that his mother, al-Khayzuran, killed him, I can see some justification for this claim; however, if you claim that anyone else killed him, I can't."

Ja'far laughed and said, "It is not unlikely that al-Khayzuran committed this crime, as is commonly said, for my father had angered her by preventing her from meddling with state affairs. But the fact is that she did so after being urged by that Persian man!" Saying this, he gnashed his teeth.

Isma'il said, "I think you mean Yahya ibn Khaled."

"Yes, I mean him," Ja'far agreed. Then he added, "The proof of this is that he was the one who objected to my father being acknowledged as the succeeding caliph. Al-Rashid had yielded to being deprived of the right of succession to the caliphate and accepted having that right transferred to me. But Yahya incited him to reject this transfer and continue his efforts until my father agreed to restore the right of succession to al-Rashid on condition that I would be the caliph after him. After my father's agreement, Yahya hastened to kill him, for, a few nights later, it was said al-Hadi died and some people claimed that my grandmother, al-Khayzuran, had killed him. However, I believe that if she really did, it was only upon Yahya's instigation. Don't you remember that Yahya was said to have been the first to know of my father's death and that he hurried at night to al-Rashid and informed him of the good news? Al-Rashid remembered this favor and rewarded Yahya with the reins of government, which were later given to his son, Ja'far, the current vizier who, as you know, is so powerful and influential that it is true to say that he and not al-Rashid is the real caliph."

Chapter 9
The Barmakids and the State

As sweat flowed down his forehead, Ja'far ibn al-Hadi spoke and Isma'il listened. He may have shared his opinion but did not think it wise to encourage it because he believed it was not at all in the best interest of the state. Rather he believed it would weaken it, and so he sought an excuse for the Barmakids.

Isma'il said, "I think that you have a poor opinion of the Barmakids. It is as if you agree with their enemies who speak evil of their deeds. You know that the Barmakids have rendered a great service to this state unequaled by any other group. I am a Hashemite, as you know, and the caliph is of my own flesh and blood; I am hurt by what hurts him, and I am pleased by what pleases him. But I believe that you have wronged these non-Arab clients, and you have forgotten their aid in organizing this state, since the time of their grandfather Khaled. Wasn't Khaled one of the staunchest supporters of Abu Muslim in transferring this state from the Umayyads to us? When Abu Ja'far al-Mansur killed Abu Muslim and the Persians and Kurds rose against him, he would have lost his power over the state had Khaled not come to his help and guaranteed him victory over them by his wise advice and not by military force. This is to say nothing of his managing government affairs and organizing its departments— deeds that have been continued by his son Yahya, and his two grandsons, al-Fadl and Ja'far. The Barmakids, my son, are the bulwark of this state and the mainstay of its splendor. And look at Baghdad that bears the traces of their good management and organization. They have established in it libraries, learning circles, barracks for the soldiers, dwellings for the sick, judicial councils, and police stations. The widespread interest in learning and philosophy that you see and the flocking of dhimmi

people[14] and others to translate the books of the Greeks and Persians are
due to the encouragement of the Barmakids, who gave funds generously
for this purpose. Wasn't Yahya ibn Khaled the first to be interested in
having *Almagest* [15] translated from Greek into Arabic? And would you
deny that he made great efforts to collect books from India and elsewhere?
Haven't the Barmakids brought physicians from India to spread the art
of medicine? These physicians are among us now, and Menke, their chief,
is the one whom Yahya advised al-Rashid to summon when he was so
severely sick. We almost despaired of saving him, but Menke treated and
healed him. The Barmakids were the ones who got al-Rashid interested in
establishing the Maristan hospital and who appointed Indian physicians
to be responsible for its administration. They also established a hospital
for themselves and appointed the Indian physician, Ibn Dihn, to be its
administrator. And are you not aware of al-Fadl ibn Yahya's important
role in the use of paper? I will never forget how the employees of the
government departments were weary of the use of leather and parchment
for their books and records until al-Fadl ordered the use of paper, and
so we established paper factories in Baghdad. If I were to enumerate the
good deeds of these Barmakids, I would be exhausted before I could finish.
And you know my solidarity with the Hashemites, my zeal for this state,
and my desire for its safety. It does not stand to reason that I would say
anything based on emotion or prejudice. I only tell the plain truth. So,
don't be deceived by the grudge of al-Fadl Ibn al-Rabi' and that of others
against the Barmakids and by their speaking evil of them, for they only do
that out of jealousy because of their inability to equal their achievements."

Ja'far listened to these words with bowed head and looked at the
movement of the water lapping against the sides of the boat as it was
sailing leisurely. When Isma'il stopped speaking, Ja'far became aware of
how annoyed he had become on hearing him praise the Barmakids, whom
he hated intensely. But he could not refute Isma'il's arguments, and he
found that the best thing for him to do was to continue speaking about
them, so he said, "Suppose they were angels who had come down from
heaven. Did they not kill my father and take away my right to rule?"

14 Free non-Muslim subjects living under Muslim suzerainty, paying a capital tax, and
receiving protection and safety. *Translator's Note.*

15 Arabic title of Ptolemy's book on astronomy, *Megale Syntaxis tes Astronomias.*
Translator's Note.

Isma'il said, "Your claim is null, or it is without proof, for nobody has ever said that Yahya ibn Khaled killed your father or took any steps to kill him in order to take the caliphate from your hands."

Ja'far replied, "That he killed him, I have no doubt—although many people don't know it. That he killed him in order to take the caliphate from my hands is a fact that you can deduce from his actions after my father's consent to designate al-Rashid as his heir apparent before me, for he hastened to kill him before I was designated as heir apparent. And when al-Rashid became caliph, he quickly designated his dissolute son, al-Amin, as his heir apparent, and I think he intended to make the caliphate mine in succession to al-Amin. But his Barmakid vizier enticed him to designate his other son, al-Ma'mun, as the successor heir apparent. Consequently, I was left with nothing." He mumbled angrily, "And, by God, if…"

Isma'il smiled and interrupted him, saying, "I am indeed surprised at how your deeds contradict your words. How can you have a grudge against this boy and yet sit with him in a gathering of wine and love? Furthermore, I don't understand this grudge of yours, for how can you attain your goal when al-Rashid is on the throne of the caliphate, surrounded by soldiers and assistants, and when the Hashemites support him and back him, and when he has already designated his two sons to succeed him in the caliphate, one after the other? Therefore, relinquish these childish thoughts. No doubt if al-Rashid were to know anything of what you harbor in your heart, your flesh would fly in pieces between heaven and earth. But I have kept your secret and will continue to keep mum about it because I want your good and hope for your return to your senses. But if you persist in what you are doing, my interest in the safety of the state will force me to sacrifice you unless I see you acting honorably. Now tell me, how do you hope to attain the caliphate?"

Isma'il's threat had a great effect on Ja'far because he respected and feared him. He felt annoyed, suppressed his emotions, and felt like choking. Tears flowed from his eyes because of his deep agitation, and he bowed his head in embarrassment. Signs of confusion were visible on his face. Then he pulled himself together and said, "My uncle, I see that you make light of me and my acts, and you think that I am not careful in what I say. But I don't ignore my powerless state in my opposition to al-Rashid with his soldiers and assistants, and I don't aspire to the caliphate now. However, I do aspire to the caliphate after him, and this is not so difficult to attain if his Barmakid vizier falls. Listen, then, to my words until the end. When al-Rashid dies, the caliphate passes to al-Amin first, and he is not fit for it. I don't see him improving in anything but his immersion in revelry, luxury, and amusement; the statesmen will not keep him. As for al-Ma'mun, he is a man of reason and determination— truth be told. But I don't think that anyone of the Hashemites likes him because of his Persians heritage—his maternal uncles are Persian. And I think you know that Ja'far al-Barmaki was the one who spared no effort to have him designated as a future caliph for his own purposes, not least of which is to take the state away from us. Wait, hear me out. The only obstacle to regaining my right to the caliphate is the existence of this Persian, who deserves to be killed, if not in revenge for my father, then for his monopolization of state funds for himself and his family. You see, their income from their estates is perhaps equal to that of the state treasury. Sahl ibn Harun, who knows these things best, informed me that the taxes levied on their estates and amenities amount to twenty million dinars per year. And you know, my uncle, that the taxes collected from all the kingdom from its farthest east to its farthest west is not much more than this amount. I have learned from the state treasurer that the total of the taxes levied by the state is about four hundred million dirhams, that is, twenty-seven million dinars. And we, the Hashemites, seek our stipends in dribbles of one thousand and ten thousand, as if we were begging. This is to say nothing of the pomp that the Barmakids have appropriated, for you can see that the horses standing at Ja'far's door are much more numerous than those standing at al-Rashid's. Who will know what the consequence of this appropriation will be when al-Rashid dies and al-Amin is what you know him to be? Will the state not slip from our hands? As for al-Ma'mun, I admit he is resolute, but I don't think he has the zeal to keep the caliphate among the people of his family and the reason is perhaps his relationship with the Persians through his mother, as well as his submission to the advice of Ja'far al- Barmaki, his educator."

Isma'il admired Ja'far's shrewdness and may have thought he was right. But his primary concern was the welfare of the state, so he said, "I don't deny the great wealth of the Barmakids, but don't forget that they spend from its proceeds to benefit the people. You know that there is no one among us who does not receive a salary or a gift from Ja'far al- Barmaki or his brothers. I have learned from their treasurer that twelve million dinars, that is, more than half their income, is portioned into specific sums kept in sealed documents, each of which bears the name of a person in the state to whom they will send it as a gift. Their wealth, therefore, goes back to the state and its people, and I don't think that the caliph acts more generously. Furthermore, removing this man constitutes a danger to the caliphate, and I think that if al-Rashid himself wanted to kill him, he would not be able to because most of the men of the state are his friends on whom he has lavished generous gifts and favors. Therefore, stop thinking this way and listen to my advice, for I value your youth and care for your life. My opinion is that you should try to get close to al-Rashid, for this will be better for you and more enduring. I will guarantee you that you will have the position you merit, and I myself will do my best to achieve that."

When Ja'far ibn al-Hadi saw that Isma'il stuck to his opinion, he pretended to accept it because he was afraid that if he angered him, Isma'il would give him away. So he said, "And what do you think will happen if I become close to al-Rashid?"

Isma'il was pleased that Ja'far was convinced and that the danger to the state would be allayed. He said, "The most that people aspire to, when becoming close to the caliphs, is that they marry their daughters. So what do you think of marrying al-'Aliya bint al-Rashid?"

Ja'far thought that such a marriage would not stand in the way of his goal—in fact, it would rather help him to achieve it. So he expressed his approval and said, "It will be a dear relationship, but al-Rashid may ask the advice of his vizier, who will not approve!" Isma'il laughed and said, "Don't think so badly of al-Rashid. He is more resolute and more courageous than you think, and I will guarantee that to you. And now, I ask you to go back to Basra and wait till you hear from me."

Ja'far said, "I will go at your bidding, but I see no harm in remaining here until this task is accomplished."

Isma'il said, "Fine. Go then now to my palace, and I will go to al-Rashid tomorrow and talk to him about this matter."

Ja'far asked, "Will you not permit me to return to al-Amin to bid him farewell and get some belongings I left with him?"

"Go, with God's protection," Isma'il said.

The sun was about to set, and Ja'far asked Isma'il to permit him to leave the boat in order to board a skiff to al-Amin's palace.

So Isma'il ordered that the boat be anchored at the riverbank, where Ja'far saw a skiff. He boarded it and returned to al-Amin's palace. The night had fallen and it was dinner time. When he came closer to the raised platform, the dogs barked. They were huge and menacing. He remained standing, hesitating between getting off the raised platform and entering the palace from the other door behind the garden. As he stood there, he noticed that the raised platform was empty. He did not hear any singing, nor did he see any light. He decided to have the skiff go around to the other door, which was some distance away.

As he was thinking, he saw a light appear on the raised platform and approach the wall. He then heard some faint noise and saw a hand stretching over the wall with a lantern. When the dogs saw the lantern, they stopped barking. Then a man appeared and Ja'far recognized him as the chief of the slave-boys, so he called to him and the man said, "Is that my lord Ja'far?"

"Yes," Ja'far said. "Shall I enter from here?"

"Wait for a moment, and I will return to you," the man replied in a low voice.

He left him and went back with his lantern. Ja'far remained standing in the skiff, waiting for him and wondering about the cause of that secrecy. After a while, the light appeared again and he heard his voice say, "Come, my lord. But please tiptoe quietly."

Ja'far was surprised at such a request. He disembarked and walked until he reached the secret door, where he was met by a man with a lantern. "Enter, my lord," he said. So he entered and the man walked in front of him with the lantern. They passed by the raised platform, and Ja'far saw that traces of the drinks and food were still visible, as if the people had left only a short while earlier. He was puzzled and thought of asking what was going on, but he refrained from doing so. The man continued to walk in front of him until he passed through the corridor and reached the middle hall in the women's apartments. He saw lighted candelabras in the corners of the hall and candles illuminating the walls, but there was no one there. He could not help asking the man, "Where is our lord, the heir apparent?" The man replied, "We are going to him, my lord."

* * *

Ja'far walked behind the chief of slave-boys from hall to hall, all of which were lit by candles on candelabras and furnished with magnificent furniture, each hall having a different color and shape. He then reached a closed door at which the chief of slave-boys stood and knocked lightly. Ja'far heard the sound of some movement, and then the door was opened and al-Fadl ibn al-Rabi' appeared, still in the attire of a drinking companion as he had been when Ja'far had left him. Al-Fadl took Ja'far by the hand and led him in, silently. Ja'far entered the room and saw al-Amin sitting on a carpet, still in the attire of a drinking companion. Next to him was a bare-faced woman wearing a cloak. Ja'far knew she was a slave-woman and noticed signs of concern on her face. He greeted them and remained standing, so al-Amin ordered him to sit down, saying, "Sit down and listen to this strange story."

He sat down and al-Fadl sat next to him. Al-Amin said, "This slave-woman has brought us news that interests you and us. She is one of our slave-women, and we have asked her to be our spy on that vizier. Listen to the news she has brought us of his treason."

Ja'far was delighted with what he heard, and turned to the slave-woman with attention and remained silent. She addressed her words to al-Amin and said, "You know, my lord, that Yahya ibn 'Abd Allah ibn al-Hasan al-'Alawi rebelled in the Daylam region against the state and that a group of Shi'a people who were hostile to the 'Abbasids supported him, wanting to take the caliphate away from them. And you know that the Commander of the Faithful, al-Rashid, sent more than one military leader to fight them. But their rebellion continued to grow, so he sent al-Fadl ibn Yahya, brother of the vizier Ja'far al-Barmaki, to fight them. When he reached Taliqan with his army and learned that the rebel leader Yahya al-'Alawi was hiding in the strongholds of the Daylam Mountains, he outsmarted him by promising him good treatment if he surrendered. Yahya believed al-Fadl's promise because he was, like him, a Shi'ite, and so he came to see him. Al-Fadl treated him well and suggested that it would be a good idea for him to accompany him to Baghdad, where he would surrender to the Commander of the Faithful. Yahya declined at first, but al-Fadl continued to insist until Yahya consented on condition that al-Rashid would write a document in his own hand guaranteeing his safety. They agreed on the wording of such a document, which al-Fadl wrote and sent to our lord, al-Rashid. The Commander of the Faithful signed it, and when Yahya arrived in Baghdad, he welcomed him, honored him, and granted him generous means of support. Then our lord, al-Rashid, heard from one of the knowledgeable people that Yahya was intending to rebel, and…"

Nodding his head, al-Amin interrupted her and said, "Yes, he continues to have evil intentions. Will the hearts of those Alids ever be friendly to us, after our mutual enmity has reached this extent? Nor will our hearts be friendly to them!"

Ja'far said, "And who knows whether al-Fadl has not colluded with his friend Yahya al-'Alawi in secret, agreeing to bide their time and then rebel together against us?"

Al-Fadl ibn al-Rabi' said, "That is what the Commander of the Faithful has come to think, for after he had given him the document guaranteeing his safety, he annulled it—as you will hear."

Looking at al-Amin, the slave-woman continued her report and said, "Yes, our lord al-Rashid annulled the document—I don't know why—but I learned that al-Zubayr's kinsfolk reported al-'Alawi, so the Commander of the Faithful ordered that he be seized and imprisoned."

Al-Amin was surprised at her words and said, "Therefore, he must now be in prison."

She said, smiling, "He is rather on his way to his family."

"What are you saying?" said al-Amin. "Who set him free?"

"The vizier, Ja'far," she said.

"And how so?" al-Amin wondered. "This is unforgivable!"

She said, "Let me tell you what I saw with my own eyes at sunset today."

He was all ears to hear her report.

She said, "The vizier was sitting in his palace in the afternoon, while the servants and slave-girls were busy doing their work—except me. I was intent on observing who was coming in and going out, and I saw Yahya ibn 'Abd Allah al-'Alawi enter alone without anyone of his entourage. I knew he had come clandestinely, so I observed him until he entered into the presence of the vizier. They sat together in a private room, with no other person. I surmised that the secret meeting was for some important matter. I went to another room separated from theirs by a closed door, but through cracks I could see what was inside. I stood there, and I saw the vizier stand to welcome al-'Alawi and have him sit beside him. He then ordered the servant not to permit anyone to enter the room. When they had settled down, the vizier asked al-'Alawi about his conditions in prison, and the man cried and complained and finally said, 'For God's sake, show concern for my condition, Ja'far, and let not my grandfather, Prophet Muhammad (may God bless him and grant him peace), be your enemy. I swear by God that I did not do anything necessitating my imprisonment.' When al-'Alawi ended his words, I saw the vizier acting kindly toward him and saying something to comfort him, which I didn't understand. But I finally heard him say, 'Go wherever you like.'"

When the slave-woman said this, al-Amin was amazed and said, "Shame on him for this brashness, or rather for this treason! How dare he release a prisoner whom my father ordered arrested? And what did he do next?"

She said, "Al-'Alawi expressed his fear of leaving prison, for he said he could be seized again and returned to prison."

"True, by God," al-Fadl ibn al-Rabi' said.

Ja'far Ibn al-Hadi asked, "How then was he released?"

She said, "He sent men of his retinue with him to take him to his safe house. I saw him leaving and praising the vizier, and I heard the vizier encouraging him and soothing him."

"So al-'Alawi escaped?" al-Amin said.

"Yes, my lord," she said, "and I tried to see you immediately in order to convey the news to you, but I could not leave earlier."

Al-Amin turned to Ja'far Ibn al-Hadi as though seeking his opinion. The latter motioned to him to let the slave-woman go. Al-Amin ordered her to go to the chief slave-woman, who would reward her. So she rose, kissed al-Amin's robe, and left.

When Ja'far was alone with al-Amin and al-Fadl, he began speaking and magnifying the danger of what they had just heard, in order to incite them to action against the Barmakids. He said, "Tolerating this insolence would be a sign of weakness!" He waited to see the reaction of al-Amin, and when he saw him burst into loud laughter, he was astonished and asked, "What makes my lord laugh?"

Al-Amin said, "I am laughing at my expectation of your surprise and shock when you hear the story that al-Fadl told me before you came."

He turned to al-Fadl as though ordering him to speak, so al-Fadl said to al-Amin, "I think my lord means the story of my lady, al-'Abbasa."

"Yes," al-Amin confirmed.

Ja'far ibn al-Hadi became more eager to hear the story. Al-Fadl began relating what had happened to him at the House of Slaves that day at dawn and what Abu al-'Atahiya told him about what he had seen and heard. Ja'far listened, totally astonished. When al-Fadl ended his story, Ja'far stood up and shouted, "Oh, what treason! How can you tolerate all this? Why don't you inform the Commander of the Faithful of this treason?"

Al-Fadl said, "Regarding the story of al-'Abbasa, no one dares tell al-Rashid about it unless he is willing to risk his life for, God help us, al-Rashid will be furious."

Ja'far said, "How can we know about this treason and not divulge it? Doing so is a further treason."

Al-Fadl said, "It will be necessary to be cunning in order to inform him of the matter, such as a hint or insinuation in the words of a songstress. As for the news about al-'Alawi's escape, it is easy to convey."

Ja'far knew that the news of al-'Alawi's escape alone was enough to have Ja'far al-Barmaki put to death, and this was what he wished for. So he urged al-Fadl to hasten in conveying this news to the Commander of the Faithful. Then he asked, "And where did the two little sons of al-

'Abbasa go? I hope you have been able to catch up with them and to take and keep them. The news has to be supported by having them in custody. Woe to the one who conveys it without evidence—his life will be short!"

Al-Fadl said, "As soon as I had heard the story, I sent a group of my men with Abu al-'Atahiya to take the two boys. They have not yet returned to give me the news, but I am confident they will succeed."

As they were talking, they heard footsteps in the opposite room. Then there was a special knock on the door that signaled to al-Amin that his slave-boy had come to deliver an important message. Al-Fadl rose and opened the door. The slave-boy entered and remained silent. Al-Amin understood that his slave-boy wanted to see him alone. Ja'far and al-Fadl understood this too, so they asked permission to leave, which al-Amin granted. As soon as they left, the slave-boy said, "A man from the Chakeriyya hirelings has just arrived." Al-Amin knew that the man was a messenger from his mother, Zubayda, for she was the first to hire servants from the Chakeriyya who went about on mules in various directions carrying her messages.

So he asked, "What does he want?"

The slave-boy said, "Our lady, mistress Zubayda, requests your presence tomorrow morning for an important matter."

"Tell him," al-Amin said, "that I will go to see her tomorrow morning, God willing."

Night had fallen, and so al-Amin went to bed.

Chapter 10

Zubayda, al-Rashid's Wife

Zubayda, daughter of Ja'far ibn Abu Ja'far al-Mansur, was the cousin of al-Rashid and his wife, whom he married in the year 165 AH (781 AD). Zubayda had first place with Al-Rashid, who preferred her to his other wives because of her Hashemite lineage and her beauty. His other wives were no more than mothers of his children.

Zubayda's original name was Amat al-'Aziz (Handmaid of the Mighty One), but her grandfather al-Mansur named her Zubayda (Dainty Cream) because of her tender skin and her radiance. She was influential with al-Rashid, who sought and often accepted her opinion.

She was the originator of several unprecedented and memorable feats in Islamic history. An example is the water system in Hejaz known as 'Ayn al-Mashash, which was a canal she commissioned that made water flow for twelve miles to Mecca across every lowland, highland, plain, and mountain on the way. She spent one million and seven hundred thousand dinars on it. This is in addition to large structures, houses, pools, and cisterns in Hejaz and in the frontiers, on which she spent thousands of dinars, aside from what she spent helping the poor. She had one hundred slave-girls who knew the Qur'an by heart, each of whom had to recite part of it every day. Their continuous recitation could be heard in her palace like the buzz of bees.

She was also the first to use gold and silver utensils studded with gems and the first to wear robes of fine embroidered fabric, each costing fifty thousand dinars. Furthermore, she had domes made of ebony, sandalwood, and silver that had curtain hooks made of gold and silver. They were lined with embroidered fabric, sable fur, brocade, and several kinds of silk—red, yellow, green, and blue. She wore sandals studded with jewels and had lighted candles of amber placed on candelabras of gold. She set many new trends as people imitated her in her attire and other things.

She had a palace in Baghdad on the western bank of the Tigris River. It was named after her but was also called the House of Repose. It was situated to the south of the Palace of Eternity and to the east of the City of al-Mansur. It was surrounded by gardens that had no equal in those days.

Zubayda had an ardent zeal for the Hashemites and harbored a grudge in her heart against the Barmakids, especially against the vizier Ja'far ibn Yahya because he disparaged her son al-Amin and gave more prominence to his brother al-Ma'mun, although the latter's mother was a slave-woman. The latest development that increased her rancor was that Ja'far ibn Yahya prevailed on al-Rashid to designate al-Ma'mun as an heir apparent along with her son al-Amin, whom she would have liked to be the sole designated heir apparent. In the year 186 AH, al-Rashid went to al-Ka'ba on pilgrimage with his sons, his viziers, generals, and judges and wanted to designate al-Amin and al-Ma'mun as his heirs apparent there; two documents recorded this and were hung on al-Ka'ba, and both al-Amin and al-Ma'mun took an oath to implement these provisions. When al-Amin was about to leave al-Ka'ba after that, Ja'far al-Barmaki stopped him and said, "If you betray your brother, may God abandon you!" And he made him swear three times to this. Zubayda kept her displeasure about this event secret but since then had waited for an opportunity to get even with Ja'far. Her grudge against the Barmakids was unequalled in hatred and rancor by any of their enemies. She spared no effort in finding out everything they were involved in, hoping to discover a mortal weakness that she could exploit. She knew about the affair between Ja'far and al-'Abbasa but not about their two boys. Had she known about them, she would not have hesitated to reveal their affair to her husband because she did not fear him, firm as she was in the knowledge of her influence with him.

On the morning of that day when uproar arose in the House of Slaves, one of Zubayda's spies pursuing al-'Abbasa's news there learned the story of the two boys and conveyed it to her. She decided to seize the first opportunity to convey it to al-Rashid, but she wanted to consult al-Amin first and so she sent for him—as was related above.

The next morning al-Amin mounted his horse and went to Zubayda's palace. Clad in black and wearing the tall headgear, he was accompanied by slaves led by a knight holding a spear, as was customary in the procession of the heir apparent in those days. The procession moved parallel to the eastern riverbank until it reached the nearest bridge; it then crossed it and moved forward on the western riverbank and approached Zubayda's palace. The people stood up for al-Amin on the way, greeting him and wishing him long life, especially the Arabs and those who supported their dominance in the affairs of state. He returned their greetings with a bright face, full of the vigor of youth and the dignity of kingship.

Zubayda was waiting for him and had prepared all means of comfort, kindness, and welcome for him on account of her strong love, for he was her only offspring and the repository of all her hopes. She ordered her slave-girls to sprinkle flowers and aromatic plants along the garden paths and made ready for him a place to sit, redolent of the sweet scent of musk and amber; this was in a room of her palace whose ceiling was a dome made of sandalwood covered with embroidered fabric, sable fur, and several kinds of bright-colored silk. Brocade curtains hanging from gold hooks were let down from the sides of the dome onto the walls of the sitting room, and on them verses of poetry or familiar wise sayings were embroidered with gold thread. On the floor of the room, there was a single expensive carpet on which were designs depicting one of the Persian kings hunting lions, which looked so real that you could almost hear the sounds of a hunting scene. On the edges of the carpet, there were verses of poetry embroidered with gold thread, and in the middle, there was a picture of a peacock whose colors were woven with silk, gold, and silver thread and whose eyes were made of sapphire.

In Zubayda's palace, there were many rooms, each with special furniture arranged in a special way. The furniture in the room that was prepared for al-Amin was Armenian. It consisted of ten pieces, including the cabinets, the cushions, the mattress-seats, and the carpet that we described above. Such furniture was worth no less than five hundred thousand dinars, without the carpet, the curtains, and the artistic inscriptions and drawings that covered the dome, the windows, and the walls, and without the gold candelabras on the sides, in which were placed amber candles of the most expensive kind, which had never been used before Zubayda's time.

* * *

Al-Amin arrived in the garden and a group of Chakeriyya servants received him and helped him dismount. The bearer of the spear then walked in front of him carrying it until they both reached the flowers spread out on the paths, whose fragrance was diffused and mixed with other balmy scents. At that point, the bearer of the spear stood aside, and al-Amin walked alone until he reached the gate of the palace, where he saw his mother standing and waiting for him. When he was close to her, she embraced him and gave him a kiss that expressed her yearning, and he kissed her hand.

Zubayda had a bright face and was of white complexion. She possessed the dignity of the Hashemites, with a certain sweetness and beauty. She had large, black eyes that showed intelligence and sharpness. Her cheeks were round and reflected luxury and affluence. Her mouth was small and smiling, and her nose above it expressed the dignity of the highborn. Her chin was of little protrusion, and there was no depression or crease between it and her collarbone. Her neck was softly round and very white, and it was smooth without any protuberance.

She was of medium height—almost tall—and a little plump. When she hurried while walking, her shoulders and hips wobbled not unlike many a person brought up in opulence. She wore a crimson-colored silk cloak that covered all her clothing and had a gilt girdle whose two edges were clasped with a buckle studded with gems. Her hair was plaited in one braid flowing on her shoulder. Around her head, she wrapped a simple headband not decorated with gems. Headbands were still being used at the time, but common women did not wear them. They were limited to the womenfolk of the houses of caliphs and princes—very much like modern fashions in every age, worn first by a notable, high-class woman and then imitated by her friends before becoming prevalent among the common people. Headbands had been invented by al-Rashid's sister to conceal a defect in her forehead, and she had hers studded with gems, as mentioned earlier. Women liked that and imitated her. However, Zubayda was too proud to imitate anyone, particularly 'Aliyya, for she was greatly aware of her own high position with al-Rashid because of her lineage, her beauty, and her discernment. So she adopted a headband that was simple and without gems, out of disdain for imitations. Nor did she ever wear a necklace, a ring or a bracelet.

When al-Amin saw her headband, he could not help smiling and said, "I see that you are imitating my aunt 'Aliyya. These headbands are beautiful, mother. But I don't see any gems on yours."

She smiled and pointed to her feet with her forefinger. He looked at her feet and noticed that she had studded her sandals with gems. So he admired her pride and her indulgence in luxury.

He walked beside his mother, not knowing where she was taking him. She went through a corridor and reached a flight of stairs she ascended, and he followed her. Then, through another corridor, they reached the room we mentioned above. He was not dazzled by the expensive furniture there, but he was surprised at the scent of musk on entering the room. He saw two rows of beautiful slave-girls at the door, wearing turbans. They had combed their hair in various fashions. They were clad in gowns and tunics and had girdles with gold and silver inlays. Their figures were attractive and their breasts were particularly prepossessing. Some of them carried bowls of musk and others bottles of perfume. At this sight, the prince could not help showing his wonder and admiration, while his mother tried to hold herself back from laughing. He turned to her, and so she laughed.

"What are all these clothes, mother?" he wondered. "I see that you have made these slave-girls into slave-boys!"

"I did that," she said, "trying to imitate you, my son. I saw that you have obtained slave-boys and embellished them excessively to look like beautiful slave-girls. So I obtained these slave-girls and made them look like slave-boys, as you can see. I have called them 'the slave-girls with beautiful builds,' and I will send them to you as a gift."

Al-Amin was pleased and thanked her. They had by now reached the sitting place prepared for them, an ebony throne inlaid with gold, in the front part of the room. Zubayda sat on an embroidered silk cushion stuffed with ostrich feathers and made al-Amin sit next to her, and she kept looking at him. She then gestured to the slave-girls and slave-boys, and they all left.

When she was alone with him, her expression changed from smiling affability to one inspiring awe and loftiness. Her shining black eyes showed intelligence, sharpness of mind, and seriousness. Then she asked, "How did you spend your day yesterday, Muhammad?"[16]

He replied, "I spent it as you would like me to, my lady: in peace and enjoyment."

"How about the night?" she asked. "Why were you hiding in seclusion?"

"Who told you that?" he said.

"The Chakeri man I had sent to you informed me," she replied. "Why were you hiding?"

He said, "It is a seclusion you would be happy to hear about. I intended to come and inform you about a secret you would be very interested to know. But, tell me, why have you sent for me?"

She was leaning on his shoulder and her hand was on his cheek, toying with the hair of his temple, as she looked at him with tenderness and love. When he told her this, she smiled and said, "I, too, have something you would be interested in knowing, and I hope that it will help you get rid of that Persian man."

He knew she was referring to Ja'far al-Barmaki. He was astonished and said, "The news I have is also related to him, may God shame him! Do you mean his story with al-'Alawi or with my aunt al-'Abbasa?"

Zubayda was alarmed; blood rose to her cheeks, and surprise was visible in her eyes. She asked. "Have you known about al-'Abbasa's story?"

"Yes," he replied, "and I was quite angry. But I don't think we can benefit from that immediately. As for the story of al-'Alawi, it can be exploited sooner."

She said, "What 'Alawi do you mean? And what is his story? I haven't heard anything in this regard."

16 Al-Amin's full name was Muhammad al-Amin (meaning Muhammad, the Trustworthy), but to those closest to him, he was known only as Muhammad. *Translator's Note.*

He sat up and related to her what he had heard the previous evening from the slave-girl. Meanwhile, she looked at him, and her eyes were sparkling with astonishment and wonder. When he finished his report, she sighed and said, "That is the punishment of anyone who makes little of the power that God has delegated to him. Your father, despite his discernment and resoluteness, has surrendered the caliphate to this Persian man, and nothing remains of the caliphate for your father but its name. However, the tyrant shall meet with the consequences of his tyranny."

He said, "I don't deny my father the right to give this vizier a free hand in matters of the state; this is necessary, because the caliph cannot take in hand all matters by himself."

With seriousness in her eyes, she said, "Giving him a free hand in government affairs may be permissible, but what is your father's excuse for letting him into his harem as an unmarriageable man (a *mahram*[17])? Your grandfather al-Mahdi employed the Barmakids and had confidence in them. But he did not go to the extent of giving them a free hand. Your uncle al-Hadi did not do anything of the sort either, and I don't think anyone would do what your father has done!" She said this, with anger showing in her face and increasing her awesome dignity.

Al-Amin asked, "What do you mean, mother, by saying 'letting him into his harem'?"

She said, "I mean that your father, God protect him, ordered that Ja'far be permitted to enter the apartments of the caliph's wives, whether at home or on a trip. Your father also permitted him to see his slave-girls and his sisters and daughters when they are unveiled, claiming that there was a 'brotherly' relationship between the two of them because they were nursed by the same woman. It is no wonder that Ja'far has shown such brazen audacity!"

She sighed but then began to fly into a rage again. There was a bowl of musk in her hand and she busied herself with crumbling its contents while talking. When she was overwhelmed by rage, her fingers trembled and the cup fell from her hand, and the fragments of musk were scattered

---

17 *Mahram*: a male of age, whose degree of consanguinity precludes marriage to certain females such as his mother and sisters, according to Islamic law. He is thus permitted to see them when they are unveiled. *Translator's Note.*

over the carpet. Al-Amin was about to collect them and asked, with a man's earnest zeal for his womenfolk, "Has he been given such a free hand in the wives' apartments that he could enter your palace and see you?"

She shouted, "No, never... Will this *mawla* dare to look me in the eye? He has never treaded on the ground of this palace, nor have I ever asked him to do anything for me—and I never will."

By this time, al-Amin had finished collecting the musk fragments and returned them to the bowl, which he then gave to his mother, saying, "What's to be done now? This man must not be allowed to do what he pleases; otherwise, we would lose control and be subjected to endless shame."

She interrupted him and said, "The greatest blame concerning your aunt falls on your father, for he permitted his vizier to enter her palace, to speak with her, and to provide for her needs. He is a good-looking young man, of clean clothes and good scent, and she had not known another man. That is like pouring oil over fire. But this does not absolve him from treason."

She returned to busying herself with the musk fragments, while looking at the carpet and staring at the woven peacock in its middle. Al-Amin remained patient, but he was dispirited and annoyed because he had not attained his desired aim, nor had he dared talk openly with her about killing the man or reporting him. He was at a loss and bowed his head in silence, and signs of perplexity appeared all over his face. His mother noticed that and hastened to soothe him by saying, "I think you would like to know my opinion about what to do with this man."

"Yes," he said, "I am at my wit's end."

She said, "Do you think we should tell your father about his sister, al-'Abbasa?"

He said, "I don't know. All I want is to have this man killed."

She laughed, put her arm around his neck, and kissed him. Motherly tears of tenderness would have flowed from her eyes were it not for the gravity of the situation she was dealing with. Then she said, "I was intending to tell him about his sister, but confronting him suddenly is not without risk, so let us now be satisfied with telling him about al-'Alawi."

She then lowered her voice, put her hand in her pocket, and got out a slip of paper she gave him, saying, "Don't think I have forgotten the need to take revenge on this client on your behalf. I will never forget his emphatic demand that you should swear an oath to implement the provisions of the document signed last year. His impudence and bad manners reached the point of belittling you in front of me. I prepared a few verses of poetry about the issue we are dealing with, and I want to have them reach your father secretly without the vizier's knowledge. We would thus inform your father of the danger threatening the state from this man; if al-Rashid does not wake up, we will resort to more effective means."

Al-Amin took the slip of paper and read the following verses written on it:

> *Tell the man to whom God entrusted His land,*
> *And who has power and supreme authority:*
> *Look, Ibn Yahya has become a ruler like you,*
> *There is no difference between you and him.*
> *He has built a house, the like of which*
> *Neither Persians nor Indians have built.*
> *Pearls and sapphire are its gravel,*
> *Amber and frankincense are it soil.*
> *We are afraid that he will inherit*
> *Your kingdom, when death takes you away.*
> *A slave will not vie with his lord*
> *Unless the slave becomes wanton.*

When he finished reading it, he was pleased with it and said, "I think it will lead to Ja'far's execution. But how will you make it reach my father?"

She said, "I will charge one of our spies to put it in your father's place of prayer, and when he sees it, he will read it. I think it will fulfill the required purpose; if not, I have more effective medicine!"

She fell silent, and then she stood up. So al-Amin stood up too, knowing that she intended to leave the room. They walked together and she said, "I think you must be hungry. Let us go to the dining room."

He said, "True, I am hungry. Will I return to my palace after eating?"

She replied, "I have been longing to see you, Muhammad. So let us spend this whole day together."

Chapter 11

At al-Rashid's Gathering

After Isma'il ibn Yahya and Ja'far ibn al-Hadi had parted company, Isma'il intended to visit al-Rashid in order to ask him for al-'Aliya's hand in marriage on behalf of Ja'far. So in the morning, he put on his black attire and headgear, mounted his horse, and headed for the Palace of Eternity. On the way, he considered the best method to broach the subject of his cousin's engagement. He knew al-Rashid's severity and rashness when he was roused to anger, and he was afraid of the consequences if the caliph should think ill of him.

As soon as he approached the palace, he saw people leaving the markets in a hurry and rushing toward the main road from the palace to the bridge. So he ordered one of the two slave-boys escorting him to investigate the cause of that commotion, and the slave-boy returned and reported that the Commander of the Faithful was going to al-Shammasiyya to attend the horse race. Isma'il perceived in this an evil omen and became sure his task would fail, for he would not see al-Rashid in the morning, nor could he see him in the evening because al-Shammasiyya was in the eastern section of Baghdad and the race would last all day long.

He dismounted and stood on the side of the road so that he could see the caliph's procession but no one would notice him. He saw the people shoving one another and moving as though they were being led unwillingly. Then he saw young menservants running and carrying bows in their hands, with which they shot slugs at the common people in the road, in order to make way for the procession; they were a group of servants called Ants.[18] Behind them were infantrymen with the state's

---

18 *Naml* in Arabic, so called because of their small size, constant movement, and great number. *Translator's Note.*

emblem, some of whom carried sharp swords in their hands and others spiked maces; behind them were men, with bows pulled taut, walking in a dignified and calm manner. The caliph came after them riding a horse dyed with henna and sitting on a gilt saddle covered with silk adorned with gold. He wore an excessively high headgear without a turban, for when the caliphs wore headgear without turbans, they chose to have them quite high and with pointed tops because they needed to be higher than the headgear of everyone else.

Al-Rashid was forty-one years old. His white face was bright and his large eyes sparkled with intelligence. His beard was light and of a chestnut color, his mustache was long and fine, and there was a smile on his lips. In his right hand, he held a scepter of ebony with a golden edge. His horse was trotting leisurely, as though it knew who was riding it. Just behind the caliph was the umbrella man, who carried an umbrella made of ostrich feathers, slanting forward on its stick in order to protect the caliph from the sun. Following them were horsemen from the special guards, then the generals and the chief state officials, but Ja'far the vizier was not with them. The race horses followed, with light saddles, and their grooms led them by their halters. One of the horses was ridden by the chief groom, a Turk who was an expert in horse training. At the rear of the procession was another group of young menservants who warded the people off.

Isma'il stood watching that procession with the eyes of a philosopher reflecting on what it all meant. He wondered at men's delusions and their preoccupations with external appearances that only disguised irrefutable truths. He looked at the elite, the generals, and the Hashemites surrounding al-Rashid, and he knew what they really believed in their hearts. Some of them hated al-Rashid and wished him dead;, others loved him and served him devotedly but only out of self-interest. He then thought of himself and of the task he had come for. Zeal for the state and desire for its safety moved his heart. He was chagrined by the failure of the task he came for on that day, so he returned home hoping to come back the next morning to see al-Rashid.

The next morning, wearing his black attire and headgear, he mounted his horse and headed for the Palace of Eternity escorted by his two slave-boys. The palace grounds had four successive walls, and the caliph's sitting room could only be reached after one passed through the gate in each of the walls, where guards from the Chakeriyya group stood with their weapons. He passed through the first gate on horseback, and the guards stood up as a mark of respect. They let him through because they knew that he was one of the leading Hashemites, in addition to the special esteem in which al-Rashid held him. He then passed through the second gate and the third, where the guards stood up and greeted him as before. But when he reached the fourth gate, one of his two slave-boys was required to lead his horse away, so he continued on foot on a wide road leading to the House of the Common People. Meanwhile, the palace slaves walked in front of him, and he followed slowly behind them until he reached the house in which al-Rashid usually received the common people. Next to it, he saw rooms in which poets, writers, and boon companions waited until they were admitted or until al-Rashid summoned one of them. He noticed that they were noisy and that there wasn't a single guard in the place, so he knew that al-Rashid was not there. He was surprised and wanted to learn the reason when all of a sudden he saw Masrur, al-Rashid's servant, speeding toward him, which caused his sword to hit his thigh. On seeing him, Isma'il was not pleased because he knew the man's boorishness and cruelty—he was originally from Ferghana. Masrur bowed to kiss Isma'il's hand, but Isma'il pulled it away and asked about the Commander of the Faithful.

"He is at the House of the Elite, my lord," Masrur said.

"Why? Today is the day when he meets with the common people," Isma'il said.

"He was about to go to the House of the Common People," explained Masrur, "when a delegation from the King of India arrived. He decided instead to meet with them in the House of the Elite to impress them more with his awe and glory."

So Isma'il walked toward that house. On his way there, he saw two rows of the caliph's Turkish soldiers standing in full array, wearing heavy armor: only their eyes were visible. He asked Masrur, "What is the matter with these soldiers? And why are they standing with their armor as though they were on a battlefield?"

Masrur said, "When the Commander of the Faithful learned of the arrival of the delegation from the King of India, he wanted to impress and awe them so that they would let their king know the power of Islam that they had seen. So he commanded that these soldiers be paraded as you see."

Isma'il was pleased that al-Rashid's wanted to display the pomp of the state, but he was overcome by his fear of the plots woven against it, and he felt ill at ease. He walked between the two rows of soldiers to the house until he was close to its door, which was high and could be reached only by a flight of wide, white marble stairs interspersed with pieces of green slabs. Guards stood on both sides of the stairs with swords in their hands. Masrur entered before him in order to inform the chamberlain of Isma'il's arrival and ask that he be allowed to enter.

Isma'il climbed the stairs following him, proceeding slowly while permission for him to be admitted was sought. Very soon, he was invited to come in; he walked down a wide corridor paved with red tiles tied together with gold braces, while the servant who invited him walked in front of him. At the end of the corridor, he saw three fierce-looking dogs with bodies as big as those of lions, tied with iron chains around their necks. Three huge men held the dogs by the chains, and their heads were uncovered. From their appearance and color, Isma'il knew they were Indians. He was afraid of the dogs' blazing eyes and huge bodies. He passed by several private rooms, hallways, and corridors where the servants stood up to honor him, until he reached a round hall whose floor was covered with expensive carpets on which lay hides of tigers and lions; on the sides of the hall were candelabras with colored candles. Isma'il stopped to read the verses of poetry and wise sayings that were inscribed on the walls, and he waited for further permission as was required for those who entered into the presence of the caliph. But the servant returned and gestured to him to go forth because someone of his stature did not need any further permission.

So he went forth to a doorway on which was a curtain of silk adorned with gold. The servant moved the curtain to the side with his left hand and gestured to Isma'il with his right to enter. He entered into a large hall, thirty cubits long and thirty cubits wide, girded by marble columns. On its wall were gold pictures of land and sea creatures, interspersed with verses of poetry and wise sayings written in gold. On the floor was a carpet of yellow silk whose maker imitated the velvet carpet of Chosroes.[19] It had pictures with resplendent colors and gold thread representing trees, rivers, birds, and fish that made the onlooker believe he was in a garden with fresh plants in which streams ran and birds sang; on the margins of the carpet, there was beautiful embroidery. The hall had a very big dome built in three tiers, each of which stood on five columns, and its ceiling was decorated with pictures and writings. In the middle of the hall, there was a curtain of Chinese silk between the two walls to screen the caliph from those who sat with him—this was the custom for sitting with the caliphs during those times, except when the caliph chose to see someone face to face with the curtain raised.

Isma'il saw chairs arranged outside the curtain for the Hashemites to sit on, but they were all empty. According to the conventions of those days, the Hashemites used to be called "Sons of Kings" or "Nobles" (Sharifs). The cushions placed between the chairs were for the elite princes and generals. Isma'il saw Indians with brocaded hats sitting on them, and they were wearing robes of Indian fabric on which were colored pictures representing some large animals, especially elephants. Around their necks, they wore necklaces of expensive gems and golden amulets representing some of their idols. The Indians sat there, awed and humbled, waiting for the command of the caliph, and in front of them on the carpet, there were swords made in their country that were called 'citadel swords' (qal'iyya). Isma'il knew that they were the delegation from the King of India and that the dog keepers he had seen in the corridor were their followers.

The curtain attendant invited Isma'il to enter if he wished or to sit on one of the chairs until al-Rashid finished with the Indians. Isma'il had heard al-Rashid clear his throat, so he knew that he was there, sitting on his throne behind the curtain; he preferred to sit down until the caliph finished with the delegation, although he was afraid their presence might prevent him from speaking to the caliph about the matter for which he

---

19 Probably Chosroes, the First. Chosroes is the Greek form of the name of two great kings of the Sasanids of Persia. In Persian, it is Khosrau, or Khusrau or Khosru, and in Arabic it is Kisra. Khosrau I, called Khosrau Anushirvan (531–579 AD) was one of the greatest Persian kings, who ruled the Sasanid Empire at its apogee during the golden age of Pahlavi literature. Khosrau II, called Khosrau Parvez (591–628 AD) was his grandson and fought the Byzantines between 623 and 628 AD in the war mentioned in "Surat al-Rum" in the Qur'an (Q. 30:2–5). He was finally defeated and then deposed and killed by his own son. *Translator's Note.*

had come. He then heard al-Rashid talking to them from behind the curtain, the curtain attendant being his interpreter; they used to select curtain attendants from among those who knew several languages for this purpose.

"What have you brought us?" al-Rashid asked the head of the delegation.

"These citadel swords that have no equal in our view," they said.

Al-Rashid ordered someone to bring him al-Samsama, which was the sword of 'Amr ibn Ma'di Karib.[20] He commanded one of his Turkish men to use it, and he did and broke with it those Indian swords, one by one. Then al-Rashid ordered that it be shown to the Indian delegation, and it was found to be without any dent, so they were bewildered and bowed their heads.

"What else do you have?" al-Rashid asked.

"We brought dogs that no lion met without being wounded by them," they said.

When Isma'il heard what they said, he was afraid to see the dogs again.

"We have a lion," al-Rashid said. "If your dogs are able to wound it, they will be truly as you said. Let the dogs go out to the lions in their cages, one of which will be released to meet them, and we will watch their fight from the window."

The curtain attendant went out and gestured to the Indians. They stood up and walked; they passed by the dogs in the corridor and took them with them. Some slave-boys led everyone outside the house, and one of them preceded them to the lion caretaker and ordered him to let out a huge lion. So he did, and it was brought to a courtyard where the Indian dogs were.

Isma'il saw the lion strut haughtily and roar, and he had no doubt that it would tear the dogs to pieces. But lo and behold, the dogs tore into the lion. Al-Rashid saw this from the window and sent word to the

---

20 'Amr was a heroic warrior and a poet of early Arab history. He lived mostly in the pre-Islamic period and died in the year 21 AH/641 AD, having adopted Islam for the last ten years of his life. *Translator's Note.*

delegation to return to the hall where they had been. They returned and Isma'il returned with them, perplexed at what he had seen the dogs do. When they returned, al-Rashid said to the delegation, "Where have you come by these dogs, and what kind are they?"

They said, "They are Suyuriyya dogs and live in our country. They have no equal in the whole world."

Al-Rashid said, "I would like to keep them. Choose whatever you wish from the rare or uncommon things of our country in return for them."

"We wish to have the sword with which our swords were broken," they said.

He said, "It is not permissible in our religion to exchange gifts by giving you weapons. If it were not for this, we would not have withheld them from you. Wish for whatever else you would like."

"We wish to have nothing else," they insisted.

"This cannot be," al-Rashid said. "You cannot have it."

He then ordered that they be given many presents and generous rewards, and they left, full of awe and in great dread of the caliphate.

* * *

As for Isma'il, his thoughts returned to the task he had come for. As soon as the caliph finished with the Indian delegation, he wanted to speak with him alone, before any of the Hashemites or anyone else came, making him lose this opportunity. After the Indian delegation left, the curtain attendant returned and invited Isma'il to enter into al-Rashid's presence, for there was no longer any reason to hold him back. He said to him, "When the Commander of the Faithful learned of your arrival, he immediately ordered me to let you in, and said, 'I would like that no one else be admitted until I finish speaking with him.'"

He then widened for him the space between the two parts of the curtain, and Isma'il looked in and saw al-Rashid sitting cross-legged on a throne of pure gold studded with jewels, placed on a platform with a canopy in the front part of the hall. The platform with the canopy was built between two of the columns of the hall covered with embroidered gold fabric. At the foot of each of the two columns, pages stood with fly whisks or kerchiefs in their hands; behind the platform with the canopy, two Chakeri men stood on its sides, each of them holding an unsheathed sword. The canopy itself was an umbrella-like structure supported by ebony columns inlaid with ivory. Its ceiling was made of black silk embroidered with beautiful golden drawings, and from its front and two sides gold crescents were suspended, and there was a golden citron hanging from each, with large gems hanging—red, yellow, and blue hyacinth—in a dazzlingly beautiful array.

Al-Rashid was sitting on the throne on the platform under the canopy, and he was wearing the clothes he usually wore when receiving visitors, be they kings or their representatives, when he wanted to awe them with the power of Islam, the majesty of the state, and the splendor of the caliphate. He had worn these clothes that day to receive the Indian delegation. On his head, he wore a short headgear with a black turban of embroidered silk, in the folds of which were gems in the shape of little rosaries. At the front of the headgear, just above the forehead, there was a gold knob studded with jewels of hyacinth and emerald from which rose wires of gold with pearls like a peacock's crest, three of which were like pigeon eggs at the root of the crest. Al-Rashid wore a black cloak over which he wore the Prophet's *burda*.[21] Anyone approaching the throne could not help being awed. As for Isma'il, he had become accustomed to this and, in any case, he was a wise and rational man who was not impressed by ostentatious appearances. And yet, he was preoccupied with the state of the caliphate. He feared its weakening, and he knew al-Rashid was severe and rash when angry.

When he looked in from between the two parts of the doorway curtain, he said in a loud voice, "Peace be upon the Commander of the Faithful, God's mercy, and His blessings."

"And peace be upon you, Uncle," al-Rashid said, moving as though he was about to stand up in honor of Isma'il. He smiled at him and added, "Welcome!"

---

21 The *burda* is Prophet Muhammad's woolen mantle, worn by the caliphs as a symbol of legitimacy and politico-religious authority. The Prophet had given it to the poet Ka'b ibn Zuhair as a reward for a poem in which he praised him. Mu'awiya bought it from the poet, and the Umayyad caliphs inherited it from him and wore it. It was subsequently worn by the 'Abbasid caliphs. *Translator's Note.*

Isma'il entered, hastening his steps to prevent the caliph from standing up. Al-Rashid rose a little from his seat, stretched out his hand, and shook Isma'il's, saying, "You have come to your own family, Uncle. Does someone like you need to seek permission to enter?"

He then beckoned to the pages, and they offered Isma'il a chair, which they placed next to the throne, and al-Rashid motioned to him to sit down as he gave him a kind and welcoming smile. Isma'il sat down and expressed his gratitude for the attention and friendliness with which he had been received. He invoked God's blessings upon al-Rashid and remained silent as was conventionally required in sessions with the caliphs, for visitors should never address the caliph first. Al-Rashid was pleased with Isma'il's observance of protocol and deference, the more so because he was aware of his pride and self-confidence owing to his high position.

"You have come to us for a good reason, God willing," al-Rashid said. "You have been away from us for many days, and you don't usually come to us unless you have advice to proffer or an important matter to discuss."

"I reside in Basra, O Commander of the Faithful," Isma'il said, "and I rarely come to Baghdad. If I thought that there was any service I could render by being with the caliph, I would have spent all the days of my life with him. But I have now come to seek a favor of him that we can add to his continuous kindnesses and abundant benefactions."

He said, "Say what you need. Your wish is my command."

Isma'il appreciated that gesture of amiability, bowed his head thankfully with his hands in his lap, and said, "Commanding is my lord's prerogative, may God make it his alone with no one to share it with. He generously bestows whatever favors he likes. If my lord will permit me to say a few words, I would ask permission to speak with him alone."

Al-Rashid beckoned to the pages and the two Chakeri men to leave, and he turned all his attention to Isma'il, his eyes sparkling with interest because he knew that Isma'il would not request to be secluded with him unless there was an important matter to be discussed.

"May I speak?" Isma'il said, looking directly at al-Rashid.

"Speak. Ask whatever you like," al-Rashid said.

He said, "It is not unknown to my lord that Ja'far, son of my brother al-Hadi, is one of our best cousins."

When al-Rashid heard Ja'far's name, he became wary of the request that might follow and that he would not want to implement. But he was kind enough to say, "Yes, he is my brother's son. Is he in need of any grant?"

"No, my lord," Isma'il said, "for the kindnesses of the Commander of the Faithful continue to be conferred on him as well as on the rest of the Hashemites—but he would like to be even more honored."

Al-Rashid realized with his perspicacity that Isma'il had come as a matchmaker, but pretended not to understand and said, "Relationship to the Messenger, Prophet Muhammad, is the greatest source of honor for him and us."

"Yes, it is so," Isma'il said, "but he would like to be closer to his uncle, the Commander of the Faithful, who is the successor of the Master of all Messengers."

Al-Rashid had no doubt, then, that Isma'il had come to ask for the hand of his daughter in marriage to Ja'far, so he quickly said, "All that you ask will be done, my Uncle, except asking for al-'Aliya's hand in marriage!"

Isma'il was surprised at this unexpected response and said, "I have come only to ask for her hand. If this is impossible, command is the sole prerogative of the Commander of the Faithful, and we obey his every wish and pray for his long life. But the freedom he bestows on me when dealing with him gives me the audacity to ask a question which, I hope, will not be burdensome to my lord."

"Speak," the caliph said, "for you have a special consideration and a right."

Isma'il said, "Is it perhaps that the Commander of the Faithful does not think that his nephew is equal to our lady al-'Aliya? Who is more of a match for her than the son of her uncle, brother of her father, the grandson of the noble king and venerable old man?" He meant al-Mansur.

Al-Rashid said, toying the scepter with his fingers, "As for equality, no person can contest it with him. But word has been given, and al-'Aliya is engaged!"

Isma'il thought it unlikely that the caliph's daughter would be engaged without him knowing. He surmised that al-Rashid had said that in order to decline his request.

"Al-'Aliya is engaged?" he said. "I did not know that. Had I known it, I would not have come to ask for her hand. Besides, I did not think anyone but her cousin could be given that honor."

Al-Rashid stirred in his seat, looked at the carpet before him, trying to conceal the agitation almost visible in his face and said, "Yes, but our vizier Ja'far requested her in marriage for Ibrahim ibn 'Abd al-Malik ibn Salih, our cousin, and we did not reject his request."

When Isma'il heard this, he bowed his head, sensing the magnitude of his failure. His anger at the extent of Ja'far's influence affected him more than his failure. But he suppressed his feeling lest he should anger al-Rashid and kept his head bowed while al-Rashid looked at him, observing his reactions and wanting somehow to assuage him. When Isma'il's silence became too long, al-Rashid said, "I am sorry to decline your request, but you know that it is not appropriate to break my word; ask any other favor for our brother's son."

Isma'il raised his head and, seizing the opportunity of al-Rashid's desire to make up for his failure, said, "My lord is right. Breaking his word is not appropriate for someone in his position. I know this because of my own bad feeling when breaking my word. I must now return empty-handed after I had promised the caliph's nephew this honor. I was hasty in my promise, but I did that only out of my desire to protect the state, for my lord knows my zeal for its security."

Al-Rashid realized what Isma'il was insinuating, namely, the desire to satisfy the son of his brother al-Hadi in order to distract him from seeking the caliphate or obstructing its policy. Al-Rashid was accustomed to hearing Isma'il say things much more frankly than that—things which no other person would dare say at all. Yet, this insinuation angered him because nothing upset him more than the smallest suggestion of meddling in his rule, even indirectly. But he controlled his anger, ignored the remark, and said, "You are well known for your zeal regarding our state, which only becomes stronger thanks to the efforts of men of wisdom and sagacious opinions like yourself—and they are few. As for my nephew, he is of my flesh and blood and I would like to please him. Is there anything else that you would request for him besides al-'Aliya?"

Isma'il said, "May God give long life to the Commander of the Faithful. I see that his courtesy toward me knows no bounds, and I am pleased that he understands what I mean. I therefore make a request to him that his nephew be given some work that will occupy him. I ask that he be appointed to rule the province of Egypt or Khurasan."

Al-Rashid was dumbfounded, surprise written all over his eyes. He shook his head in astonishment and said, "And this too is not possible, my Uncle; for I promised my vizier yesterday morning that the province of Egypt would be given to Ibrahim. As for Khurasan, I promised a few days ago to give it to the vizier himself. I have kept this news secret and have not informed anyone. If you were not Isma'il, I would not have divulged it to you."

Isma'il was disconcerted by his successive failures and bowed his head in silence and deep thought. But he knew it was necessary for him to be frank about his suggestions, so he returned to his natural way of speaking freely. He became oblivious to his situation and his fear of untoward consequences if al-Rashid became angry. So he said, "The Commander of the Faithful will, I hope, permit me to reveal to him what is in my heart and speak with him simply as Harun ibn Muhammad, I being simply his cousin Isma'il ibn Yahya." He cleared his throat and sat up, while al-Rashid resigned himself to wait patiently for what he had to say as he stared at him.

Isma'il continued, "You know my great zeal for the safety of this state and my deep desire that this ring remain on Harun's finger and this *burda* on his shoulders. You know also what thoughts may be in your nephew's mind. I know his weakness and inability to achieve his aims. But good politics require us to avoid all causes of dissension that may give our enemies an opportunity to attack us—and they are many. Among them are the Byzantines in Constantinople and the Umayyads in al-Andalus.[22] I believe they are unable to succeed, but wisdom requires us to support one another and to be united. This is easy for al-Rashid, if

22 Al-Andalus is the name that the Arabs gave to the Iberian Peninsula (Spain and Portugal) when they ruled it from 711 to 1492 AD and achieved a high degree of civilization in the region. *Translator's Note.*

he uses his intelligence and shrewdness and distracts those of his relatives with ambitious designs by making them serve his state instead of leaving them free to challenge him."

Al-Rashid promptly hastened to interrupt him to prevent him from continuing to speak at length and disclose more than he had done—for then he would not be able to control his feelings—so he said, "We would have liked to appoint our nephew as governor of Egypt if it had not been for the promise that it would be given to Ibrahim. Do you have for me any suggestion in this matter?"

Overcome by pride and independence of opinion, Isma'il quickly said, "I have one suggestion."

"What is it?" asked al-Rashid.

With his palms on his knees as though he was ready to stand up, Isma'il said, "That you designate him as caliph after Muhammad al-Amin and 'Abd Allah al-Ma'mun. Do that as a gesture of amiability and as a means to gratify him."

When al-Rashid heard his words, he laid down the scepter from his hand and put it on the throne's seat and suddenly rose and stepped down to the carpet. His movement was so impetuous that the *burda* slipped from his shoulders and was about to fall, and he became distracted from his surroundings and oblivious to Isma'il's presence near him. He rearranged the *burda* on his shoulders and began to walk up and down the hall. Isma'il stood up and realized that staying there was risky and useless, and decided that disclosing what was in his heart should be left for another occasion: al-Rashid was standing up and that was one of the signals caliphs gave for dismissal. But he did not want to leave before making sure that al-Rashid would not think ill of him, so he said, "I think that the Commander of the Faithful has regretted the freedom he had permitted me in order to speak unrestrainedly in his presence. I believe I have been presumptuous taking more liberty with him than I should have, and so I discussed subjects that are none of my concern!"

Al-Rashid had stopped and pretended he was reading two verses of poetry engraved on the wall of the hall. When he heard what Isma'il said, he turned to him and gave him an affected smile that did not conceal his anger and said, "Isma'il has a special standing with us that you know, and he has the merit of giving us advice and counsel. Don't be disturbed by my sudden standing up. If I am angry, my anger is not directed at you; for how can I be angry at an elder of the Hashemites and a wise man of the 'Abbasids? For, in spite of my desire to honor you, I was sorry that you did not ask me for something that I could deliver on."

Isma'il realized that in these words the caliph was trying to conceal his anger and pretend to be civil, so he said, "I thank my lord for his graciousness and his good intentions. It seems the man's bad fortune brought about this circumstance. Fortune has its ups and down, but this is a time when it did not favor him. Will my lord allow me to leave now, and we will postpone this matter to a more propitious time than this one?"

Al-Rashid was pleased and said, "Fine, my Uncle. You may leave."

So Isma'il left, walking backwards in front of al-Rashid as was the custom when leaving meetings with caliphs. When he reached the curtain, he departed while al-Rashid was still standing and looking at him, seething with anger and filled with a desire to be alone.

Isma'il left the palace and mounted his horse immediately, regretting that he had come. His two slave-boys escorted him on foot, not knowing the anger that raged in his heart and the regret that afflicted his mind: the state's condition was all the more precarious on account of all the different parties with their conflicting purposes. He reached his palace at noon. He found Ja'far ibn al-Hadi waiting for him and, on being asked what had happened, related to him some of the news. He told him about al-Rashid's apology for declining to accept his marriage to al-'Aliya and exaggerated the caliph's apologies, in order not to upset Ja'far. He did not tell him about having asked on his behalf for the province of Egypt or for the heir apparent position. He ended by saying, "I am sorry for my failure, and al-Rashid is sorrier than I am, but we can really do nothing about that. So be patient and be reasonable, and we shall seize a more auspicious occasion, for al-Rashid has a high opinion of you."

Ja'far was not unaware that Isma'il was toning down the effect of the news on him but he went along and said, "I accept your request, but do you know the reason for al-'Aliya's engagement to Ibrahim?"

"No," Isma'il said. "But the vizier has an audacious familiarity in his relations with the caliph, and 'Abd al-Malik has similar relations with the vizier. So 'Abd al-Malik may have approached the vizier and asked him to intercede for the engagement of al-'Aliya to his son Ibrahim, and al-Rashid accepted his request."

Ja'far ibn al-Hadi said, "If it were as simple as that, it would have been insignificant. But I will tell you what really happened and that will surely demonstrate to you what I had told you about the disdain these non-Arab clients have for the caliph and his family. A spy of mine in Ja'far al-Barmaki's house told me that this vizier was in a pleasure gathering with his boon companions; he was wearing silk and was daubed with perfume and so were all his companions. He ordered his chamberlain not to admit anyone but 'Abd al-Malik ibn Bahran, his butler. The chamberlain heard the name 'Abd al-Malik but did not hear the name ibn Bahran. Our cousin 'Abd al-Malik ibn Salih was waiting for an opportunity to speak with the vizier concerning some of his needs, so when he heard about that gathering, he went to the vizier's house. The chamberlain told Ja'far al-Barmaki that 'Abd al-Malik was at the door, and Ja'far thought he was ibn Bahran. So he ordered that he be admitted. 'Abd al-Malik entered, wearing his black attire and headgear, and saw the people there in the attire of drinking companions. When Ja'far saw him, his face became ashen—and you know that 'Abd al-Malik does not drink wine. But when he saw that situation, he took off his black attire and headgear and asked for the attire of drinking companions. He entered and greeted everyone and said, 'Have us share in your merriment, and do with us as you have done with yourselves.' A servant came and clothed him in the attire of drinking companions. He then ate with them and was brought a liter of wine, so he drank it and said to Ja'far, 'By God, I have never drunk wine before today.' So Ja'far gave him more wine. He was brought perfume and he daubed himself with it, and he drank and caroused with them in the best manner, and Ja'far's embarrassment was gone. When 'Abd al-Malik wanted to leave, Ja'far said to him, 'Name your needs, for I cannot give you enough things in return for what you have done.' 'Abd al-Malik said, 'The Commander of the Faithful bears a grudge in his heart against me; I request that you remove it from his heart and restore his good opinion of me.' Ja'far said, 'Consider it done: the Commander of the Faithful has become satisfied with you and his feeling against you has gone.' 'Abd al-Malik said, 'And I have a debt of four thousand dirhams.' Ja'far said, 'Consider it done: it has been paid on your behalf, for the amount is ready. But as it is from the Commander of the Faithful, it is more prestigious coming from the caliph and more indicative of his good feeling toward you.' 'Abd al-Malik said, 'And I would like to raise the rank of my son, Ibrahim, by his marriage to an offspring of the caliph.' Ja'far said, 'Consider it done: the Commander of the Faithful has married him to al-'Aliya, his daughter.' 'Abd al-Malik said, 'And I would like that his position become noted by having a flag above his head.' Ja'far said, 'Consider it done too: the Commander of the Faithful has appointed him governor of Egypt.' Look at this audacity that is as repugnant as al-Rashid's approval of it. Ja'far did all this as a reward for 'Abd al-Malik's drinking of wine, and we blame our cousin al-Amin—despite his young age—for his drinking and consider him a profligate man. But this is true profligacy, and you are not unaware of its harm to the kingdom. Yet, al-Rashid did what Ja'far wanted without caring about the effect of all this in weakening the kingdom."

Isma'il listened to Ja'far Ibn al-Hadi and was about to burst with anger, but he gave a brief answer pretending to make light of the story. He said, "This is what the spy told you, and his report is certainly not without some exaggeration. At any rate, keep our discussion secret and be patient. We will see what happens."

Ja'far Ibn al-Hadi was silent more out of respect than conviction.

Isma'il said, "Go to Basra, and I will follow you in two days."

"Fine," Ja'far said, bidding him farewell and pretending he was making ready to travel. He disappeared for one day, and then went to see al-Fadl ibn al-Rabi' at home. Al-Fadl was still thinking of a way to report the news of al-'Alawi to al-Rashid. Muhammad al-Amin had informed him once more about the story of his mother, his conversation with her concerning al-'Alawi, and her feelings against the Barmakids. Al-Fadl was not ignorant of all that. So when Ja'far ibn al-Hadi came to see him, he welcomed him and listened to what he had heard about 'Abd al-Malik ibn Salih and the marriage of al-'Aliya, and about all this being an indication of the caliph's weakness and the tyranny of the Barmakids. He urged him to report the news of al-'Alawi to al-Rashid.

Al-Fadl said to him, "I have prepared everything."

Ja'far asked, "Have you found someone who would convey the news?"

Al-Fadl replied, "We have no one but Abu al-'Atahiya, for you can buy him with money and he is close to the caliph."

Having remembered something he had forgotten, Ja'far asked, "Did he return from tracking the two boys?"

"He did," al-Fadl assured him, "and he will keep them in a safe place until they are needed."

Ja'far Ibn al-Hadi was delighted and said, "By God, Ja'far al-Barmaki has been cornered. Now see what you can do to convey the news to al-Rashid. I am leaving Baghdad as my uncle Isma'il insisted that I do, and you are equal to the job."

"Rest assured," he said.

Ja'far bade him farewell and left, thinking that he had instigated al-Fadl against the vizier and used him for his own purposes, whereas al-Fadl believed that he had used Ja'far ibn al-Hadi for his purpose, for if the Barmakids fell, the vizierate would return to him. Meanwhile, he was not unaware that Ja'far ibn al-Hadi bore a grudge against al-Rashid and that he was only striving to restore the caliphate to himself. That is why al-Fadl was making Ja'far believe that he was striving to help him get the caliphate, but in truth all he cared about was regaining the vizierate, without caring whether his vizierate was in the service of al-Rashid or another caliph. Intentions differed, plots varied, and efforts contradicted one another, but the goal was the same and shared by all of them—namely, to overthrow the Barmakids by any means possible. And if God wants something, He prepares its causes.

Meanwhile al-Rashid, alone in the hall, was unhappy at the manner in which Isma'il had left him, notwithstanding his high position and exalted rank. He began to think about their conversation and repeated in his mind what he had told him; he concluded that he could not have said anything else. He walked up and down the hall, burdened with concerns. He thought of his vizier, and realized that the influence, esteem, and power he had attained was greater than that of his own Hashemite cousins. Then he returned to his reason and realized that he was bound by circumstances; for the vizier had the reins of government in his hands

and ran state affairs with wisdom and proficiency. He spared al-Rashid
its preoccupations and burdens. Furthermore, they had strong bonds of
allegiance and affection for each other, and the vizier's father, Yahya, had
rendered him a great service for he was instrumental in placing him on
the throne of the caliphate by his good planning. But then al-Rashid
questioned his own high opinion of his vizier as his doubts returned
because of his knowledge that Ja'far was partial to the Shi'a of 'Ali and
because of the many people who had criticized him—even though he
realized that their criticism was based on their jealousy.

While walking in the hall and thinking, he turned by chance to
the throne and saw the scepter that he had laid on it. He went to take it,
and his sight fell on a slip of paper behind the cushion. He picked it up,
unfolded it, and read it. He found that it contained the verses that his
wife Zubayda had read to her son Muhammad al-Amin. When he reached
the following verses,

> We are afraid that he will inherit
> Your kingdom, when death takes you away.
> A slave will not vie with his lord
> Unless the slave becomes wanton,

blood gushed to his head and his anger flared. Thinking deeply, he
looked at the slip of paper and read it again, confused, thinking he had
left it there. His thoughts turned again to Ja'far al-Barmaki and his
wealth, power, and tyranny. He pondered that they reached to such an
extent as to permit him to give the caliph's daughters in marriage to
whom he pleased, the governorship of provinces to whom he liked, and
to grant funds without consultation, fearing no power or objection.
He said to himself, *It is time for you, Harun, to wake up from your slumber
and look into the problem of this "helper" and his presumptuous conduct for
he will soon stretch out his hand to grab my powers, God forbid.* He jumped
with the scepter in his hand as though he was attacking an enemy,
saying:

> When wings grow on ants so that
> They can fly, their ruin is due soon.

He looked around and saw the bliss and pomp that surrounded him. He imagined that the caliphate, at his death, would pass on to Ja'far al-Barmaki. He knew that his son al-Amin was weak and that his son al-Ma'mun was stronger but sided with the Persians because he had been brought up in the bosom of Ja'far and grew up to love the Shi'a. If the caliphate passed to al-Ma'mun while Ja'far was alive, it would go effectively out of the hands of the 'Abbasids. He, therefore, regretted that he had asked Ja'far to educate al-Ma'mun and had neglected what should have been his most important priority: namely, the survival of the state in the hands of the 'Abbasids. He then remembered how Ja'far had urged him to designate al-Ma'mun as heir apparent and how he had kept insisting until he accepted. He imagined that Ja'far had done that in order to transfer the caliphate to the Shi'a after it left al-Amin's hand. He gnashed his teeth in regret and said, shaking his head:

> *The correct opinion appeared clearly to me, but*
> *I deviated from the path that was more judicious.*
> *How can milk be returned to the udder*
> *After it had flowed and become divided loot.*
> *I am afraid things will be wry after being straight,*
> *And the rope will be unraveled after being well twined.*

Again, he steadied himself and thought deeply and objectively about the realities on the ground. He became afraid of Ja'far al-Barmaki because he knew he had many people who liked him and supported him, among whom was a large group of elite statesmen, some of whom were Hashemites who received abundant gifts and favors from him. These concerns continued to echo in his mind as he paced the hall with his hands behind his back. At one point, he stood in front of the curtain and read the verses embroidered there in gold thread:

> *Beware of matters which, if their income*
> *Is plenty, will be restrained regarding sources.*
> *And it is not appropriate for a man to absolve himself*
> *When there is no man among all the people to absolve him.*

After reading the verses, he pulled himself together and returned to his senses. He looked at the slip of paper in his hand and said, "Perhaps the writer of these verses was one of the enviers of Ja'far, for they are numerous. At any rate, I will be patient and will wait for an opportunity to discover the truth."

* * *

He spent a while longer thinking about these matters, sometimes standing still and at other times walking, still wearing that magnificent attire. Suddenly, the chamberlain entered and said, "Poets and boon companions have been waiting at the public gate since morning. Today is the day for them to see you. Will my lord allow any of them to enter?"

When al-Rashid heard his words, he came to as if waking up from a deep sleep. He was at a loss, because he was in no mood for poetry or revelry. He preferred to be alone. But if he dismissed the poets, people would think he was worried, and he was too proud for that. So he said, "Who is at the gate, among those mentioned?"

"They are many," the chamberlain said. "Some of them are people with stipends and flowing incomes who live in Baghdad, and others are people who have come from remote parts of the country seeking gifts."

Al-Rashid said, "Dismiss those coming from remote parts now, and we will permit them to enter some other time; ask the treasurer to give them generous rewards and to please them. Who is at the gate among the people with stipends?"

The chamberlain replied, "Among scholars, there are al-Asma'i, al-Kisa'i, and Abu 'Ubaida."

Al-Rashid gestured with his hand as if interrupting him and said, "Forget the scholars. Who else?"

He said, "Among the poets are Abu Nuwas al-Hasan ibn Hani', Abu al-'Atahiya, and Marwan ibn Abi Hafsa; and as for..."

Al-Rashid's face shone when he heard the name of Marwan, because he liked his poetry's criticism of the followers of 'Ali. But he did not have an inclination to hear poetry or literature that day; he knew that nothing but singing could clear his mind, so he said, "Call in only those three poets and admit them to the hall of drinks. Are there any boon companions or entertaining singers at our gate?"

"There are singers," the chamberlain said. "I have seen among them some of the friends of our lord Ibrahim ibn al-Mahdi, the brother of the Commander of the Faithful; they are of those who follow his method of singing, such as Ibn Jami', Ibn Nabih, Ibn Abi al-'Awra', and Yahya al-Malaki. I have also seen some of the friends of Is'haq al-Mawsili who are admirers of his method, and I heard them discussing which of the two methods of singing was better."

Al-Rashid interrupted him and said, "Forget these singers. I am not inclined today to meet them and hear a debate about methods of singing. Summon Barsuma, the reed player, as well as Abu Zakkar, the blind fiddle player, and Husain, the buffoon. As for singing, I would like to hear the songstresses of the palace." He bowed his head for a while, and then said, "But that will not be good enough unless Ibrahim al-Mawsili is there. Summon my servant, Masrur."

The chamberlain gestured in obedience and left. Moments later, Masrur came in with his sword and all his crudeness, and he greeted the caliph.

"Go to Ibrahim, the singer, at once," al-Rashid said to him.

Masrur remained standing still, so al-Rashid knew he wanted to speak and said to him, "What is the matter with you? Why don't you go?"

He said, "I don't know where I can find Ibrahim now, for the Commander of the Faithful has permitted him to be alone with his family one day per week... And it is today."

"Go, bring him wherever you may find him," said al-Rashid.

He obeyed and left. Then al-Rashid clapped and a servant appeared, and he said to him, "Bring me the man responsible for clothing." He meant the man who helped him wear his clothes, so the servant brought him the man and al-Rashid said to him, "I intend to have a gathering with drinking companions. Clothe me with the appropriate attire." The man left and soon returned with several pages carrying parts of that attire. It consisted of an embroidered cape woven of gold thread; a gown with a wide, red sash; and a small embroidered turban. These made up his summer attire for such gatherings. Other slave-boys came, some of whom carried incense burners with aloe and ambergris, and others carried bowls of perfume. The man responsible for clothing al-Rashid started taking the jewels off the caliph's turban and undoing it, disrobed him of his *burda* and his robe, and clothed him with the gown and sash, the cape, and the small turban. When the man finished clothing him, al-Rashid went out a door of the hall leading to the women's houses. He continued to walk from one corridor to another and from one house to another until he reached a house whose inner courtyard was paved with marble and whose inner walls were clad with embroidered fabric woven of gold thread. He then reached a hall whose floor was similar and whose walls were similarly decorated with embroidery, and in it a throne of sandalwood was placed for him. In the middle of the hall, a curtain of the same embroidered fabric with beautiful figures was let down. All around the hall, there were cushions of embroidered fabric, but nobody was sitting on them because the poets usually sat in the other section of the hall with the curtain separating them from him.

When al-Rashid sat there and the slave-boys stood in front of him, he remembered that he had not eaten since morning. He ordered the man responsible for serving food to bring him some food. So a cloth was spread out for him, on which the food was traditionally served: he was first served broth to invigorate his body and then stews of greens; these were followed by chickens, grilled pigeons or partridges, and several kinds of fish, spiced meats, and legumes. He was then offered flat pies stuffed with meat and fat spiced with pepper and ginger, followed by sweet honey pies and almond cakes. Finally he was offered nuts to munch on after the meal. He ate, but he was anxious. When he finished, he heard a lute playing a tune that he had not heard before.

He listened and the sound pleased him. He knew it was coming from the gallery behind the curtain, and he felt gradually relieved of his depression while enjoying that strange tune. From its delicacy, he realized it was the voice of a slave-girl, and he shouted, "Who is singing for us from the gallery, may God bless her?"

"This is Qaranfula (Carnation)," the answer came from behind the curtain, "and her voice is as pleasant as her scent."

Al-Rashid recognized the voice that answered him—it was Husain, the buffoon, and he shouted at him, "Woe to you! What Qaranfula?"

He answered, "She is a slave-girl whom our lord, the heir apparent, sent to the Commander of the Faithful this morning as a gift. Sing,

Qaranfula. The caliph is thrilled with your voice. I wish I were in your shoes, for that would spare me the blows and the slaps."

When the caliph heard this buffoonery, he laughed and all those who heard him laughed too. The buffoon continued, "This is my lot for being close to the caliphs: I cry and they laugh. I wish my good luck would help me become a carnation or a rose so that people might smell me and hear my voice or take pity on my skin. But I am afraid my wish will be granted, and my good fortune will then go away and confusion will set in and destiny will convert me into a watermelon or a morsel of broth meat. I will then be eaten by people and they will enjoy me, but I will end in the darkness of their innards—and what an end! Sing, Qaranfula, sing! I beseech God that He may keep me as I am for it has been said, 'Better the devil you know than the one you don't!'"

Al-Rashid roared with laughter, and everyone there guffawed. Then they all fell silent, waiting for al-Rashid's reaction. None of the boon companions or the elite, who would usually be sitting with him on his side of the curtain, was with him; only the slave-boys and the pages standing there to serve him or fan him could see his face. He was silent for a moment, trying to hide one of his concerns that had pestered him that morning. Then he said, "I knew that this songstress was new when I first heard her singing and her lute playing, despite the many other songstresses we have in this palace. Woe to Ibrahim al-Mawsili! Where is he?"

The chamberlain said, "Masrur has gone to track him, and he has not yet returned."

Al-Rashid said, "Put up a curtain for this songstress, and add her to the best songstresses in our palace who have learned this art from Ibrahim—and bring the drinks."

* * *

There were three hundred songstresses in al-Rashid's palace; among them were players of the lute, the harp, the guitar, the mandolin,[23] and

---

23 The musical instruments used by the Arabs in 'Abbasid times differed from those used in the modern West, although their names may suggest similarity. The Arabic names mentioned here are *al-'ud* (similar to a medieval European lute), *al-jank* (similar to a medieval European harp or lyre), *al-mizhar* (similar to a medieval European guitar), and *al-tunbur* (similar to a medieval European bandore or a mandolin with a long neck). *Translator's Note.*

other musical instruments. They differed in their standing with al-Rashid depending on the degree of their beauty and their artistic perfection in his view. These were in addition to two thousand slave-girls who did not sing but were concubines. His servant, Masrur, was the one usually responsible for the concubines and the songstresses, but the caretaker of the slave-girls deputized for him when he was not available.

The man responsible for drinks brought the table of drinks with all the necessary paraphernalia such as pitchers and cups of crystal, gold, and silver that were engraved with beautiful engravings, which we described earlier during al-Amin's gatherings. As for the drinks in such gatherings, these were usually several kinds of wines made from fermented grape juice, brewed dates, apples, apricots, or other delicious fruits, in addition to drinks made from fermented solutions of honey, molasses, or other products.

When the songstresses were organized and ready to sing, the server of drinks went around with the pitchers of drinks and offered them to al-Rashid. He drank a little, while screened from the songstresses by the curtain and from the poets by another curtain. With the songstresses were Barsuma and Abu Zakkar. Whenever one of the songstresses sang a song that al-Rashid knew and was thrilled to hear, he called out to her by name.

He then ordered the chamberlain, "Tell al-Hasan ibn Hani' to recite his poetry."

When the poet was told of al-Rashid's order, he read verses he had prepared. He actually recited them in a grandiose, theatrical, and affected manner as was the custom of poets in the gatherings of caliphs, and al-Rashid was thrilled.

"And you, O Ibn Abi Hafsa," he shouted.

"At your command, O Commander of the Faithful," responded Ibn Abi Hafsa and began to recite a poem he had composed, praising al-Rashid and critically alluding to the followers of 'Ali. This reminded the caliph of the concerns that he had almost forgotten.

"That's enough on this," he said. "Ask Abu al-'Atahiya: Is he still maintaining his asceticism and his renunciation of poetry?"

Abu al-'Atahiya replied, "O Commander of the Faithful, the kinds of music and singing we are now hearing have hit asceticism with a devastating catapult. Someone has spoken truly when he said, 'Singing is a magical spell against adultery.'"

Al-Rashid liked his words and laughed, saying, "This indeed is real poetry. Recite a couple of verses."

"At your command," Abu al-'Atahiya said. "I will say what will come to my mind in a moment, for I abandoned composing poetry a long time ago."

At that moment Masrur entered. When al-Rashid saw him, he shouted at him, "Woe to you, where is Ibrahim?"

"He is at the door, my lord," Masrur said. "I have brought him from the farthest corners of the earth."

"Let him in," al-Rashid said, "so that he may be close to these songstresses in order to teach them and help them."

Ibrahim entered and offered his greetings. Ordering him to sit down, al-Rashid said, "We think we have inconvenienced you by asking you to come unexpectedly today, preferring our pleasure to your rest. Excuse us."

Ibrahim was embarrassed by this civility on the part of the caliph and said, "We are the servants of the Commander of the Faithful. When he asks us to serve him, he honors us and raises our status."

Al-Rashid interrupted him and said, "Listen to the new singing." Turning to the woman who was handling the curtain, he said, "Ibrahim, the master of singers, likes to listen to that new singing."

"Sing, Qaranfula," the slave-woman shouted.

When Ibrahim al-Mawsili heard her name, he smiled and said, "Qaranfula is here? This songstress is indeed rare with regard to her mellow voice and perfect art. I have long wished I could make her join the songstresses of the palace. She is one of the white slave-girls whom I taught singing and one of the best regarding her skill and perfect performance."

Al-Rashid said, "Our son, Muhammad, gave her to us today as a present, and I have not yet seen her face."

"Her face is beautiful, my lord," said Ibrahim.

Husain, the buffoon, shouted from behind the curtain, "We praise God because her teacher taught her singing only, and he did not teach her beauty."

Al-Rashid laughed and ordered the server of drinks to pour a glass for Ibrahim and said, "Husain is charming. Drink this, Ibrahim."

Husain, the buffoon, shouted from inside, "May God bless the Commander of the Faithful because he was fair to me and his singer. He described me as being charming, and gave Ibrahim a glass to drink, as if charming people don't drink lest they should become more high-spirited and fly!"

Al-Rashid laughed and said to Ibrahim in a low voice, "Damn him! He threw a stone and hit two persons, for he unknowingly considered me lacking in charm and high spirits."

The buffoon heard him, so he tried to correct his mistake and said, "I ask the Commander of the Faithful's pardon. Denying me drinks has intoxicated me, and so I have become confused, and I have spoken haphazardly without thinking. But a person needing something knows what he needs, and that is why my words refer to Ibrahim and only to Ibrahim."

Ibrahim laughed and said, "Rest assured, Husain, for your words have registered with me. Now, leave me alone!"

Al-Rashid then said, "Let us hear, O Qaranfula!"

So she began to play her lute alone and sing, and-Rashid expressed exaggerated words of appreciation for her voice. Her friends among the songstresses were jealous, including one who had a favored position with al-Rashid. The caliph then heard some uproar behind the curtain, followed by laughter, so he asked, "Why are the songstresses laughing?"

The woman handling the curtain replied, "The songstress, Diya', says that the Commander of the Faithful admires Qaranfula, who knows only one or two songs that she is accustomed to singing. If he orders one of the poets to compose a couple of verses for her to sing impromptu, we will see..."

"Well said, well said," al-Rashid exclaimed. "Abu al-'Atahiya, come up with one or two verses that you have composed now."

The poet said, "I am at your service, Commander of the Faithful, but if I say something, will you guarantee my safety?"

Everyone was astonished at his question, especially al-Rashid, but he thought he was saying that in jest, fearing the songstresses, so he said, "Yes, you will be safe."

The poet persisted, "And will you reward me, O Commander of the Faithful, with a grant different from that of the other poets, because I have not composed poetry for a long time?"

Al-Rashid became more astonished at these conditions, but he still thought the poet was joking, and he said, "And we will reward you."

Abu al-'Atahiya continued, "And will you permit me to see your face alone?"

Al-Rashid was annoyed at the poet's conditions, but he tolerated him and said, "We will do that too. Now, speak."

"Don't be surprised, my lord, at my audacity," the poet pleaded, "for it has been said

A slave will not vie with his lord

Unless the slave becomes wanton.

When those present heard this verse, they thought the poet was referring to his audacity in setting conditions for the caliph in a way that was unprecedented. But as soon as al-Rashid heard the poet's words, he remembered that he had read them an hour earlier on that slip of paper. He felt ill at ease and realized that Abu al-'Atahiya would not have ventured to say this unless he wanted to reveal something he held in his heart, especially after requiring that he see his face, which was a way of requesting a meeting with him.

Al-Rashid's mood changed, and he forgot the music he was enjoying. His sole concern now became learning the secret of that slip of paper. He immediately stood up, and all those present stood up without understanding what was going through his mind, for they knew nothing of the background of the poem. He clapped and Masrur came. Whispering to him, the caliph ordered him to reward the poets and the songstresses and to bring him Abu al-'Atahiya alone. He sought the gathering's permission, and they all left, and the former din in the hall was transformed into silence and gravity.

Masrur then entered holding Abu al-'Atahiya by the neck, thinking he was the cause for changing everyone's joy into grief. Masrur had no doubt that al-Rashid would order cutting off the poet's head.

As for Abu al-'Atahiya, he had ventured to embark on this momentous act out of his greed for the large amount of money that al-Fadl ibn al-Rabi' had promised him. He planned this method, believing it not improbable that having composed the poem for Ja'far's mother, she had sent it to be placed on the caliph's throne in the House of the Elite. Abu al-'Atahiya thought that al-Rashid must have read it, since a reference to only one verse made him want to know more; if al-Rashid asked him for more information, he decided to relate to him the story of the release of al-'Alawi. But he did not feel the danger he was exposing himself to until he saw the caliph's gathering change from singing and commotion to gloom and silence. His heart raced, and he became afraid for his life, especially after Masrur had seized him by the neck and brought him to al-Rashid. His turban was slanting on his head, his beard was disheveled, his hands were trembling, and his knees were knocking against each other so that he could hardly stand up. When he saw al-Rashid, he fell at his feet and began kissing them, and he was overtaken by sobbing. Masrur was sure, then, that Abu al-'Atahiya was guilty and that he would soon hear the caliph's order to kill him. He stood with his hand on the hilt of his sword and his eyes fixed on al-Rashid's lips.

When al-Rashid beheld the terror that had overtaken Abu al-'Atahiya and saw his cringing and earnest supplication despite being given a promise of safety, he pitied him and said, "Don't worry, Abu al-'Atahiya! You are our poet, and we honor poets. Stand up and don't be afraid."

As soon as he heard these words, the poet stood up, folded his arms, and lowered his head, keeping his eyes staring fixedly on the floor. His knees and hands were still visibly shaking. Then he heard al-Rashid order Masrur to leave, and he looked sideways at the man and, when he was sure he had left, his heart was reassured, and he raised his eyes to al-Rashid with humility.

146

Al-Rashid reclined in his throne and gestured to Abu al-'Atahiya to sit down, so he sat kneeling on the carpet, tears still shining in his eyes. "Don't be afraid, Abu al-'Atahiya," the caliph said, "you are safe."

"Am I safe, O Commander of the Faithful?" the poet asked in a choking voice.

"Yes, you are safe if you believe me," said al-Rashid.

"Am I safe from you and your vizier?" the poet asked.

"Don't ask too many questions," al-Rashid said. "If the Commander of the Faithful says you are safe, you should have no fear."

Abu al-'Atahiya heaved a deep sigh and calmed down, and he said, "My lord will know that I have embarked on this difficult act out of my wholehearted dedication to his service."

Weary of waiting, al-Rashid asked, "Tell me, how did you know this poem, and who told you about it?"

"No one told me about it," the poet said.

"How, then, did you know it? Is it, perhaps, of your own composition?" the caliph asked.

"Yes," the poet said.

"What made you compose it?" asked the caliph.

"What made me compose it," the poet said, "is a matter I had learned about, and I knew that no one of your retinue would dare inform you about it. I devised this ruse to make it reach you, and I hope I have not hurt myself and my family by doing so."

"Don't worry," the caliph said. "What *is* this matter? And what has our vizier to do with it?"

Abu al-'Atahiya replied, "He alone is the one responsible for it, my lord, and I will relate it to you. If the facts prove me wrong, then my blood is to be shed with impunity."

"Tell me the story," the caliph said, "and don't be afraid."

So Abu al-'Atahiya related the story of al-'Alawi and his release by Ja'far al-Barmaki, to the very end. As he spoke, his voice trembled and faltered but al-Rashid listened attentively and remained composed.

When he heard the full story, he asked, "Are you sure of the truth of this story?"

"If I was not sure," Abu al-'Atahiya said, "or rather, if I was not positively certain of the matter, I would not have exposed my life to this great danger."

Ja'far's relationship with al-Rashid was so close and his standing so high that al-Rashid did not want his poet to know that his interventions could sow discord between them. He thought it wise and resolute to induce him into thinking that he had committed errors in his story, so he laughed and said, "I have no doubt that you have come forth to reveal this matter because of your zeal for the state, and that is why you deserve being thanked and rewarded. But you have taken the trouble to do all that in vain, because our vizier did not do anything by himself and on his own, for he released al-'Alawi only on my advice."

When Abu al-'Atahiya heard this, he was at a loss and was overcome by embarrassment. But he was reassured, at least, that his life was safe and that he would receive the money that al-Fadl had promised him. However, he was afraid of Ja'far al-Barmaki if ever he were to know that he had reported him, so he said, "I thank God that what happened was done in accordance with the advice of the Commander of the Faithful. I am reassured about the life of the vizier. But I have become afraid of him for my life if he ever hears that I have conveyed to you this story, for he will think I am one of his enemies."

Al-Rashid interrupted him, saying, "Don't be afraid, for I will keep it secret from him. Be reassured." He said that and stood up, so Abu al-'Atahiya stood up too, having calmed down. As for al-Rashid, his suppressed anger gave him such pain that it almost felled him. But he was able to conceal the feelings in his heart. He was not unaware that Abu al-'Atahiya was not acting alone. But he was satisfied with what he had heard. He clapped, and Masrur came in quickly like a flash of lightning. Al-Rashid said to him, "Take Abu al-'Atahyia and order our treasurer to give him one thousand dinars, then set him free."

"I hear and obey, O Commander of the Faithful," said Masrur as he took hold of Abu al-'Atahiya and went out with him.

When al-Rashid was all by himself, he became full of anxiety, and his suspicions returned to him. He remembered the conversation between himself and Isma'il that morning and how he had driven him away disappointed, in spite of his family relationship and high esteem—all in consideration for Ja'far al-Barmaki. He thought: "How could Ja'far dare do such an unexpected act and release a prisoner whom I had entrusted to him?" He was firmly persuaded now of the accusations that Ja'far was loyal to the followers of 'Ali and preferred them to the 'Abbasids. When this thought came to him, he raged with blind anger and became unaware of his surroundings. He began to walk up and down the hall aimlessly, talking to himself and saying, *Am I in a dream? Can Ja'far commit such treason, when I loved and honored him so much, when I raised his status and handed him control of government affairs and gave him a free hand in all matters of the state? Is it conceivable that what I heard about him from enviers is true? Why does he betray me and release an enemy I entrusted him with in spite of his knowledge of my hatred for the followers of 'Ali? And how dare he do that without fear for his life? This too is not conceivable unless the man is bereft of reason, for he knows what Harun will do when his anger is aroused!*

Chapter 12

Al-Rashid and Ja'far

Al-Rashid was unsettled and spent the next hour talking to himself before he decided that the best thing to do to clear his suspicions would be to ask Ja'far himself about the truth of the story. If it was true, he would quickly take his revenge. So he controlled his anger, for, in spite of his impetuous temper that could lead to severe violence, he had a strong will and was able to suppress his feelings and curb his passions. He clapped and Masrur came, and he said to him, "Summon the man that brings me food, and then go to the vizier and ask him to come to me."

"What shall I tell the vizier?" Masrur asked.

"Tell him," replied the caliph, "that the Commander of the Faithful would like him to come and have dinner with me tonight, and don't say anything more."

"I hear and obey," Masrur said and left.

The sun was about to set, so when the man responsible for food came in, al-Rashid told him, "Prepare a table at which I will have dinner with the vizier."

The man gestured in obedience and went out. Al-Rashid remained alone, and his troubling thoughts returned. Wanting to think of other things, he sought to amuse himself until Ja'far arrived, so he decided to go out to the palace garden for a stroll. He ordered someone to bring him a cloak, and a slave-boy came and helped him put on his sandals. He then went out to the garden and walked aimlessly between the trees and fragrant plants.

He soon found himself beside the cages of the wild animals, one of which had a lion al-Rashid often played with; when he saw it, he felt drawn to it by the natural human interest in seeing a lion or any other wild animal in a cage.

Perhaps the reason was an admiration for its strength, a wonder at its appearance, as well as a desire in his soul to emulate its qualities. The sight of wild animals excites a man's choleric temperament—and much more so if he is angry!

Al-Rashid stood at the cage and ordered the caretaker to feed the lion, so he brought a sheep that he had slaughtered and cut into small pieces, and he threw the lion a piece. The lion jumped at it and devoured it in one mouthful and stood waiting for another. Al-Rashid ordered the man not to throw another piece, and the lion began to roar and walk to and fro in the cage, its tail curved like an arch on its back as it looked at the caretaker with sparkling eyes while the caretaker teased it the with pieces of meat from a distance. When it felt the food was slow to come, the lion began hitting the bars of the cage alternately with its head and with its claws, staring at the piece of meat in the caretaker's hand and roaring and baring its fangs while the caretaker laughed. Meanwhile, al-Rashid was beginning to share the lion's anger. He frowned increasingly and his facial expression became more contorted, and he found that he almost wanted to attack the caretaker, imagining he was partaking in the lion's anger—because his feeling toward Ja'far was akin to the lion's toward its prey.

However, animals of prey cannot subdue their feelings, so they become angry and excited in their cages. But a rational human being can control his anger and restrain himself from attacking his prey, even if it is in front of him.

Al-Rashid was thinking about that and the caretaker was waiting for his order to throw the piece of meat to the lion, when the lion filled the air with a roar that awakened al-Rashid, so he gestured to the caretaker to throw the piece to it. The lion pounced on it and kept roaring until the man threw the third piece, then the fourth, and the others until the lion was finally satiated. It then lay down, its head between its front legs, and was quiet, but its eyes continued to sparkle and fury was still visible in them.

Al-Rashid spent one hour there until his spirits were raised. He became increasingly sure of his belief that a self-possessed and composed man who had political power and restrained his anger was a rational lion, and he wanted to be that kind of lion that night.

When the sun set and shadows became darker on Baghdad's palaces and gardens, al-Rashid returned to his palace. He walked between the trees in his embroidered robe and turban. The slave-boys made way for him out of respect, having noticed his anger and some of them knowing its cause, although al-Rashid thought his secret was well kept.

As he walked, he heard some clattering, neighing, clanking, and uproar at the gate of the palace, so he knew that Ja'far's procession had arrived. He continued to walk, and when he reached the door of the House of the Elite, Masrur met him and told him that the vizier was waiting for him inside.

* * *

Al-Rashid entered the hall. The candles on the gold candelabras were lit and the place was redolent of the scents of incense and perfumes. He sat on the throne and, a few moments later, the chamberlain entered to ask permission for Ja'far to enter. Al-Rashid said, "Let the vizier enter with no hindrance."

Ja'far entered, wearing a headgear and a cloak, as was his custom when coming for a meeting with the caliph, this being the official attire of the 'Abbasids. Ja'far was not at ease with regard to this invitation at the end of the day, and he feared that his enviers had slandered him after Abu al-'Atahiya had discovered his secret and had seen his two sons with their mother.

When Masrur had invited him to come to al-Rashid, he had asked him what the caliph wanted, and Masrur had replied, "I don't know." When he did not notice any suspicious signs in the man's face, Ja'far set off in his elaborate procession in which there were a few strong horsemen devoted to him. They entered with him until they reached the fourth gate in the palace grounds, which was accessible only to him and the Hashemites and similar elites. Ja'far dismounted and headed for the House of the Elite, while Masrur walked silently in front of him. He then entered the hall with an affected smile, pretending he was at ease, but he was not really calm in his heart of hearts.

When he approached, al-Rashid welcomed him and smiled, saying, "I wish you had come in clothes like mine, for our gathering is a pleasure gathering." He invited him to sit down next to him on the throne's wide seat. Ja'far returned the caliph's greeting and sat next to him politely, having regained his composure and feeling reassured. They began to converse, and al-Rashid treated him kindly and amiably.

"I have invited you because I like your company," was one of the things al-Rashid told him. "I have been bored all day after having received the Indian delegation."

He told him about the castle swords that the delegation had brought and their strong Suyuriyya dogs that had attacked the lion.

Ja'far said, "May the Palace of Eternity ever remain the source of pride and power, and may the Commander of the Faithful always remain strengthened by God's support and have kings and potentates humbly seeking his friendship."

However, Ja'far's heart was full of fear of al-Rashid and of the possibility that he might know that the marriage with al-'Abbasa had been consummated and of his intention of fleeing if their secret was uncovered. Each of them posed as a friend of the other, but each harbored a grudge against the other in his heart. They continued this charade until mealtime, when the dinner table was filled with all kinds of meats, birds, and condiments, and all sorts of legumes and fruits. The slave-boys stood carrying pitchers of water and cups of drinks. They both sat to eat, al-Rashid expressing his excessive amiability toward Ja'far and offering him food from the various bowls, even feeding him with his own hand, giving him one meat pie after another and one apple after another. He displayed a cheerful attitude, conversed joyfully with him, and laughed with him until he touched on the subject of al-'Alawi and asked, "What happened to al-'Alawi whom I entrusted you with?"

Ja'far said, "He is still in the same situation, O Commander of the Faithful. He is still in prison as you ordered."

"Is he still there?" al-Rashid asked, smiling.

"Yes, O Commander of the Faithful," Ja'far said.

"By my life?" al-Rashid pried.

Ja'far immediately realized the significance of the question. He was dumbfounded and surprise was visible all over his face. He said, "No, by your life. I set him free because I found he was not dangerous. I extracted assurances and promises from him that he would not repeat any of his prior misdeeds."

Al-Rashid laughed and offered Ja'far a peach he was holding in his hand, and he said, "God bless you! You have done what I hoped you would do, and no more than what I had in mind."

Ja'far was pleased with al-Rashid's genial civility, especially when he moved to another subject of conversation and continued to joke with him as though nothing had happened.

When they finished their dinner, the servants brought them vessels in which they washed their hands, and they sat for an hour conversing with each other. Finally, Ja'far asked permission to leave, which al-Rashid granted, walking with him to the hall's door to bid him farewell. After he saw him off, he gnashed his teeth and said to himself, *May God kill me if I don't kill you!*

As for Ja'far, al-Rashid's flattery did not fool him, and his welcoming behavior did not deceive him. He left the palace feeling that he was in danger. He realized that the mention of al-'Alawi was not made by accident or by mere coincidence. He knew that al-Rashid's intention was not to set the man free as he claimed. How could he believe that? For when al-'Alawi had been free, he had a safety document in al-Rashid's handwriting and with his seal, which al-Rashid made continued efforts to rescind until he finally annulled it and tore it up. He then ordered that the man be arrested and imprisoned because he feared him. How could he be fooled by al-Rashid's claim that he intended to release the man when he knew al-Rashid's character and his excessive secretiveness? However, he pretended to be at ease, and they parted after making reciprocal insincere statements, each thinking he had deceived his friend when in fact both were deceivers and deceived.

After saying good-bye to Ja'far, al-Rashid began to think of the surprises of that day. He remembered Isma'il's visit in the morning and how he had disappointed Isma'il and had not met his request to protect

Ja'far's relationship with him. He also remembered what he later learned about his vizier's arrogation of authority and his release of al-'Alawi, which made him begin to think of killing him. He realized he had ill-treated Isma'il in spite of his wise advice and good intention, so he decided to meet with him to inform him of what Ja'far had done and to tell him confidentially that he intended to have him executed. He was certain of Isma'il's sincerity, a certainty he did not feel regarding any other member of his family or any one of the men of his state. But his feelings did not go so far as to think he should apologize to Isma'il for disappointing him. He felt uneasy and thought there was nothing better than hunting to drive away his distress.

In the morning, he called his servant Masrur and commanded him to tell the hunting party to prepare themselves to accompany him to the land of Dujail, near Baghdad. Then he asked, "Do you know the place where Isma'il ibn Yahya is staying?"

"Yes, my lord," Masrur said.

"Go to him," al-Rashid said, "and invite him too. But don't upset him with your boorishness!"

Masrur asked, "And what shall I tell him if he asks me what the Commander of the Faithful wants from him?"

"Tell him," the caliph said, "that I intend to go out hunting and that I would like him to be with me."

Masrur gestured in obedience and went to the falconers, the lynx-men, and the partridge-men as well as to the men responsible for organizing the hunt and the chase, and he ordered them to the land of Dujail. They had maps, and they knew the roads to that place and did not need to be given directions.

Dujail was a piece of land several parasangs[24] long by an equal number of parasangs wide with a semicircular fence on one side made of posts set at equal distances and tied to one another by ropes and wires to form a strong, impenetrable barrier. The custom in hunting was for the advance party to chase the animals to be hunted and force them to flee in front of them into the brush and the thickets within that semicircular

---

24 A parasang (*farsakh* in Arabic, *farsang* in Persian) is an ancient unit of distance equal to about four miles. *Translator's Note.*

barrier, where they were surrounded and cornered by closing the open side with their horses, lynxes, and dogs; they continued to close in on the animals until they made them back into the barrier where they had no escape. When the animals were confined to that area, the caliph and the elite accompanying him arrived and hunted the animals they wanted.

Al-Rashid's custom when he went hunting was to spend part of the day wandering on his horse in the outskirts of Baghdad and the surrounding plantations and villages until he knew that the animals had been cornered and the time of hunting them was at hand; he would then go to the area and start chasing some of them in person or he would watch the falcons, hawks, and lynxes and how their owners used them in the hunt. On that day, he went hunting only to create an opportunity to speak with Isma'il.

On being invited by al-Rashid's messenger to join the caliph in the hunt, Isma'il dressed in his special hunting attire, mounted his horse, and went to the Palace of Eternity. Al-Rashid was waiting for him in the hunting procession, which is different from other processions of the caliphs. As soon as he approached the palace, Isma'il saw the men managing the hunt going out with their hawks, falcons, and lynxes, dressed in light clothes and some wearing felt caps. Many men with their hunting animals were milling around. One was playing with his hawk and urging it to catch a bird flying overhead, but when the hawk prepared to fly, the man held it back. Another man was leading his lynx with an iron chain, a third was inciting his dog to capture prey. He tried to make it believe the prey was behind a tree, but the dog would not move because it did not smell the prey. Chaos reigned with a discordant mixture of sounds—neighing, barking, growling, clattering, clanking, rattling, and rumbling. Isma'il rode past all that until he entered the second of the palace's gates, where he was met by Masrur, who said, "My lord should not dismount, because the Commander of the Faithful is going out in his procession, and he ordered me to tell you that."

So he waited on his horse until he saw al-Rashid in his light clothes riding his horse and surrounded by horsemen in the hunting procession. He could not help dismounting, but al-Rashid quickly said to him, "Mount, my Uncle, and bring your horse next to mine."

Isma'il did so and wanted to ride behind al-Rashid out of politeness as was the custom when accompanying mounted caliphs. But al-Rashid invited him to ride his horse parallel to his own, saying, "Isma'il ibn Yahya is not a person who is required to follow this protocol. I have invited you to come with me only to enjoy your company."

So Isma'il invoked blessings upon the caliph and rode beside him. Al-Rashid ordered Masrur to give word to the men responsible for the hunt to proceed with their work at Dujail as usual. Then he and Isma'il rode on, but they did not converse. They continued in silence until they had gone out of Baghdad and approached its outskirts and gardens. Al-Rashid then got hold of his horse's bridle and turned around, a motion that the horsemen of the procession understood meant that he wanted them to go away; they dispersed and he and Isma'il continued to ride on. When they were alone, al-Rashid looked at Isma'il with visible concern and asked, "What did you think after you left me yesterday?"

"Nothing," Isma'il said, "except that I continued to pray for you to have long life and for your rule to remain strong."

"That is what I know about you," the caliph commented. "Yet if you had reproached Harun and criticized him, I would not have blamed you; for I did not show you the proper respect that is due to you. I hurt you for the sake of a man who neither showed the proper respect that is due to me nor to the 'Abbasids."

He said this and turned around as though he was afraid that someone might hear him. Then he pretended to smooth the embroidered silk covering of the front of his saddle and stretched out his hand on the horse's neck, combing it with his fingers and looking for Isma'il's reaction.

Isma'il realized what al-Rashid was talking about and surmised he wanted to harm Ja'far. This grieved him because he knew it would harm the state, so he ignored the matter and thanked al-Rashid for his high opinion of him and said, "I think that the Commander of the Faithful honors me excessively, and far be it from him to do anything that deserves blame! But even if he did, he is above all blamers. However, what displeases me is that he is dissatisfied with his helper. If he tells me openly what he would like to do and permits me to speak candidly, this will be an additional act of confidence in me."

Al-Rashid interrupted him, saying, "I think you pretend not to know, my Uncle. Someone like you does not fail to understand what I would like to do."

Isma'il said, "If what I think is right, al-Rashid is complaining of his vizier."

Al-Rashid said, "Are you astonished at my complaint of a man to whom I handed control of my state and to whom I gave a free hand in running my affairs and those of my family and relatives and who then began to make efforts to bring about my demise?"

"God forbid!" said Isma'il. "Your vizier, O Commander of the Faithful, is only one of your helpers, and he fully devotes himself to you—this is what I know about him."

They were talking while their two horses were moving parallel to each other among high trees with thick branches shading the roads. They were far from the city and were heading to no specific place when they came across a country estate with people, cattle, and buildings. They went around it until they reached its gate. Al-Rashid looked at its threshing floor and the abundant yield of grain on it and at the livestock grazing freely around it. He turned to Isma'il and asked, "To whom does this estate belong, Isma'il?"

Isma'il knew that it belonged to Ja'far al-Barmaki and that al-Rashid wanted to use it to buttress the truth of his criticism of the man, so he said, "It belongs to your brother, Ja'far ibn Yahya."

Al-Rashid sighed and said, "If I ask you about the rest of the estates in this suburb, you will give only the same answer. That is because the one you called my 'brother' has given his relatives possession of all the estates and gardens surrounding Baghdad. Do you see how we have made these Barmakids rich and how we have impoverished our own children and neglected them, to the extent that the country has become theirs, their processions have become more magnificent than ours, and their wealth has become greater than ours? Now if these are their estates near the city, think how many more they have in the other cities!"

These words troubled Isma'il because of their implications for protecting the security of the state, which was always his primary concern.

So he said, "The Barmakids are only your slaves and servants, and their estates and all their possessions belong to no one but you!"

Al-Rashid did not expect Isma'il to defend a man who, only yesterday, had been the cause of his failure. This increased his respect for him, but he did not like his method of defense. Like every angry autocrat, al-Rashid wanted Isma'il to agree with him on his intended plan.

"I see that you have a high opinion of my enemies," al-Rashid said, looking at him with the look of a headstrong tyrant, bursting with anger. "You think they are my slaves, whereas the Barmakids in fact consider the Hashemites to be their slaves. They believe that they themselves are the rulers of the state and that every favor the Hashemites have is only an act of kindness bestowed by the Barmakids."

Isma'il decided to stop defending the Barmakids at this point lest al-Rashid's anger become directed at him, so he said, "The Commander of the Faithful knows his servants and slaves best."

Al-Rashid realized that Isma'il, fearing his anger, had not frankly told him what was on his mind. He wanted to know Isma'il's opinion, so he said to him, "I have not asked you to accompany me for pleasure, my Uncle, nor do I know you as a man that complies and agrees with me for fear of my anger!"

Isma'il was perplexed, and he hesitated whether to respond or remain reticent. Although he knew the esteem in which al-Rashid held him, he was cautious about how freely to speak, fearing the caliph could change his mind and turn against him. He knew that no one had attained as much power and influence as Ja'far, to the extent that al-Rashid had come to call him his brother and to call Ja'far's father, Yahya, his father; and yet the moment he suspected him, the man's very life became endangered. So Isma'il remained silent, and he continued to think deeply as he rode next to al-Rashid, not knowing where he was being led.

He looked up and found that he was at the city gate. He said, as though waking up, "I see that we have returned to Baghdad. Where is the hunt?"

Al-Rashid said, "I only used the hunt as a pretext to talk to you. Yet I heard nothing from you other than what all the people we know and act hypocritically toward us tell us. But you are the elder of the Hashemites and their wise man, and I accept no dissimulation or blandishment from you."

Isma'il said, "Thank God, the Commander of the Faithful thinks well of me. But I have not heard a frank question from him so that I may respond with a frank answer."

Al-Rashid's procession had by now returned and preceded him as he entered Baghdad, so he said to Isma'il, "We are now entering Baghdad, and we shall soon enter the Palace of Eternity; there, we will sit together alone and we will talk."

Isma'il became apprehensive of the consequences and remained silent until they entered the palace. They dismounted and walked to a private room. Al-Rashid sat on the throne and invited Isma'il to sit next to him, so he sat with a lowered head waiting for what the caliph might say.

Al-Rashid began by saying, "Tell me what is on your mind. Don't you think that these non-Arabs have become presumptuous toward us and have taken exclusive possession of the state and its funds to our detriment?"

"Yes, indeed," said Isma'il. "They have done so obeying the orders of the Commander of the Faithful. If he had ordered them otherwise, they would also have done as he commanded."

"Did I order them to take exclusive possession of everything and utterly disregard me?"

Isma'il did not immediately respond, hesitating whether to say frankly what he believed concerning the meritorious services of the Barmakids to the state or to go along with the caliph's words. He finally decided to offer his independent opinion, so he said, "Having been honored by the high opinion that the Commander of the Faithful has of me, I ought not to withhold from him any of my thoughts. The Barmakids are, indeed, the slaves and clients of our lord—there is no disagreement about that. But the Commander of the Faithful is the most knowledgeable of all people about the good deeds that the Barmakids have done in the service of the state, right from the time of their grandfather Khaled who was in the service of your grandfather al-Mansur, who recognized his merits and gave him precedence and, later, did likewise with his son Yahya and his grandson Ja'far. Al-Rashid is not unaware of the fact that these persons have had a good effect in serving his state and in organizing its administration and all its affairs. This is in addition to their glorious feats in raising the light of learning and enhancing its causes by giving precedence to philosophers and bringing physicians from India and Persia to Baghdad. They built the hospital and built up the city of Baghdad; they introduced the use of paper and were interested in the translation of books. They have done all this, only because al-Rashid was satisfied with it—and I am afraid to speak at length on this subject."

As Isma'il spoke, he kept observing al-Rashid's reactions and thought he noticed a certain annoyance caused by his praise of the Barmakids. It was as if nothing pleased al-Rashid except what supported his determination to do away with them. To redress the situation, he therefore said, "On the other hand, I don't deny that they have taken exclusive possession of the state funds, for man is greedy by natural disposition. But I know that they spend on the poor most of the money they earn from their proceeds."

Al-Rashid laughed grudgingly, shook his head, and said, "They don't do that out of magnanimity and charity, but they buy parties and they will soon mobilize soldiers against us."

"God forbid," Isma'il quickly said.

Al-Rashid interrupted him and said, turning fully toward him, "Why not? Our vizier, whom you have called my 'brother,' is siding with the followers of 'Ali against us."

Isma'il was startled and said, "He sides with them?"

"Yes," the caliph said. "He released Yahya ibn 'Abd Allah, whom I ordered to be arrested."

"He released Yahya al-'Alawi?" Isma'il said.

"Yes," al-Rashid repeated. "He released him. There is no doubt about that. He himself admitted the matter to me."

Isma'il found that it was no longer possible for him to defend the Barmakids. He was now sure that al-Rashid's anger was motivated by his ill feelings toward the Shi'a of 'Ali. He said, "This is insolent forwardness and presumptuous cheekiness! Do you think he did that on purpose and with malice?"

"Whatever his purpose was," al-Rashid said, "I will not tolerate this act of his."

Isma'il asked, "What is to be done, my lord?"

Al-Rashid said, "What is to be done? It is legally permissible to execute him—that's it."

Isma'il was alarmed at the caliph's haste and said, "If the Commander of the Faithful kills his slaves, he is indeed their owner. But he is more knowledgeable than I am of the consequences of such an act. He has just said to me that the Barmakids buy parties."

Al-Rashid and Isma'il bowed their heads in thought. Al-Rashid then raised his eyes and asked, "What does our cousin think?"

Isma'il said, "Don't you think that you can separate him from his parties by giving him a position far away from Baghdad?"

Al-Rashid's face shone at this remark, and he said, "That is what I have decided to do. I will appoint him to govern Khurasan. Once he is out of Baghdad, we will think about what to do with him."

Isma'il was pleased that al-Rashid accepted his advice, and he said, "This is an excellent course of action."

"It is a right course of action," al-Rashid said. "After that, we will look into his problem." He then turned to him with full attention and said as he stared at him, "Know, Isma'il, that I have revealed this secret of mine to you only because I have great confidence in you, and I order you to keep it secret. No one knows about it but you. If anyone gets to know the reasons for my actions, I will know that only you could have revealed it. Do you understand?"

Isma'il was astonished at this threat. When he heard al-Rashid addressing him in that tone, he realized why advisers of kings had to go along with what they wanted and flatter them; otherwise their lives were in danger. So he said, "God forbid that I reveal your secret, O Commander of the Faithful."

Al-Rashid then shifted in his seated position, and Isma'il knew that it was time for him to leave; he stood and asked permission to leave, which was granted. He left, greatly distressed at what he had just heard and concerned for the well-being of the state on account of al-Rashid's change of heart; he went home to wait for what the caliph would do. On the next day, he learned that al-Rashid had sent for Ja'far, and when the vizier came, the caliph sat him on his right-hand side and honored him. He spoke with him for one hour and gave him gifts, among which was a slave-boy from the caliph's crops of special attendants—one of the best and most handsome and pleasant, who was an intelligent scribe and accountant. Isma'il also learned that Ja'far was very pleased, and he wondered at al-Rashid's ability to suppress his inner feelings, despite the intense pressure he endured and the hasty anger to which he was inclined. He might have thought that al-Rashid had forgiven Ja'far and that his anger against him had subsided—but he knew that al-'Alawi's release and al-Rashid's hatred for the Shi'a were continuing to make al-Rashid fear for his rule.

Two days later, Isma'il learned that al-Rashid bestowed robes of honor upon his vizier and gave him the governorship of Khurasan. He thought that the caliph had pardoned him, and he hoped that grudges would thus end and things would return to their former normality. He thought especially so when he found out that Ja'far was happy with this governorship and hastened to send his assistants and his men to precede him to al-Nahrawan, outside Baghdad. They went there, pitched their tents, and began to prepare for the trip to Khurasan, which was quite far and required them to have lots of provisions. When Isma'il learned of Ja'far's departure, he thought of visiting him to bid him farewell and to try to smooth any lingering hard feelings he had for al-Rashid by resorting to an idea that occurred to him.

As for Ja'far, all the caliph's gifts and honors did not eliminate the inner ill feelings that he harbored toward al-Rashid. But he thought that being governor of Khurasan would give him some relief. He decided to get in touch with al-'Abbasa to talk her into coming with him to Khurasan. On the day when robes of honor were bestowed upon him, he returned to his palace in al-Shammasiyya. It was only one of the palaces that belonged to the Barmakids in that neighborhood; they had several palaces there, the most famous being that of Yahya ibn Khaled at the al-Shammasiyya Gate and another at al-Bardan Gate. In that year, Ja'far was living in his palace at the al-Shammasiyya Gate. His palaces were no less magnificent than those of al-Rashid. The poem that Zubayda had slipped to her husband is description enough:

> *He built the house that no Persians*
> *Or Indians have ever built the like of.*
> *Its gravel consisted of pearls and rubies,*
> *And its soil, of ambergris and incense.*

With its splendid furniture and its other household effects, the magnificence of Ja'far's palace and of others like it that belonged to the Barmakids rivaled those described earlier in the Palace of Eternity, al-Amin's palace, and the House of Repose (Zubayda's palace).

Ja'far returned to his palace, hardly believing that he had been appointed governor of Khurasan, although al-Rashid had promised this several times before. So he thought that either al-Rashid had no grudge against him or that he appointed him as governor of Khurasan because he feared for the state if he remained in Baghdad. He was therefore encouraged as this led him to consider that al-Rashid was weak, and his own fear of the caliph was allayed.

On his return to his palace, he ordered his household manager to prepare for the journey to Khurasan and to inform his superintendent of slave-girls and slave-boys and his scribe to be ready on the next day. He entered the palace full of admiration for the slave-boy whom al-Rashid had given him as a gift, for he was of good manners and extreme beauty. He took him to a hall whose furnishings were sky blue in color because, according to ancient beliefs, he believed that this color was a good omen and a source of delight and joy. The slave-boy entered and proceeded to entertain him. Suddenly the chamberlain came and announced, "Isma'il ibn Yahya is at the door."

Ja'far stood up to receive him, brought him in, and made him sit in the place of honor in the room as an acknowledgment of his high rank and because he trusted him, his pure intentions, and his sincere manner of speaking. When talking to him, Ja'far realized that Isma'il wanted to talk to him privately, so he asked everyone in the hall to leave and remained alone with him giving him his full attention.

"My sire," Isma'il said, "you are about to leave for a province which is of abundant wealth and vast regions. If you were to give some of your estates to the offspring of the Commander of the Faithful, this would make your position with him more favorable."

When Ja'far heard these words, he immediately thought that al-Rashid had sent Isma'il to mediate such an action. His feelings of disdain for al-Rashid and his perceived power over him increased, and his grudge against him grew. Also he began to think that he would escape from his grip by moving to Khurasan before al-Rashid's possible discovery of his affair with al-'Abbasa.

Ja'far held Isma'il in high esteem. He had often mentioned in front of him the services of the Barmakids to the state, and Isma'il had agreed with him. So he said, "By God, O Isma'il, your cousin would not have made his mark if it were not for me; nor would this state have been established if it were not for us—the Barmakids. Is it not sufficient that I have taken upon myself to remove all his worries about himself—his children, his retinue, and his subjects? I have filled his treasuries with money and have continued to manage all important matters for him—and yet, he turns his eyes to what I have saved for my children and for my descendants after I die, and the greed of the Hashemites creeps into him. By God, if he wants me to give away anything of that, evil consequences will quickly befall him!"

Isma'il regretted having come to see Ja'far, and he was afraid that his conversation with him would be reported to al-Rashid, who might then suspect him of having revealed the secret he had entrusted him with. So he changed the course of the conversation with Ja'far and seized an opportunity to seek his permission to leave, which he did.

Ja'far returned to his senses after Isma'il had left and realized that he was wrong in criticizing the Hashemites, knowing that Isma'il was one of them. He feared he might reveal what he had heard to al-Rashid, and there would thus be no reconciliation between the two of them. He became all the more determined to escape with al-'Abbasa and their two sons. He clapped and his servant Hamdan appeared. He depended on him and trusted him, so he told him what he had decided. "We are leaving for our camp at al-Nahrawan tomorrow," he said. "Go now and tell 'Utba to inform her mistress al-'Abbasa to be ready to travel, and I will send someone to bring her to me. Do you understand?"

166

"Yes, my lord, I understand," Hamdan said and left quickly.

* * *

During all these events and after her last meeting with Ja'far, in which she had heard him promise to go to Khurasan, al-'Abbasa was continually thinking of his wish and hardly believed it could be realized. She preferred living in a humble hut with her husband and two sons in safety and security to living in those magnificent palaces in continuous danger and under constant observation, especially after Abu al-'Atahiya had discovered her secret and had seen her sons with his own eyes. Fearing that the news would reach her brother, al-Rashid, she did not feel safe. Every time she saw two persons whispering to each other, she imagined they were speaking about her. Whenever she saw a group of horsemen passing by her palace, she assumed they were coming to arrest her. Only meeting with her servant 'Utba gave her relief, for she disclosed her fears to her, and 'Utba tried to calm her down and give her hope.

Then one day she learned that al-Rashid had appointed Ja'far as governor of Khurasan. She saw the people running in the streets to attend the appointment ceremony, and she leapt for joy. She waited several hours for Ja'far's messenger, to no avail; then she learned that Ja'far's assistants and men had left for al-Nahrawan, but his messenger still had not come. It occurred to her that he might have been distracted from her, and she suddenly doubted his sincerity—for lovers are often insecure and full of suspicions. She intended to complain to 'Utba, who was sitting with her on the balcony, where she had waited for Ja'far only a few days ago. Suddenly, she saw Hamdan approaching, wearing the attire of her palace servants. She sent 'Utba to meet him and bring her his message. When he saw 'Utba, he told her why he had come and insisted that she inform her mistress to be ready to travel. She should take only light things with her and disguise herself as a slave-girl so that when Ja'far's messenger came to take her, he would need to say no more than one word. When 'Utba informed her mistress about that, she cried with unmitigated joy, and she ordered her to bring Hamadan to her so that she might hear the good news directly from him. He entered and stood politely.

"In what state did you leave your master?" she asked.

"He is well and sends you greetings, my lady," he replied.

"When do you think we will leave here?" she asked.

"Perhaps tomorrow morning," he replied.

She turned to 'Utba as though reminding her of the two boys, al-Hasan and al-Husain.

"As you know," 'Utba said, "they are safe with the two servants. When we leave Baghdad, we will send someone to bring them from Hejaz or from wherever they would be, and you will be rid of these fears."

Al-'Abbasa heaved a deep sigh of relief but joy was not visible on her face. She dismissed Hamdan and entered her room, and 'Utba began to make ready for the trip. It was late afternoon, the sun was about to set, and al-'Abbasa was alone in her room. Her reaction soon began to make itself felt. She became depressed and overwhelmed by her emotions. She imagined herself fleeing from her palace and from her own brother, abandoning that palace with all the comfortable amenities she had been accustomed to: its halls, its gardens, its furniture, its servants, its slave-girls, and everything else in it. Indeed, she did prefer living with her loved one in a hut to living alone in a palace. But human beings are creatures of habit and comfort, clinging to the things they are familiar with and finding it hard to give them up—the more so for her, who was brought up in a palace that she had rarely left. But whenever she imagined being with Ja'far and her two sons, she calmed down. Then her fear of her brother's wrath would overwhelm her as she imagined that on learning of her flight he would be so angry that he would dispatch armies to find her. And these apprehensions would almost dissuade her from fleeing! She continued to struggle with her emotions and to hope for some deliverance. Then she remembered a servant of hers, Urjuwan, who was a trustworthy man who had kept her secrets during her anxiety attacks. She had made him chief servant at her palace and used to find solace in his company during her times of trouble and anxiety. So she decided to have him accompany her in her escape. She called 'Utba and asked her, "Where is Urjuwan?"

"He is here, in the palace," 'Utba replied. "Shall I call him?"

"Yes," said al-'Abbasa. "I think we should have him accompany us."

'Utba went out and returned with Urjuwan. He was of a dark complexion, for he was originally from the land of the Berbers in North

Africa. He had grown up in the palace of al-Mansur, and the caliph drew him close to him. Urjuwan was tall, mostly because of his long legs, as was the case with eunuchs. At that time, he was about fifty years old, and if it were not for the scarcity of hair on his face, his gray hair would have been visible and his mature age would have been noticeable; but one could rarely tell the age of eunuchs by just looking at them.

Urjuwan had brought up al-'Abbasa since her childhood, and he was devoted to her service; she was familiar with him and trusted him. When summoned, he stood in front of her, and she looked at him with tears in her eyes. Seeing her crying, he cried with her and said in his friendly voice and foreign accent, "What is your command, my lady?"

"We are about to travel," she said, "and I would like you to accompany us."

"I am your slave and at your command," he said.

"Do you know where we are going?" she asked.

"Wherever you like to go, I will go with you—even to death," he said.

"God bless you, Urjuwan," she said. "Help 'Utba in packing our effects, and she will give you the news."

"I hear and obey," he said and went out with 'Utba, who related to him what they were doing, so he began to prepare for the trip.

Chapter 13

Al-Rashid and his Wife

Al-Rashid was more secretive than he had appeared to be to Isma'il. In spite of his great confidence in him, he did not tell him what he intended to do to Ja'far for releasing al-'Alawi without his permission. He had only appointed him as governor of Khurasan in order to test him and observe his reactions. He gave him the handsome servant as a gift so that he would be the caliph's spy who would report to him Ja'far's every word. In fact, this servant was standing by when Isma'il visited Ja'far, and he heard their conversation and immediately reported it to al-Rashid. When his letter reached al-Rashid, he became sure of Ja'far's disloyalty, and his fear of him returned. He was sitting on his throne when he read the letter, and he jumped off his seat with alarm and thought that events were moving too quickly to permit much time for reflection. He believed that if his vizier left Baghdad, he would slip away from him, for the people of Khurasan were under Ja'far's control and it was easy for him to make them rebel against the caliph. When al-Rashid imagined this, his heart throbbed and he was at a loss; he began to pace to and fro in the room as if he had been afflicted with some madness. He felt a need for a heart-to-heart talk with a confidant, but he no longer trusted Isma'il after hearing about his conversation with Ja'far and his friendship with him— even though he did not harbor any ill will toward him. He felt a need to find someone who would go along with him without arguing with him as Isma'il had done.

He spent a whole hour hesitating until he was fuming with rage. Then it occurred to him to consult his wife Zubayda about the matter. He loved Zubayda and respected her and felt blessed that, contrary to custom regarding women in those days, he could talk and consult with

171

her about such matters notwithstanding her enmity toward Ja'far. Once he decided to consult her, he felt at peace again. It was near sunset, so he called Masrur and ordered him to prepare a nag for him to ride secretly to her palace, the House of Repose, accompanied by no one but Masrur.

When the nag was ready, he disguised himself and set off. Masrur walked behind him. When he came to the House of Repose, the guards did not recognize him, but they recognized Masrur, so they opened the gate for them. They entered the garden, and al-Rashid dismounted and ordered Masrur to precede him to Zubayda and tell her that he was coming. When she was told, she realized that al-Rashid must have some important reason for coming at this hour. She went out to receive him in the hall, in which she had received her son Muhammad a few days earlier. The candles were lit, and they made it look more resplendent. Zubayda wore her best clothes, perfumed herself, and received him in the most welcoming manner, wearing her necklaces of jewels, her gem-studded pins in her hair, her beautifully shaped and adorned brooches on her bosom, and even her bejeweled sandals. Her reception was very cordial and warm. Al-Rashid smiled at her, despite his intense anger, as he sat on the bed. He seated her beside him and held her hand. Although he busied himself with looking at her jewelry, which the lit candles made more radiant and glamorous, she noticed the rage concealed behind his smile. She ignored it and continued with her welcoming words.

"Welcome to the Commander of the Faithful," she said. "He has delighted me with his presence and honored me with his visit. Will he order any food or drink?"

"I have not come to you for food, my cousin," he said.

"God willing, I pray that some good wind brings you here," she said.

He thrust his hand in his pocket and took out the letter that his spy had sent him, and he handed it over to her without saying a word. She took it and read it while he kept observing her and evaluating her reaction. When she finished reading it, she returned it to him and started laughing.

"I see that you are laughing," he said. "It is as if you have not read the letter!"

"Yes, I did," she affirmed.

He said, "I don't think you will understand its content unless I tell you what this Persian man has committed."

When she heard his words, she thought he had come to find out about al-'Abbasa's story. Ignoring this, she said, "What has he committed?"

He said, "He has released al-'Alawi, whom we had succeeded in arresting with great difficulty. But hardly had we imprisoned him and thought we had become safe from his evildoing, when Ja'far set him free. You can see from the letter that this slave has become so arrogant that he is a threat to us. Who will guarantee that if he goes to Khurasan, he will not be tempted to rise against us and rebel? Khurasan will then slip out of our hands. Advise me, for I feel I am blessed by consulting you."

Zubayda laughed, but her laughter was mixed with sarcasm and disdain. Nobody in the world but she dared do that in the presence of al-Rashid because she knew he loved and respected her and because she had the advantage of kinship and the power of love on her side. Her influence in this particular instance was that much stronger because she had often advised him to desist from surrendering to Ja'far and his relatives. But he had not listened to her and attributed her negative attitude to her jealousy of them. So now when he came to complain of the consequences of his former actions, she gave him the look of a victor and said, "O Commander of the Faithful: in relation to the Barmakids, you are like a drunken man drowning in a deep sea. If you have woken from your drunken state and if you have been saved from drowning, I will tell you something much more serious than that. But if you are still in your former state, I will leave you to your own devices."

Her tone greatly affected al-Rashid, and if it were not for his feelings of respect and love for her, he might not have been able to prevent himself from striking her. Instead he said, "What has happened, happened. Tell me now if there is any 'thing' that is more serious than this?"

She replied, "The matter that I am referring to has been concealed from you by your vizier, and it is more difficult than the situation you are in—and uglier."

Al-Rashid's anger increased as he raised his voice, "Woe to you, what is it? Speak."

Looking away from him, she said, "I deem myself too exalted for even talking about it. But summon Urjuwan, the servant. Be severe with him, and give him a thorough drubbing to unnerve him, and he will confess everything to you."

Al-Rashid, about to fly into an even greater rage, stood up and enquired with surprise, "Urjuwan, the servant of my sister al-'Abbasa?"

"Yes," she said. "The servant of your sister al-'Abbasa."

"Where is he?" he asked.

She clapped, and one of the Chakeriyya men standing at her door came in.

"Go at once," she ordered, "and summon for us Urjuwan, the servant, from the palace of al-'Abbasa."

He obeyed and went out. Al-Rashid waited for Urjuwan as though he was on tenterhooks while Zubayda sat in front of him. Neither of them uttered a word.

Urjuwan knew all about his lady's secret and the cause of her forthcoming travel. He was always concerned about her comfort and devoted to give her satisfaction.

Good-hearted eunuchs are a blessing to their masters. They forget themselves and are totally dedicated to serving their master with all their abilities. Perhaps this is because they don't get married, so they are not attached to any woman or child; their emotions are thus focused on their masters. They rejoice when their masters are happy, and they are saddened when their masters are sad. Their loyalty and dedication are such that they endure any suffering caused by the actions of their masters, whatever those actions may be.

Urjuwan was one of the most good-hearted and most devoted people in the service of al-'Abbasa. She treated him exceedingly well because of the comfort he afforded her and the services he provided her, especially the ways in which he helped Ja'far enter and leave her palace. For his part, Urjuawan was increasingly attached to her.

On that night, he was busy indoors preparing for the trip to Khurasan when the servants called him. He went out and saw a Chakeri man waiting for him at the door, and he immediately knew he was a messenger from Zubayda.

"What do you want?" he asked the man.

"Come to our lady, Zubayda," the man answered.

"Now?" Urjuwan asked.

"Yes, this minute," the man urged.

"Wait, so that I may first tell my lady," Urjuwan said.

"There is no need to tell her," the man said, "for only a word or two will be exchanged before you return."

Urjuwan believed him and left without telling al-'Abbasa or anyone else.

As for al-Rashid, he became impatient while sitting and waiting. So he got up and walked in the courtyard while convulsed with rage, wondering what the serious matter was that Zubayda refused to tell him and which the eunuch would reveal. Suddenly it crossed his mind that it might be a scandal touching on honor. His thoughts were interrupted by the sound of footsteps in the garden. The Chakeri man had returned with Urjuwan. Al-Rashid went into the room, which Zubayda had left in order not to hear his conversation with the eunuch.

The Chakeri man entered and said, "Urjuwan is at the door, O Commander of the Faithful."

Al-Rashid ordered, "Bring me the sword and the leather execution mat."

The Chakeri man brought them, and al-Rashid spread the leather execution mat nearby and put the sword beside him. Then he said, "Where is Urjuwan? Bring him in."

When Urjuwan heard the angry voice of al-Rashid, he was terrified. He entered, his knees knocking with fear, and he stood there meekly. When he saw the leather execution mat and the sword, he could hardly remain standing and did not dare raise his eyes from the floor. Al-Rashid gestured to Masrur to dismiss the servants and the Chakeriyya men and to close the doors so that no one would know what was happening in the room. He then looked at Urjuwan and said, "If you don't tell me the truth about the story of Ja'far, you will have no escape from being killed."

Urjuwan knew that the caliph was asking him about the affair of Ja'far and al-'Abbasa, but he remained silent. Even if he wanted to speak, his tongue would not have let him because of the intense fear gripping him.

"What is the matter with you?" al-Rashid screamed. "Speak or else! Here is the leather execution mat and here is the sword." Then he shouted, "Masrur!"

That uncouth man appeared in a wink. Al-Rashid gestured to him, so he unsheathed the sword and stood next to the leather execution mat waiting for the caliph's orders. When Urjuwan saw that, he knelt at al-Rashid's feet and began to kiss them and cry. Al-Rashid then spoke gently to him and said in a calm voice, "Tell the truth and don't be afraid. What do you know about Ja'far and the people of the palace? Speak—immediately."

His voice choking and his tongue stuttering because of fear and weeping, he said, "Safety, O Commander of the Faithful!"

Al-Rashid replied, "Yes, you will be safe if you tell the truth. If you don't, we know everything, and we will kill you with this sword."

He wanted to keep his lady's secret and sacrifice himself for her, but human weakness in the face of death overcame him—it is an instinct that overcomes great men in similar situations, let alone a eunuch slave, however strong his loyalty may be. He rationalized that al-Rashid had only asked him about something he already knew; if he denied his knowledge and was killed, his death would be of no benefit at all to his lady. But if he confessed and remained alive, he might be able to save her or serve her. These considerations raced through his mind in a flash, but he felt the pangs of his conscience if he were to disclose his lady's secret. His mouth was dry, and he stammered because of the frightful dilemma he faced.

Noticing his hesitation, al-Rashid commanded, "Speak, or I will kill you!"

Urjuwan said in a faltering voice, "Ja'far married your sister al-'Abbasa seven years ago, and she gave birth to three sons of his: one is six years old, another is five years old, and the third ... lived for two years ... and died recently. The two sons ... were sent ... to the city of the Messenger ... and she is ... preg...nant ... with the fourth." He then choked.

Al-Rashid listened to his words and simmered with rage. "How come you know this and have not told me?" he demanded.

Urjuwan took heart at this question and replied, "You yourself permitted your vizier to enter into the presence of your family, and you ordered me not to prevent him any time he wished to come, by night or by day."

Gnashing his teeth, al-Rashid yelled, "I did order you not to prevent him at any time, but why did you not inform me the first time he came?" Turning to Masrur, he barked, "Cut off his head!"

Masrur took hold of him with an iron fist and dragged him violently to the leather execution mat as if he was personally avenging himself. Urjuwan fell to the ground, shouting, "Safety! Safety!"

Masrur did not give him a chance to ask a third time lest al-Rashid should accept his plea and pardon him. Masrur was a harsh, bloodthirsty man who took pleasure in the sight of blood and boasted about the number of those he executed and about the speed with which he killed them. He quickly gave Urjuwan a blow of the sword on his neck and severed his head from his shoulders.

Al-Rashid turned his face away and asked about Zubayda. He was directed to her room and entered it, mad with rage. She was sitting on her bed with a lowered head, deep in thought. When she saw al-Rashid coming, she prepared herself to get up, but she did not. As for him, he did not pay attention to anything because of his wrath.

With a trembling voice, he said as his beard quivered and his color paled: "Did you see what Ja'far has done to me? And how he has dishonored me and scandalized me among the Arabs and the Persians?"

She replied in a quiet voice and a composed manner: "This was predictable. You have allowed a young man with a handsome face, beautiful attire, fragrant presence, and a gigantic view of himself to enter into the presence of the daughter of one of God's caliphs. She has an even more beautiful face than he does, she is more immaculately dressed, and has a sweeter fragrant presence than him. This is what you get when you add fuel to fire!"

"Are you still rebuking me?" he said. "By God, we shall obliterate this shame with blood!"

His threat pleased her, and she wanted to strengthen his determination to take revenge on Ja'far. Pretending to be busy folding the edge of her sleeve embroidered with gold thread, with anger and reprimand clearly visible in her eyes, she said, "What I am most afraid of is that your feeling of brotherly affection will overcome you when you see him and that you will forgive him."

Al-Rashid felt the reprimand in her words and the hidden censure they contained concerning his disregard of her advice on previous occasions. But he felt he was too important to tolerate any criticism from anyone, whoever he or she may be. He restrained his feelings and said, "Enough, my cousin. We have now to be cautious in suppressing this scandal and, by God, I will kill anyone who knows about it. And I hope to erase the crime committed by my sister and my vizier, whom I used to call my brother."

Among all people, she was the one who knew his character best, the conflict of his emotions, and his hesitation. She felt he was about to leave, so she stood up and tried to keep him with her; but he declined and said good-bye, not paying her any further attention, either because he was ashamed or because he was angry. So she held him by his hand and stopped him, saying, "Wait a minute. Wouldn't you like to know where the two boys are?"

"The two boys?" he said, startled. "Are they not in Medina?"

"No," she said. "They are in a nearby place that I know, and I can bring them over whenever you like."

"Here, in Baghdad?" he asked.

"Yes," she said.

He freed himself from her and shouted, while still in the room, "Masrur!"

Masrur appeared in a flash, so al-Rashid said to him while Zubayda was standing by, "Have you seen anything tonight?"

"No, my lord," he said, and to affirm his extreme loyalty in keeping secrets, he added, "I am deaf and blind."

Al-Rashid ordered him to bring the nag and Masrur obeyed. When the nag was brought, he mounted it and headed for the Palace of Eternity, Masrur running behind him. Part of the night had elapsed, and al-Rashid was lost in thought all the way, having become very disturbed on account of al-'Abbasa's affair and the strong feelings of agitation it evoked in him. He continued thinking of the gravity of what had happened and felt that his kingdom, his power, his wealth, and all the world's comforts he had acquired did not alleviate the oppressive burden of that disaster. He thought of bringing his sister over or of going to her in order to have her executed. But he was afraid of the ensuing scandal, so he waited patiently for the next day.

Chapter 14

Al-Rashid and his Sister

Al-'Abbasa was unaware of what was being plotted because she was busy with preparations for the trip to Khurasan. 'Utba was beside her, doing her best to put her mind at ease and give her hope. She was preparing all that would lead to her lady's happiness after she had left Baghdad and was living in Khurasan, where her husband would be the master of the house. However, whenever al-'Abbasa thought rationally, she realized that she was exposing herself to a great danger that might lead to bloodshed. But whenever she obeyed her heart's desire and imagined being together with her husband away from it all and occupied with bringing up her two sons under the protection of their father, she was happy and her face brightened. Then her brother's potential knowledge of the affair and his resulting anger would intervene, and she would return to her depressed mood. As she oscillated between elation and depression, a thought occurred to her that allayed her anxiety and gave her hope: to live in Khurasan with her husband and two sons under an assumed name and withhold her story until God would decree what He wished.

As she was entertaining these thoughts, she saw 'Utba running toward her visibly surprised and disturbed. Her heart began to race and blood rose to her face. In view of the dangers surrounding her, unexpected events and unusual sounds would quickly sow panic in her heart. On seeing 'Utba in this state, she shouted at her, "What is the matter?"

"Urjuwan!" she said and fell silent.

"What happened to him?" al-'Abbasa said, aghast.

"I don't know where he is!" 'Utba said.

"Is he not in the palace?" al-'Abbasa asked. "Look for him. Perhaps he is in one of the rooms preparing some travel equipment."

'Utba was about to go out, but then had second thoughts, so she returned and stood perplexed, with her head lowered.

Al-'Abbasa became even more frightened and asked, "What is the matter with you? Has anything happened to him? Tell me where he is!"

"I don't know, my lady," she said. "The servant has informed me that he went out of the palace and…"

Interrupting her, al-'Abbasa said, "He went out of the palace? Why would he go out at such a late hour? Where did he go?"

"I don't know…" 'Utba said, choking.

Al-'Abbasa insisted. "Woe to you! Tell me where he is!"

"I think that he went to the House of Repose," was the answer.

"The House of Repose?" al-'Abbasa shouted. "To Zubayda? What business does he have there?"

"I learned that a Chakeri man had come and asked for him in haste, and he did not give him enough time to ask you for permission to leave."

Al-'Abbasa bit her lip, lowered her head for a moment, and then said, "A Chakeri man had come and asked for him… What do you think for?"

"I think he went for a terrible thing!" 'Utba said.

"Terrible?" al-'Abbasa said. "Why? It may be for a trivial thing."

"No, I think he went for a terrible thing," 'Utba repeated, "Because the Commander of the Faithful is there tonight."

Al-'Abbasa was alarmed and shouted, "The Commander of the Faithful is there? And who told you that? Tell me… You have greatly disturbed me, 'Utba."

She said, "I learned this from a spy of ours at the Palace of Eternity who came here an hour ago and told me that al-Rashid mounted his nag and went to the House of Repose with that accursed servant, Masrur. I did not pay any attention to the matter at first, but when I found out that

Urjuwan had gone there, I was terrified and I came directly to you... I am really afraid of the consequences, my lady!"

Al-'Abbasa lowered her head in silence. A great fear began to take hold of her. She thought of what she had just heard and was troubled. She then said, "Why are you afraid of the fact that my brother is there? At any rate, we are ready to travel tomorrow."

'Utba said, "You are right. I have finished the preparations. When Urjuwan returns, we will leave immediately—if we see any need for hastening our departure."

Al-'Abbasa said, "But the vizier ordered us to wait until he sends us his messenger."

"We shall see," 'Utba said. "I will send out a eunuch to bring us news of Urjuwan."

"Yes, do that," al-'Abbasa said, turning away from her and going to the balcony where she usually waited for Ja'far's messenger. 'Utba went out to send the eunuch.

* * *

Al-'Abbasa stood on the balcony as her eyes scoured the road, but darkness obstructed her sight. Whenever she saw a specter, she thought it was Ja'far's messenger.

Overcome with worry, she waited until midnight. Then when she realized that 'Utba should have returned some time ago, she thought of sending someone to fetch her. Suddenly, she saw her running toward her with tears flowing from her eyes. Her hair was in disorder, her face was pale, and her lips were white.

"What is the matter with you, 'Utba?" al-'Abbasa shouted. "Why are you crying...? What happened to you?"

'Utba quickly held her by the hand and pulled her to the edge of the balcony. Trembling with fear, she said to her, "Go, my lady. Get off this balcony. Save yourself!"

"What happened?" al-'Abbasa asked. "Has the spy returned? What did he say?"

"He returned," she said, "but his return was of no use to us. Get off this balcony and hide somewhere in the road until I send for someone to accompany you to my lord, the vizier. Come on, get down."

Al-'Abbasa was surprised and said, "What happened? Speak."

She said, her voice trembling and faltering, "The Commander of the Faithful...my lady...The Commander of the Faithful..." She gestured with her hand toward the inside.

Al-'Abbasa understood that al-Rashid had arrived at the palace. She realized her brother would not have come to see her at midnight unless there was an important reason, and she felt that this heralded impending trouble for her. At first she was greatly alarmed and stood up. Then her dignity returned. She felt too brave to run away, especially because she was not sure that this would guarantee her safety. She steadied herself, trying to calm down and control her trembling hands. As she struggled to regain a semblance of composure, her good sense and judgment returned. She remained in her seat while 'Utba continued to pull her by the edge of her clothes and urge her to escape from the balcony and down to the road. Then she heard the sound of footsteps. She pulled her clothes away from 'Utba's hand and said, "Leave me alone. I want to see my brother face-to-face and hear what he has to say." Then she thought of her husband and whispered to 'Utba, "Send a fast man to the vizier to warn him of what has happened so that he can take his precautions and avoid falling into a trouble like ours, for the coming of my brother in this manner at this hour of the night portends an impending evil."

She descended from the balcony to the house and met al-Rashid as he passed in a corridor heading toward her. He wore a simple robe with a large cloak over it—for he had come in disguise. He had gone to his palace hoping to postpone dealing with this matter to the next day, but his anxiety and sleeplessness distressed him greatly, so he decided to come and see her with Masrur, fearing she might learn of his anger and run away. He did not expect her to be up and awake—and least of all, preparing to travel.

As for her, she took heart and welcomed him, saying, "My brother has honored me by his visit."

He did not answer her but continued walking to a secluded room of hers where they usually met whenever he visited her. She followed him, her knees trembling, but she was in control of her emotions. Her fear had left her—for the expectation of a disaster is often worse than its occurrence. Courage sustains people of value and dignity facing imminent danger, and so it was with her. She felt strong enough to discuss the matter with her brother, and if she were killed after that, she would not be sorry for having lived.

'Utba walked behind her, weeping and stammering. Al-'Abbasa directed her to go and do the task she had charged her with. As she followed her brother, she saw the servant, Masrur, in the corridor of the house; when he greeted her respectfully, she did not respond. She continued to walk behind al-Rashid until he entered the secluded room and sat down. She saw intense anger in his face; it was as though sparks of fire flew from his eyes. She ignored that and stood in front of him, waiting for what he would do.

He ordered her to close the door, which she did; then she stood facing him boldly as never before, so he quickly said, "I see that you are wearing travel clothes, 'Abbasa. Where are you going?"

She said, "To where I will see no brother and where I will fear no injustice."

He was struck by this surprising boldness; he had expected her to cringe before him and implore him. His anger intensified, but he remained patient in order to hear what she would say, so he asked her, "Do you know why I have come to see you when everyone is asleep?"

"No," she said.

He said, "Why do you answer me with such impudence?"

She said, "You asked me a question, and I gave you a truthful answer."

He said, "It is too late for that after the disloyalty you have committed."

She said, "I don't know that I have committed any disloyalty; if you had asked me this question earlier, my answer would have been the same."

He said, "Were you not the sister of the Commander of the Faithful?"

She said, "Yes, indeed. And I am his sister, still, as far as I know."

He asked, "Does someone like you betray her brother with a man from the *mawali*?"

She replied, "I have not betrayed my brother or anyone else."

He said, "Is this the way you answer me? Your affair has become well known, and you have publicly humiliated me by the treason you have committed."

She said, "What affair do you mean, Harun? Perhaps you consider truthfulness to be treason?"

He said, "I mean your affair with Ja'far, who did not respect my honor and did not fear my power."

At that point, she wanted to talk to him in a soft manner to assuage his anger in the hope he would be kind to her and spare her. So she said, "The vizier has not violated your honor, nor did he intend to harm you. Be kind, my brother, and do not be hasty in your judgment."

"Don't call me brother," he shouted. "I wash my hands of you."

"Wash your hands of me if you wish," she said. "But that man has not committed any crime."

"Woe to you!" he said. "Are you still trying to cover up what I know? I know everything. Your treacherous servant, Urjuwan, told me your secret. If you deny it, your two sons are witnesses to it."

When she heard her two sons mentioned, she became tender and protective. She imagined that if she was contrarian, he would harm them. So she became meek and her determination weakened. She was overcome by her tenderness and found it easy to humiliate herself and beg to save her sons. She knelt at the knees of al-Rashid and wanted to speak, but her tears came first. He thought she intended to confess as a prelude to seeking forgiveness, so he turned his face away from her and said, "You now know that I know the truth of your story, so you think you must confess and seek my sympathy—but this is impossible! For someone who commits an act like yours, there is no punishment but death."

She held back her tears, pulled herself together, and said while still kneeling, "I am not seeking your sympathy for myself, for I have committed no crime, but I am asking you for a right which, I think, you will not deny me."

"What right do you mean?" he asked.

She replied, "Please calm down, O Commander of the Faithful—and I don't say, 'O my brother,' lest I anger you. Calm down, and I will mention this right to you."

He showed some tolerance and said, "Speak."

She said, "Did you not make a contract with Ja'far agreeing that he would marry me, and was that contract not legally valid?"

He said, "Yes. But I made that contract so that you could see each other, and nothing beyond that."

She said, "But is a contract with such terms ever valid? And is it treasonable to implement the prescriptions of the law?"

"Don't equivocate," he said. "You both knew when the contract was written that its intention was that you would enjoy seeing each other, and nothing beyond that. It was only done because I wanted to sit with you both together, because I loved you both and I enjoyed your conversation. Is this the reward of love?"

He shook his head and gnashed his teeth.

She said in a soft voice, "Does the Commander of the Faithful think that we were better off before the contract than after it?"

Interrupting her, he said, "There is no doubt about that, for you were once the person most loved by me, and now you have become the most hated of devils."

"Why?" she asked. "Is it because we have done what God has permitted and you have forbidden? Isn't obeying God worthier than obeying the Commander of the Faithful?"

When he saw that she was making compelling arguments, his anger grew because he realized she was right—and not because she had accused him of intending to harm her unfairly. But custom overcame his nature, for he was accustomed to hearing nothing but agreement, followed by implementation of his wishes, whether right or wrong.

So it was with all people with absolute authority, especially in those times, when there were many flatterers who curried favor with the person in power by praise and incitement, heedless of the consequences. So the ruler would become tyrannical in his thought, his speech, and his deeds, no longer aware of the need for truth and objectivity to influence his actions. Thus he would justify doing for himself what he could not accept for others, believing he was made of a different clay than all other human beings and that all his actions were justified.

No, al-Rashid is not to be blamed if he insisted on finding fault with al-'Abbasa and ignoring her strong arguments, because he grew up having his commands always executed. Autocratic behavior became part of him: it ruled his mind and his opinions, especially when he was angry. When he heard al-'Abbasa's argument, he resorted to his personal authority and said, "But I prohibited both of you, and you both disobeyed me; whoever disobeys the Commander of the Faithful should be duly put to death."

She said, "If it is inevitable that you consider what we did an act of disobedience, then I must say that I am the one who was disobedient and not he, and there is no..."

Rebuking her vehemently, he cut her off and with rage in his voice said, "I see that you love him and that you want to bear the burden for him?"

She replied with sorrow in her voice, "Yes, I love him. If it were not for that, I would not have disobeyed your command regarding him. Yes, I love him; I believe that he deserves my love and the love of the one who is greater than I am, because he is special among all people. He has done deeds that have raised his rank over his peers, and only the Commander of the Faithful is higher than him, and no one else." She said that, having regained her pride, as her eyes shone and her cheeks blushed, as though she was ashamed of her declaration, which was not expected of women at that time, especially in the presence of the caliph.

Al-Rashid said, "Woe to you! Do you admit in my presence that you love him and that you prefer him to all others, even to all the Hashemites? However high you may raise his esteem, he is only a non-Arab client. Don't argue with me about what cannot be changed—he is definitely going to be put to death!"

When she heard him threatening to kill her husband, she trembled and began feeling weak. It was easy in those circumstances for her to humiliate herself for the sake of saving her beloved and her two sons. Patiently bearing her suffering, she resorted to kind words and pleaded with him, "Harun, my brother Harun! Rather, Commander of the Faithful! If you have renounced me now, remember that al-'Abbasa was once your sister and that you both played together and loved each other when you were little. Listen to her and hearken to her intercession for the vizier, for he is your vizier and has not been remiss in serving you. Will you put him to death when he has not committed an offense? And if someone must inevitably be executed, kill me. I am the one who did wrong, not he."

Laughing in disdain, he said, "You too will be put to death. And so will your two sons, so that I may erase this shame from existence!"

When she heard him threatening to kill the two boys, she shuddered, stood up, and shouted in a choked voice, "You will put them to death...? What is their crime? They are innocent children, two angels who know neither what is legally permissible nor what is legally forbidden. I beseech you by God to have pity on them." She then put her hand on her bosom, saying, "My sons... Oh! O Commander of the Faithful, have pity on these two children."

She said this, her voice faltering and choking on her tears. Al-Rashid was about to relent and have pity on her. His feelings of brotherhood and fatherhood stirred in him but not enough to overcome his anger and desire for vengeance. This was especially so because he thought that his vizier had only sought to have children from al-'Abbasa so that his sons would have Hashemite blood. That would entitle him to assume the caliphate, which was limited to Qurayshi descendants in those days. He heard his sister's imploration and fought his own emotions, especially when he heard her defend the two boys. He knew they were innocent, but he thought they would be a danger for him if they remained alive. He answered her, "I will put them to death in order to eradicate this shame from existence."

She returned to cringing before him seeking his compassion for the two boys, and she said while weeping and sobbing, "Have pity, my brother...yes, my brother... For you *are* my brother... Remember, we were both born of one mother's womb... And if you still consider our act to be treason, kill both of us but spare the two boys, for they are innocent."

He said, "They are the fruit of the crime you both committed, and nothing can erase this crime except killing all those involved."

When she realized that seeking his compassion would be of no avail, her pride and her dignity returned to her. She wiped her tears, gave him a look that pierced his heart, and said, "Do you still consider our act to be a crime, when we only obeyed God's command?"

"Don't try to change my mind," he said, "for you have both disobeyed the Commander of the Faithful and must be duly punished." He stood up as if intending to leave, but she stopped him and said, "You have embarrassed me, O Harun, and you have forced me to say things you are not accustomed to hear from me or from anyone else. How dare you forbid us from doing something that you permit for yourself?"

He chided her vehemently, his hand on the hilt of his dagger, and said, "Has your insolence reached the point of accusing me of an act like yours?"

She said, "Yes, I say this and I fear no blame. What you charge us with is only to have fulfilled the terms of a lawful marriage that you yourself contracted and signed. But I remind you of the numerous slave-girls and concubines in your palace, whom you enjoy and have pleasure with and find nothing wrong in that, believing the law allows you this. How can you then forbid me from exercising my right in one lawful marriage? Isn't this injustice? Don't you give and receive slave-girls as gifts, in tens and in hundreds? Your own wife, Zubayda, gave you ten of the most beautiful slave-girls as a gift. She did so without believing that this was demeaning for you or her, nor a crime either. And yet you both believe that what I did is a crime. If your sister now seeks your compassion, you get angry and threaten to kill her, her husband, and her two innocent children. You don't accept a mother's intercession, even though she has agreed to be put to death to spare them."

When he heard her words and saw her audacity, he could no longer tolerate looking at her. He scolded her vehemently and said, "I see that your insolence has gone beyond all limits. I made a mistake in giving you an opportunity to speak. My patience has run out, and it is time that I am finished with you." Then he called, "Masrur."

The cruel man from Ferghana entered, with his sword on his side. When al-'Abbasa saw him, she was sure that her death was now near and asked for God's protection. She turned to al-Rashid and said, "I am now to be killed inevitably, and there is no one to drive away this judgment from me; if you did not believe what I have told you about myself, I plead that you believe me with regard to Ja'far, for he does not deserve being put to death when he has committed none of the crimes you accused him of—and be kind to the two children." She said that and was choked by tears.

As for al-Rashid, he shouted to Masrur, "Have you locked all the palace doors and confined its residents?"

"Yes, my lord," he said.

Al-Rashid asked him, "Where are the two servants and the laborers whom you brought?"

"They are all nearby," Masrur said. "Shall I call them in?"

"Call in the two servants only," al-Rashid commanded.

Masrur went out and returned with the two servants, who were carrying a large crate. When al-'Abbasa saw this, she became certain that she was about to be executed. She turned to her brother and saw that he was looking away from her. He gestured to Masrur, and the man approached her with the unsheathed sword. She said to her brother, "Do you still persist in wanting to kill me? Don't you fear God for such an act? Do you kill me because I obeyed God and disobeyed you? You, men, permit yourselves things that you forbid for your wives. Is it fair that your palace is full of hundreds of concubines and slave-girls, and yet you kill me because of a man whom I married in accordance with God's law and His Prophet's tradition? I don't mind dying after I have met with you and discussed your accountability." She then lowered her voice and said, "But I do mind that you commit a similar act with my dear husband and my beloved two sons." She then turned her face toward the road to Hejaz, where she thought her two sons resided, having been accustomed to inhale their aroma from that direction, and she said, "Farewell, O Hasan and Husain. God be with you." She then turned her face toward al-Shammasiyya as if wanting to talk to her beloved there, but Masrur intervened with a quick blow of his sword that killed her. Al-Rashid was looking away and wished he was not there to witness her killing because he loved her very much.

When she fell dead on the floor, Masrur beckoned to the two servants, and they put her body in the crate. Then in came the laborers, ten strong men who carried pickaxes and palm-leaf baskets and who had bared their arms and lower legs. Masrur ordered them to dig in the middle of the secluded room, so they did until they reached water; then he said, "That is enough. Now bring the crate." They brought it and lowered it into the pit, and then he ordered, "Now cover it with soil." So they did, using the soil they had dug up, and afterwards they leveled the floor as it had been before being sent out of the room by Masrur. After he and al-Rashid left the room, he locked the door and al-Rashid took the key and ordered him to guard the palace and not let anyone go in or out of it and to arrest anyone who tried to enter it. Then he said, "Take these servants and laborers, give them their wages, and meet me at the palace." Masrur understood that the caliph was ordering him to kill them, so he did. He put their bodies in sacks weighed down with rocks and pebbles and threw them into the Tigris River. He returned to the Palace of Eternity and saw that al-Rashid was there and unable to sleep. Al-Rashid asked him, "Have you done what I ordered you?"

"Yes," said Masrur. "And I paid everyone his wages."

Al-Rashid gave him the key to the secluded room and said, "Take this key and keep it with you until I ask you for it."

Masrur took the key and said, "I hear and obey."

Morning was approaching, and al-Rashid said, "This is Thursday morning, and it is the day when Ja'far, the vizier, goes out in a procession, so stay close to me."

Masrur bowed in obedience.

Chapter 15

The Death of Ja'far

Ja'far al-Barmaki was unaware of what had happened. He was preparing for the trip on the next day, having decided to leave earlier after his conversation with Isma'il. It was necessary to say good-bye to the caliph before leaving for Khurasan, as was the custom of governors before going out to their newly assigned provinces. Everything was ready, and nothing remained to do except to mount the horses and leave. When he decided to bid farewell to al-Rashid, he called his servant Hamdan and said to him, "We are leaving today. Don't you know that?"

"Yes, I do, my lord," Hamdan said. "Shall I go to my lady, al-'Abbasa, and bring her here, or shall we join you at al-Nahrawan?"

Ja'far was pleased with the man's quick thinking and alertness. He smiled and said, "I think both of you should join me at al-Nahrawan. There is no need to hurry to her now. It is better for you to postpone that until after I bid the caliph farewell."

"It is for you to command, my lord, "Hamdan said.

Before noon, Ja'far went out in his ceremonial procession surrounded by horsemen and the cavalcade. When he reached the Palace of Eternity, he was admitted with the customary pomp and magnificence. He thought to himself, "This is the last time I enter these gates to meet a man who does not level with me, and with whom I do likewise, whenever we see each other. When I will be the Governor of Khurasan, I will be among my own people and supporters. I doubt we shall meet again, except if he were to come to fight me there." He soon reached the House of the Elite and dismounted.

Al-Rashid was sitting to meet people; they entered in accordance with their ranks, they greeted him, and then they left. Finally Ja'far entered and greeted the caliph, and al-Rashid responded in a welcoming, cheerful manner, seating him in his assigned place, nearest to the caliph. As usual al-Rashid began to converse with him in kind words. Letters arriving from the various regions were brought to him, which Ja'far read to him and al-Rashid signed. Then Ja'far looked at the caliph and thanked him for the welcoming reception, adding, "The Commander of the Faithful has overwhelmed me with his favors, and he has raised my position and assigned me to the governorship of the largest province of his state; for this, it is my duty to thank him."

Al-Rashid smiled and said, "You are my brother, and if I divide my kingdom between you and me, I will give you half of it."

Ja'far pretended to be embarrassed by this high praise; he sat up politely in his seat and said, "I am a client of the Commander of the Faithful, and all the favors to me from him are beneficent graces on his client." Then he added, "And if the Commander of the Faithful has sent me far away from his company and presence, I still remain his slave and I will shed my blood in obeying and serving him."

"God bless you," the caliph said, "and it is doubtless that I will miss your good counsel, for you assumed the affairs of state on my behalf for a long time, and you even relieved me from taking care of many of my personal matters."

When Ja'far heard these words, he stirred because they were the same as the ones he used the day before with Ismail. His conscience pricked him as he became worried that his earlier words to Isma'il had reached al-Rashid. But he considered it unlikely that Isma'il would have conveyed them to al-Rashid, and it never crossed his mind that the handsome slave-boy had written them to the caliph. He therefore said to al-Rashid, "Whatever effort a slave may exert in the service of his master, it is neither out of benevolence on his part nor out of graciousness."

He waited for al-Rashid's command to go out to Khurasan, because courtesy required that the caliph should initiate speaking on this subject. When he did not hear anything on this, Ja'far said, "Will the Commander of the Faithful permit me to leave?" He did not mention Khurasan so that his sentence would convey merely his request to leave the caliph's presence and go home.

Al-Rashid said, "Have you prepared yourself to leave to your new post?"

"Yes, my lord," he said.

"And do you intend to leave today?" al-Rashid asked.

"If the Commander of the Faithful so commands," he replied.

Al-Rashid wanted to delay Ja'far so he could put him to death while he was still in Baghdad. Even then, he was still hesitant because he knew the power of the parties supporting the Barmakids, even among the Hashemites themselves, the majority of whom liked him. He felt that executing Ja'far required caution and deep thought—not like the case of al-'Abbasa. So he said to him, "And have you checked your horoscope today?"

Ja'far said, "No, my lord."

In those days, they used to consult their horoscopes and believed that good fortune and ill fortune were written in the stars in accordance with the hours of the day. The homes of influential and respected persons had astrolabes with which horoscopes could be read. Al-Rashid himself had one perfectly made astrolabe he inherited from his grandfather, Abu Ja'far al-Mansur, who was greatly interested in astrology and astrologers. The astrolabe was placed on an ebony shelf studded with ivory, next to the throne of al-Rashid so that he could use it when needed. He himself had some knowledge of this art, and Ja'far al-Barmaki was even more knowledgeable than he was. Al-Rashid took the astrolabe from the shelf and ordered the chamberlain to summon one of the resident astrologers who, with other craftsmen, lived in the Palace of Eternity as was the custom of the caliphs in that age. So an astrologer was brought in.

When the astrologer entered, al-Rashid asked him, "How much of the day has passed?"

The astrologer said, "Three hours and a half."

Al-Rashid said to him, "Calculate the ascendant."

The astrologer did, while al-Rashid was himself calculating it and looking at Ja'far's star in it. He then turned to Ja'far and said, "My brother, this is an hour of ill fortune as I can see that an event will happen. It is more suitable for you to postpone your journey till tomorrow, which is Friday. You will pray tomorrow and then travel on your day of good fortune. You will spend the night at al-Nahrawan and, early on Saturday, you will take to the road. This will be better for you than traveling today."

This postponement was hard for Ja'far to accept. He took the horoscope and calculated the ascendant himself. Even if he had reached a different conclusion than al-Rashid, it was not acceptable to verify words or find fault with them in the presence of caliphs.

So Ja'far said, "You are right, O Commander of the Faithful. This hour is an hour of ill fortune, and I have never seen a star with greater burning or with a narrower orbit in the zodiac than my star today. The view of the Commander of the Faithful is correct."

He remained waiting for a signal dismissing him, as was the protocol of caliphs. When al-Rashid moved, Ja'far stood up and left, and he headed for his palace. The people, the generals, the elite, and the rank and file honored him and showed their respect inside the palace, on the sides of the street, and everywhere—unaware of his real situation and of the danger that surrounded his life.

Ja'far left the Palace of Eternity, hardly believing that he would have an independent position in Khurasan, that he would live in peace with his relatives and supporters, that he would have al-'Abbasa and their two sons with him, and that he would escape from the conspiracies at the caliph's court and from the danger that surrounded him.

When he reached his palace at al-Shammasiyya, he sent for Hamdan, and when the man came, he informed him of the postponement of the journey to the following day. He told him to take care of al-'Abbasa by staying at al-Shammasiyya after his departure and to go to her palace with the mounts when darkness fell; he would then take her to al-Nahrawan with all those she wanted to take with her, or he would travel with her beyond that place so that she would be safe. Ja'far knew that al-'Abbasa would take 'Utba and Urjuwan with her. He then took off his clothes and sat down.

* * *

When al-Rashid had come to al-'Abbasa's palace, she had ordered 'Utba to send word to Ja'far to warn him of the threats endangering his life, so he could escape and save himself. When 'Utba went to the room of the slave-girls and servants to send one of them on this errand, she found that the palace was surrounded by guards and that going out was impossible. She was greatly concerned and returned to her room, trembling with fear for her mistress after having witnessed al-Rashid's visit. She began to realize what was happening and became certain that her mistress was facing great danger. When 'Utba learned that al-'Abbasa had been killed, she cried and lamented; she realized that she too would soon be in mortal danger. But she gave little importance to her own life after her mistress was gone, and her concern was to convey her mistress' message to Ja'far because she did not doubt he would be killed after al-'Abbasa. She began considering her options but found no simple solution. Her confusion worsened and the day dawned as she was wandering from room to room, weeping and lamenting.

Slowly she realized that weeping would serve no purpose and that the best thing she could do was to try and escape from the palace. If she succeeded, she would save her life and would inform Ja'far about what had happened; his escape would be a consolation for the loss of her mistress. She suddenly thought of Abu al-'Atahiya, knowing that he was the cause of all these misfortunes. She cursed him and remembered his love for her and how he had asked the caliph for her hand but she had refused him. She now imagined that if she could see him and feign her love for him, he might find a way to take her out of the palace, for she knew the influence poets had. If she left the palace, she would have a chance to reach Ja'far. She also remembered Abu al-'Atahiya's love for money, of which she had plenty. She thought that if she failed to win him over by love, she would make use of money—and she was pleased with this idea. But the problem now was that she did not know where Abu al-'Atahiya was.

It occurred to her that money overcame all difficulties and softened the harshest of hearts. So she took a necklace of jewels that belonged to her mistress and that she had prepared for the journey to Khurasan. She disguised herself as a stranger and wore her veil and her sandals, and went out heading for the gate of the palace. She found the gate locked, so she knocked and called for the doorman who used to be on duty at the gate during her mistress's lifetime. Nobody answered her, so she knocked again and the wicket was opened. A man looked out of it who, she knew, was a guard belonging to al-Rashid's troops.

"Where is the doorman?" she asked him. "Why have you locked all the doors and confined us?"

Closing the wicket and turning away, the guard said, "Stay inside. There is no way out."

"Why not?" she inquired.

"Stay inside," he shouted. "And don't talk too much. The palace is locked by order of the Commander of the Faithful."

She hit one palm with the other in dismay and said, "Woe to me! What brought me here?"

Her ruse worked. The guard thought she was not one of the palace's people, so he opened the wicket, looked at her, and saw that she was overly disguised.

"I beseech you by God," she said. "Open the gate for me so that I may go on my way, for I have not committed any offense, nor am I one of the people of this palace."

"Why are you here?" he asked.

She answered, "I came yesterday with an important matter to be delivered to our lady, al-'Abbasa. Then darkness fell before I could leave, so I stayed overnight with one of the slave-girls. I now intend to go back to my master lest he should consider me a slowpoke and think ill of me."

"And who is your master?" he asked.

"My master is Abu al-'Atahiya, the poet of the Commander of the Faithful," she replied.

As soon as he heard his name, he recognized him because of his fame, for poets in those days were the highlight of the caliphs' gatherings.

"And what important matter did you bring from him?" he asked.

She pretended to be afraid of disclosing it, and she remained silent.

"Why don't you answer me?" the man inquired.

"I was sent by him with an important matter to be delivered to our lady, al-'Abbasa...and... and...Open the gate for me, and don't delay me, may God guard you."

The guard did not doubt that she was telling the truth, but he wanted to banter with her, so he said, "You came with an important secret matter, so stay here and keep your secret." He closed the wicket.

She shouted, "In the name of God, open the gate and don't harass me! My delay of last night is sufficient, and I expect it will lead to bad consequences. Things will be worse if I am late today too."

He opened the wicket again and said, "I will not open the gate unless you tell me the secret that you brought."

She said, "You are toying with me when you have no worries in your heart while I am very anxious. If you don't believe my words, our lady al-'Abbasa is my witness. Don't you believe her?"

Her pretense of naivety strengthened his belief in her truthfulness, but he remembered al-Rashid's strict orders. He was afraid to let her leave and bear this responsibility, so he said, "This is not my concern. I have been ordered to prevent the people of this palace from leaving—and that's it."

He wanted to close the wicket, but she held it and tried to open it, saying, "If I tell you why I came here, will you let me go?"

"Why did you come here?" he asked. "Speak."

She answered, whispering, "I think you know that Abu al-'Atahiya has stopped composing poetry."

"I know that," he said.

"And I think you know," she added, "that he likes money."

"Yes, he is famous for that," he said.

She said, "When he needs money, he composes poems secretly for some princes. Yesterday, he composed a poem praising al-'Abbasa and gave it to me to deliver to her. I carried it to her yesterday evening, and she gave me a reward and honored me by letting me stay here overnight—I wish she hadn't." She shook her head.

"And what was the reward?" he asked.

She pretended to be afraid of revealing it and she did not answer.

"Are you not going to tell me?" he asked.

Replying in a tone of someone who was afraid and seeking sympathy, she said, "Here it is."

She thrust her hand into her pocket and took out the necklace. It sparkled in her fingers and shone like the sun. The guard put out his hand to take it, but she quickly put it back to her pocket.

"Let me see it," he said.

She gave it to him, pretending to be concerned about it. He took it and began to turn it over and admire it, saying, "It is precious. But do you think I will let you go by just looking at this necklace, when I don't own as much as one of its jewels?"

She said, grumbling, "I am interested in getting out. That's all."

When he saw her so eager to get out, he said, "If you want to go, then go—alone, without the necklace."

"What shall I tell Abu al-'Atahiya?" she asked.

"Tell him," he said, "that al-'Abbasa did not give you anything."

This pleased her, but she wanted to outfox him and said, "But he will not believe me. I think I should be fair to you both: I will give you half of the reward, and I will carry to him the other half."

The guard accepted and immediately cut the necklace, took the larger part of it, and gave her the rest, saying, "This much will be sufficient for you. If you accept my way of dividing, you can go; otherwise, stay inside."

She lowered her head to think for a moment, then said, "I would rather leave, and I will consider myself as having received nothing from her."

Pleased to have the jewels, the guard opened the gate and said, "Go out. But take care and don't tell anyone; otherwise, you will most certainly be killed."

She went out, hardly believing she had escaped. She jumped for joy and hoped Ja'far could be saved. The guard was more joyful than she was. The sun had risen by then, and, paying attention to nothing else, she hastened to hire a donkey and rode it to the palace of Ja'far at al-Shammasiyya Gate.

* * *

We left Ja'far at his palace, having taken off his clothes to rest. Then it seemed to him desirable to have a session for the morning draught, which was a gathering held in the morning for drinks. It was as if he wanted to bid Baghdad farewell. So he ordered the session, and the table was prepared and the drinks were brought. He asked who of the singers was in the palace, and he was told "Abu Zakkar, the blind man, is here." He said, "Bring him." The singer entered, the curtain was set up, and Ja'far summoned some of his singing slave-girls and those who played musical instruments. Abu Zakkar began to sing, and the slave-girls accompanied him and played their lutes. Ja'far began to drink, thinking that the people were unaware of his troubles with al-Rashid. It was likely they knew more than he himself knew, especially the singers, for they came to know people's secrets by attending gatherings of pleasure in which drinks were served. When those in the gatherings rejoiced and were thrilled, indications of their inner feelings were fully revealed; the singers pretended to ignore them and kept them secret, fearing for their lives. Despite al-Rashid's suppression of Ja'far's affair, his singer al-Mawsili knew the secret, and it was said that al-Rashid asked him in one of the gatherings, "What are the people gossiping about?" and al-Mawsili said, "They say that you will arrest the Barmakids and will appoint al-Fadl ibn al-Rabi' as your vizier." Al-Rashid chided him and said, "Go away, woe to you!"

A similar case was that of Abu Zakkar, the blind man, for his blindness encouraged those who attended a gathering in which he was present to say more than they did in the presence of others; therefore he was fully aware of the danger that Ja'far was in and sometimes referred to it in his songs, references that only the people in the know understood.

When Ja'far asked him to sing on that day, he sang the following:

Don't be surprised, for every man
Will be visited by death, sooner or later.
And every provision he makes will, one day,
Be depleted even if it may last for some time.
If you could be saved from Time's events, I would have
Redeemed you with inherited possessions, new and old.

When those present heard his song, they understood him to refer to no one but Ja'far. Hardly had Abu Zakkar finished singing his song when the door was opened and the chamberlain entered. Ja'far asked him, "What is the matter?"

He said, "Masrur, the servant of the Commander of the Faithful, is at the door."

When Ja'far heard Masrur's name, he was alarmed because he always found him uncouth and insufferable. But he had no choice but let him in. When he entered, Ja'far asked him, "What brings you to us?"

He said, "My sire, accompany me to the Commander of the Faithful."

Ja'far was disturbed by this invitation and said, "Woe to you, Masrur. I have just left his presence. What is the matter?"

He said, "He has received letters from Khurasan that he wants you to read to him."

Ja'far was a little reassured, and he stood up and said to himself, *I thought I met this man in Baghdad for the last time this morning, and here I am, meeting with him one more time. 'There is no power or strength but God's.'*

He asked for his clothes and for the black attire and headgear that he wore; he put on his sword and ordered that mounts be prepared. He then left and the gathering dispersed.

As he was going out of the hall, with Masrur in front of him, the chamberlain came and stood where Ja'far could see that he wanted to speak with him confidentially. So Ja'far approached him and asked him what he wanted. The chamberlain said, "'Utba, the servant of our lady, al-'Abbasa, is at the House of Women, and she asks to see you."

He thought she had been sent by al-'Abbasa to ask about the journey, so he said, "Tell her I will return soon."

The chamberlain said, "She asks to see you *now.*"

So he thought of seeing her and asking her what she wanted, but he was afraid that Masrur would notice that and inform al-Rashid about it. He stood there for a while, hesitating, and then he remembered Raihan who knew about all the details of the journey. So he said to the chamberlain, "Let her see our slave-boy, Raihan, and let her ask him for whatever she wants."

The chamberlain gestured in obedience, and Ja'far walked out until he reached the courtyard of the palace. He then mounted his horse and moved in a procession of his horsemen and slave-boys, heading for the Palace of Eternity. Masrur was on a horse in front of everyone, and Ja'far was in the middle of the procession in his black attire and headgear, surrounded by a select group of horsemen, most of whom were Persians who would protect him with their souls. They passed through al-Shammasiyya and came to the bridge; they crossed it and approached the square in front of the Palace of Eternity. When they reached the gate of the palace, Masrur dismounted and told the horsemen of the procession to stop there. Masrur then entered; Ja'far, accompanied by his slave-boys, followed him without realizing that his horsemen had been stopped outside the palace, because his mind was preoccupied with the caliph's invitation. When they had entered, Masrur gestured to the doormen, and they locked the gate—as they had agreed earlier. Then they entered the second gate, and Masrur asked the slave-boys to remain outside. After Ja'far entered, Masur locked the gate behind him. When Ja'far entered the third gate, he turned around and saw that he was all alone, with not one of his men with him. He regretted having gone out at that hour.

In the courtyard of the palace, Ja'far saw a Turkish pavilion that Masrur had set up there by order of al-Rashid, and it was surrounded by forty black slave-boys. Ja'far thought that al-Rashid was waiting for him in it, so he entered but saw no one there; he only saw a sword and a leather execution mat on the floor. He then became certain of what awaited him. He stood there, his knees shaking, and was overwhelmed by fear. He had a sensation of how weak he was, for he knew Masrur's cruelty and that, if he wanted to resist him, he did not have the strength to defeat him; he knew, at any rate, that he was besieged in that place. So he resorted to kind words and said to Masrur, "My brother, what is the matter?"

Masrur laughed in disdain and said, "Am I now your brother? In your home, you usually address me by saying, 'Woe to you!' You know the problem... God will not grant you a respite, nor will He forget about you... The Commander of the Faithful has ordered me to cut off your head and to carry it to him now."

When Ja'far heard these words, he shuddered and his blood almost froze in his veins. Perhaps drinking had made him weak. The reader may have expected to see Ja'far, the vizier, firm and composed in this situation as great men would be. But indulging in luxury and intoxicants weakens one's heart and emasculates one's resolve, and a person so self-indulgent loses the ability to endure adversity. This was the case of Ja'far that morning, so when he heard Masrur speaking rudely to him, he fell at his feet and kissed them, saying, "My brother Masrur, you know how much I have honored you to the exclusion of other slave-boys and men of the retinue. All your needs have been met by me at all times. And you know my high position in relation to the Commander of the Faithful and how he entrusts me with secrets. Perhaps he heard something about me that is false. Here, I will give you now one hundred thousand dinars before I rise from this spot. Let me go free."

"There is no way, ever, to do that," said Masrur.

"Take me to the Commander of the Faithful," pleaded Ja'far, "and let me stand in front of him. Maybe, if he sees me, he will have pity on me and he will pardon me."

Shaking his head, Masrur said, "There is no way, ever, to do that. And I have learned that there is no way, ever, that you may remain alive."

Ja'far persisted and said, "Refrain from executing me now and go to him and tell him that you have finished doing what he ordered you to do, and listen to what he will say; then return to me and do what you please. If you do that and if I am not put to death, I will share with you my blessings and my possessions, and I will appoint you as general of the armies—to this, I call upon God and His angels as my witnesses."

When Masrur heard these promises, he was pleased. It occurred to him that al-Rashid's order to kill Ja'far might have been given in a moment of uncontrolled anger and that when the caliph's anger subsided, he might regret it and then pardon him. If this were so, there was a possibility for him to acquire all this promised wealth and be appointed to that high post. He lowered his head in thought. When Ja'far saw him lowering his head, his hope to live was revived, and he waited for what Masrur would do next; he then heard him say, "I will do that." Saying so, Masrur untied Ja'far's sword and belt, took them away, and ordered some of the guards standing there to watch him, and he went out.

When Ja'far was alone and able to think for himself, he turned around and saw nothing but the sword and the leather execution mat. He regained his reason and realized that there was no escape from death because he knew the causes that had motivated al-Rashid to kill him, and he knew the mutual hypocrisy and reciprocal deception they both practiced in their relationship with each other. He became certain that al-Rashid knew about his relationship with al-'Abbasa, and he remembered 'Utba's urgent desire to see him. He regretted having left her to wait for his return, for she might have come to warn him or to alert him of the impending danger he would face. His fear intensified and it was as if he was seeing death face to face. His sorrows rose and in his imagination al-'Abbasa's image presented itself as she was on the day when he parted with her for the last time after exchanging promises to flee together to Khurasan. He thought that escape with her and their two sons could have been possible if he had traveled the day before or if he had spoken with 'Utba before going out. He became deeply depressed and was overcome by weeping. He wished he could see al-'Abbasa before he died and kiss his two children before this eternal separation from them. He began to say to himself, *Alas! How sorry I am for you, my beloved! And how eager I am for a kiss from my two sons! I have spent my life wishing for one hour to play with them as fathers play with their children. When I had begun to think that this hour was close, lo and behold, it became as distant from me as eternity. And you, my wife in accordance with God's law—although your brother claims the contrary—you have exposed yourself to danger for my sake, and you had to face the anger of your tyrannical brother. What will be your fate if your brother will know of our affair? He will inevitably kill you—if he hasn't already. I wonder, did 'Utba come to announce your death to me and to warn me of my impending death? Perhaps this is what has happened, and you are worthy of such magnanimity. I have experienced your devotion, your dedication, and your love for me more than once. If you have died before me, I now desire to follow you; if you are still alive, you will inevitably follow me, for your brother has not hastened to kill me unless he knows our secret. God knows, we have only obeyed love and the law.*

He fell silent for a moment, holding back his tears, and then he said, *And our two sons? O Hasan and O Husain! Where are you now? Do you know what happened to your parents at the hands of your tyrannical, hard-hearted uncle?* Saying this, he choked and his voice was stifled. All of a sudden, the door was opened. He was startled and became aware of himself, so he stopped talking and his eyes stared fixedly at the door. Masrur entered and his face was frowning, so Ja'far knew that he had not succeeded and was about to ask him what happened when he heard him say, "I went to the Commander of the Faithful. When he saw me, he asked me about you and I said to him, 'I have executed your command.' He said, 'Bring me his head immediately.' "

When Ja'far heard his words, he put up a robust front and said, "Do as you please. But I have one question to ask you, so give me a truthful answer as I am in the last moments of my life."

"What is your question?" asked Masrur.

"What happened to al-'Abbasa?" Ja'far asked. "Tell me the truth and don't be afraid of being reported, for the one who hears you is going to be killed."

Masrur said, "She was killed."

"Killed?" Ja'far screamed. "Then, hasten to kill me. I have no desire to live."

Hardly had he ended his words when Masrur struck Ja'far's neck with his sword, cut off his head, and carried it to al-Rashid with blood gushing from it.

* * *

Al-Rashid had planned a stratagem to bring Ja'far into the Palace of Eternity and seclude him in the Turkish pavilion. He had ordered Masrur to set up the Turkish pavilion that morning, just after Ja'far had left the House of the Elite. Al-Rashid continued to walk to and fro in the hall after Ja'far had left and thought hard before deciding to embark on that momentous act. He hesitated between acting quickly and proceeding cautiously because he knew that many people loved the Barmakids and would die to support them. But after his constant anxiety and his long sleepless nights, he could not eat or drink without increasingly thinking of vengeance. His anger grew and he was afraid that if he postponed killing Ja'far, the latter would know about al-'Abbasa's death. He would then prepare himself to react, and matters could then spin out of control with uncertain results. Al-Rashid loved Ja'far very much, for they had grown up together; they were very close, associating without reserve like brothers. When he thought about all that and began to feel his kind side surfacing, al-Rashid caught himself as he remembered his anger at his power being usurped and his honor stained. And he resolved on killing Ja'far.

He spent some time tossing all these thoughts around as he walked alone in the hall until he became lost in his thoughts. If anyone had entered the hall at that time, he would have seen al-Rashid walking alternately quickly and then slowly, lowering his head and staring, scratching his chin, shaking his finger to threaten and menace, or gesturing as if to ask for respite from his hesitation. He was not paying attention to the embroidered tapestries hanging on the walls of the hall nor to the embellished multicolored carpets on the floor—it was as if the only color he saw was black. He sometimes stood for a moment in front of a tapestry to read its poetic verses or to look at the artistic forms covering it; he sometimes read a verse or a paragraph, but did not absorb its meaning so immersed was he in his thoughts and apprehensions. He happened to stand in front of a column near his throne and read the following verses, which urged him to accomplish his task and strengthened his determination:

> I wish Hind would fulfill what she has promised
> And heal our souls of what they have endured.
> I wish she would be tyrannical for one time—
> Only a weakling is one who is not tyrannical.

He had hesitated between being bold and being restrained, but after reading these verses, boldness got the better of him. He decided on execution and shouted, "Masrur!" The man entered in a flash, and al-Rashid ordered him what to do—as was explained earlier. Al-Rashid remained in the hall, waiting on tenterhooks for Masrur's return. When Masrur came back conveying the ruse that Ja'far had planned in the hope that he would be forgiven, al-Rashid sent him back and ordered him to kill

Ja'far as quickly as possible. So Masrur returned to the Turkish pavilion, cut off the vizier's head, and carried it back to al-Rashid, grasping it by the beard so that it was upside down, blood oozing from its jugular veins and flowing onto the cheeks, the eyes, and the hair.

Al-Rashid was sitting on the throne as Masrur entered carrying the head, threw it on a cushion in front of the caliph, and withdrew to a corner of the hall. When al-Rashid saw the head, he felt the danger dissipate, but he could not suppress his chagrin. He turned pale and emotions were astir in him. He remembered the good old times of affection they had shared. He looked at the head for a moment, while carrying an ebony scepter inlaid with ivory; he poked the carpet with it and then talked to the head, saying, "O Ja'far, have I not treated you as I treat myself? O Ja'far, you have not treated me in the same way, you have not duly acknowledged my right, you have not kept the bonds of loyalty to me, you have not looked into the consequences of matters, you have not pondered the vicissitudes of time, and you have not taken into consideration the change of fortunes. O Ja'far, you have betrayed me by dishonoring my family and you have demeaned me among the Arabs and the Persians. O Ja'far, you have wronged me and have wronged yourself—and you have not contemplated the outcome of your deeds." Al-Rashid spoke these words and poked the carpet with his scepter or knocked Ja'far's teeth with it, while Masrur was standing there, listening and watching. If he had a heart, it would have been broken, but this was an insensitive and crude man.

While al-Rashid was addressing Ja'far and blaming him in these words, with Masrur not daring to move or say anything, they heard the sound of footsteps coming quickly toward the door and approaching ever more closely; they then heard someone knock on the door and say, "Peace be to you, O Commander of the Faithful. Shall I enter?"

Al-Rashid was startled, for he recognized the voice of Isma'il ibn Yahya. He gestured to Masrur to take away the head and leave quickly; he did so and left through a side door of the hall. Isma'il did not wait for al-Rashid's response and entered.

Al-Rashid looked toward the door and saw Isma'il entering with a look of surprise on his face. He was wearing a headgear whose turban he had not wound neatly, his beard was not combed, and he was not as well dressed as one ought to be when meeting with the caliph.

When al-Rashid saw him entering, he pulled himself together, returned his greeting, and gestured to him to sit down. Isma'il sat on a chair, far from al-Rashid, and he was breathing heavily. Al-Rashid stood up, walked to him, and tried to smile in welcoming him. But agitation overcame him and he was not able to hide his feelings and put up a brave front.

When Isma'il saw al-Rashid standing, he stood up too, out of politeness. But the caliph ordered him to sit down and sat next to him, having realized that Isma'il would not have come at that hour but for an important reason. He asked him directly the purpose of his visit, and Isma'il said, "I have come to you to intercede, O Commander of the Faithful; if you decline, then I am here to ask you to delay your order."

Al-Rashid realized that Isma'il had come to intercede on behalf of Ja'far, and he was surprised that he had discovered the matter in spite of the caliph's effort at concealing all information. In fact, Isma'il had received the information from Raihan, Ja'far's slave-boy, when 'Utba relayed news to him that morning. When she had not been able to see Ja'far, she conveyed the news to Raihan. Ja'far's procession had already left, and Raihan did not dare to follow him lest Masrur should suspect him. He was at a loss what to do, but then he agreed with 'Utba to go to Isma'il because of his friendship with Ja'far. Raihan then quickly went to see Isma'il and found him sitting in the garden of his palace, where he told him what had happened. Isma'il put on his clothes quickly and went to the Palace of Eternity. He asked about al-Rashid and was told that he was alone in the House of the Elite. He entered, not knowing of Ja'far's death, for it did not occur to him that al-Rashid would act so quickly.

When al-Rashid heard Isma'il's words and knew he was interceding with him on behalf of Ja'far, he affected ignorance and said, "Your intercession is accepted and what you order will be implemented."

Isma'il was delighted at the good news and said, "May God give long life to the Commander of the Faithful. I have come to intercede with you for your vizier, Ja'far."

Nodding his head, al-Rashid said, "You have come too late, my cousin, for the sentence has been carried out."

"Was Ja'far killed?" Isma'il said in alarm.

"His treason has killed him," the caliph said.

"You killed him, O Commander of the Faithful?" Isma'il said, aghast, "You killed your vizier, the one responsible for your seal and the rule of your state?"

"I will not give you a long explanation, O Isma'il. This vizier of mine was killed by his own betrayal. If you, as a Hashemite, knew about his offense, you would have killed him yourself before I did."

Isma'il thought that the caliph was referring to Ja'far's loyalty to the Shi'a of 'Ali by releasing al-'Alawi, an issue that they had both discussed only recently. He believed that Ja'far did not deserve to be put to death, for he knew that his enemies had defamed him, so he said, "Didn't the Commander of the Faithful decide to send him off to Khurasan in order to consider later what should be done with him?"

Al-Rashid said, "Yes, I decided that; then I thought that his staying here under our sight would better preserve our rule and facilitate our intended action, because if he were to go to Khurasan, he would be among his relatives and parties that supported him. The people of Khurasan still continue to bear a grudge against us, ever since my grandfather al-Mansur killed their commander, Abu Muslim al-Khurasani. Yes, they will be unable to oppose us, but they will worry us. The sound opinion is therefore to take steps to prevent danger before it occurs."

"The opinion of the Commander of the Faithful is sound," Isma'il agreed, "but the enviers of Ja'far are many; they have vilified the Commander of the Faithful and multiplied his offenses, and their defamation of him is exaggerated. The Commander of the Faithful quickly killed him because of his desire to preserve the caliphate of the Hashemites. However, keeping him alive would have been better for the state, but the matter is decided and done now."

When al-Rashid heard the allusion to those who defamed him, he wanted to milk Isma'il for all the information he knew about them in order to seek revenge and avoid the harm they would do, so he said, "Are you sure of that? Who are these people who are slandering me?"

Isma'il was on the point of telling him what he knew of the efforts of Ibn al-Hadi, al-Fadl ibn al-Rabi', and others but he kept his tongue and pondered the matter. He believed that if he did tell him, he would encourage disunity and weaken the state, when he was the one who desired its preservation and its strength. If Ja'far were alive, he thought, the danger of giving such information would have been small. But now that Ja'far was dead, naming those who slandered him and reporting their words and deeds would just be further slander; he regretted what he had said and decided to keep the information to himself and said, "That you killed Ja'far is one of two misfortunes; but if I mention the others to you, I would be driving the state into another misfortune. I wish that the Commander of the Faithful would exempt me from that, for he knows about my desire for preserving the safety of this state. You have not listened to me in my bid to absolve Ja'far of any offense, so don't demand of me now to defame others. If there was any benefit to doing this, I would not withhold the information. So listen to me on this matter and know that I withhold the information for the general good of the Hashemites, just as my attempt to absolve Ja'far was for the same purpose. I beg al-Rashid not to consider my refusal to give information as disobedience. If he considers it to be so, he can take vengeance on me, and I will not be unwilling to give up my life."

Al-Rashid venerated Isma'il and believed in his sincerity and his noble intentions. He valued his life and did not want to lose him, so he said, "Your life is dear to us, O Uncle, and far be it for us to have a poor opinion of you. And if you disobey us, you would only do so for a higher good and in our own interest. As for Ja'far, if his offense had been limited to confronting the state and his support of the Shi'a, we would have endured him and would have watched out for him as we did in the past, because his siding with the Shi'a is not new. But he committed what is much more heinous than that. He committed an offense which, if you knew, would have impelled you to kill him yourself before I did. Don't ask me what he committed, for I am keen on keeping it a secret, so much so that if I learn that my right arm knew about it, I would cut it off." He said this, with his anger rising, his facial expression gloomy, and his lips trembling so that his beard quivered. He then shook his head and said, "Ah! If I could kill him again, I would!"

Isma'il was awed by al-Rashid's wrath, and he understood perfectly well the allusions about Ja'far that he heard; the affair of al-'Abbasa had come to his knowledge, such as it was, and it was contrary to his beliefs. But he pretended not to know about it. Even if he thought there was an opportunity for him to speak, he would not have spoken lest the conversation lead to useless argument. That is because he knew about al-Rashid's zeal for family honor and his desire to preserve the good reputation of the Hashemites. So he remained silent.

They then heard the call to noon prayer, so al-Rashid stood up. Isma'il stood up too, asked permission to leave, and left.

Chapter 16

Al-'Abbasa's Sons

Al-Rashid ordered his servants to bring him water for his ritual ablutions. He performed them before going to the mosque, where he led the people in community prayers and returned to the palace. He sent some of his elite forces to arrest Ja'far's father, Ja'far's brother, and all Ja'far's children. He declared their palaces and houses to be ownerless, so his men took possession of the slave-girls they found there and took them to be their own servants, except Raihan and 'Utba, who preferred to follow Ja'far; both were killed as they resisted those who came to loot. Al-Rashid then sent Masrur to Ja'far's camp at al-Nahrawan, where he took possession of all the tents, weapons, and other things there.

By Saturday morning on 1 Safar, 187 AH (29 January, 803 AD), al-Rashid had killed one thousand of the Barmakids and their retinue, and he spared those of them who returned to their homeland. He imprisoned Ja'far's father (Yahya ibn Khaled) and Ja'far's brother (al-Fadl ibn Yahya), and he ordered that the body of Ja'far al-Barmaki be crucified on the Baghdad bridge.

When he was satisfied with all this, he told his wife Zubayda what had happened. She approved but remembered the two boys and said, "You have done what people of strong resolve do, and you have saved the caliphate from its enemies, but what have you done with the two boys?"

He lowered his head to think, but she quickly said to him, "If you really want to erase the shame that has blemished us all, you must fully remove its trace, for these two remaining boys will be a continuing source of disgrace."

"Do you know where they are?" he asked.

"If you would like, I will tell your servant where they are," she said.

"Tell Masrur about that," he said.

She told Masrur where they were hiding, and al-Rashid went to his palace and sat waiting for them to be brought to him.

Al-Fadl ibn al-Rabi', with the help of Abu al-'Atahiya, had hidden the two boys in a house on the bank of the Tigris River and left guards with them to protect them. Masrur went there and took them to the Palace of Eternity after killing Riyash and Barra, the two servants who took care of their upbringing.

When Masrur brought the two boys, he took them to al-Rashid, who was sitting on a cushion alone. The two boys entered hopping gleefully and laughing, their faces overflowing with joy, innocence, and purity; they thought that Masrur had brought them to a festival or a banquet. When al-Rashid saw their beauty, he became depressed and sorry for the harm that would be done to them, for he knew that they were innocent and pure. But he was determined to erase all trace of the disgraceful crime from existence. He pulled himself together and called the two boys; they ran to him and threw themselves on him, and they looked with interest at the magnificent furniture in the hall and its radiant colors.

"What is your name, O apple of my eye?" he asked the elder.

"Al-Hasan," replied the boy.

"And what is yours, my dearest?" he asked the younger.

"Al-Husain," he answered.

Al-Rashid admired their manner of speaking and their Hashemite eloquence. He thought of the grave act that he was about to do, being a father who loved his children and considering that the two boys were of Hashemite blood. It was agonizing for him because of the affection arising from their relationship to him, and he continued to hesitate for some time while the two boys played with him and rumpled his beard and his collar, and tender love was about to overcome him. But he remembered what he was planning to do and was afraid that emotional weakness would get the better of him, so he decided to have them killed in such conditions that neither his eyes would see it nor his ears hear it. His conflicting emotions and his sorrow and pain stirred within him, so he burst into tears. He cried and sobbed and became unable to talk, and the two boys could not understand why he was weeping. He looked at them, with tears bathing his eyes, and said, "Your beauty is dear to me, may God have no mercy on whoever wronged you." Then he said, "Masrur, where is the key that I gave you and ordered you to keep?'

"I have it, O Commander of the Faithful," Masrur said.

"Bring it to me," the caliph ordered.

Al-Rashid then summoned a number of slave-boys and commanded them to go with Masrur to that room and dig a deep pit in it. He motioned to Masrur to kill the two boys and bury them in it. He did all that while weeping so profusely that Masrur thought the caliph had pity on them and would soon change his mind. But the caliph wiped his eyes, got up, and gestured to Masrur to proceed; Masrur obeyed and took the two boys to the room. He later returned and informed al-Rashid that he had killed them and buried them there and that he had also killed the men who helped him do that.

Al-Rashid ordered that the Barmakids should not be mentioned on any occasion and that not one of those who had been left alive should ever be asked for or given help on any matter. Consequently, they wandered aimlessly in the country, and people cited their catastrophe as an example of a tragic ending, giving them as examples of persons known for their wealth and generosity. Their enemies were given free scope to maltreat them. They assumed key positions in the state, especially al-Fadl ibn al-Rabi', who became the vizier with the authority to handle all the affairs of state.

The End

The Caliph's Sister
Study Guide [25]

1. Who was Jurji Zaidan?

Jurji Zaidan was a famous Arab writer. Born in 1861, he grew up in Beirut, Lebanon, where as a teenager he helped his father run a small restaurant. When he was nineteen years old, Zaidan enrolled at the Syrian Protestant College, now American University in Beirut. However, after taking part in a student strike, he decided to leave the university. He soon left his native Lebanon and moved to Cairo, Egypt. Once settled there Zaidan began a long career as a writer and journalist. In 1892 he established a magazine called *Al-Hilal* (The Crescent Moon), which is still being published to this day. He wrote twenty-two novels, all of which were published in serialized form in the magazine. *The Caliph's Sister* is one of them. In addition to the novels, he also published books and wrote articles for his magazine on a wide variety of topics, including the history of Islamic civilization and the history and development of languages, as well as political, social, educational, and ethical issues. He thus played a very important role in making Arabic readers more aware of the important events in their history and in developing a sense of national identity. He died in 1914.

2. What is a historical novel?

A historical novel is a type of fiction that makes use of important events from history and the people who took part in them in order to provide readers with a vivid portrayal of life in previous eras. Among

---

25 Roger Allen and Issa Boullata provided input for parts of this study guide. Neither is responsible for any remaining errors.

the prominent writers of historical novels are Sir Walter Scott (d. 1832) whose novels include *Ivanhoe* (set in twelfth-century England) and *Rob Roy* (set in Scotland just before the Jacobite rising in the eighteenth century); Russian author Leo Tolstoy (d. 1910), whose enormous novel *War and Peace* describes Russian society before and during Napoleon's invasion in 1812; and the American writer James Fenimore Cooper (d. 1851), whose *The Last of the Mohicans* portrays the role of Native Americans during the 1757 war in the North American colonies. This type of novel often provides the reader with a sense of what it was like to live in the historical period and region in question, but it also brings the events to life by revealing through conversations how the people involved in those events interact with each other and share their views and emotions.

In Zaidan's case, his twenty-two novels are set in various historical periods spanning the whole of Islamic history, beginning in pre-Islamic times (*Fatat Ghassan* first published in 1897/98) and continuing through the Ottoman Empire (*Al-Inqilab al-'uthmani* published in 1911). They all include a love story that shows how ordinary people manage to respond to the important events surrounding them. In *The Caliph's Sister* the two lovers are actually important historical figures—al-'Abbasa, the sister of the fifth 'Abbasid caliph Harun al-Rashid, whom he held in great affection, and Ja'far al Barmaki, al-Rashid's Persian vizier and favorite companion. Their love story is interlaced with the fall from favor of the famous Barmakid family during the reign of al-Rashid.

This novel is the second of four novels[26] that Jurji Zaidan wrote that were set in the early 'Abbasid caliphate. The first, *Abu Muslim al-Khurasani,* is set in the context of the founding of the 'Abbasid dynasty. The caliph al-Mansur had relied on the critical support of Abu Muslim from the Khurasan to found the 'Abbasid dynasty but had executed Abu Muslim after his accession. The current novel, the second in the series, recounts the events leading to Ja'far's execution and the fall of the Barmakids during the reign of the fifth 'Abbasid caliph. The third novel, *The Caliph's Heirs—Brothers at War: The Fall of Baghdad,* opens shortly thereafter before Harun al-Rashid's death in 193 AH (809 AD) and is

---

26 *Abu Muslim al-Khurasani* and *The Bride of Ferghana,* the first and last of Jurji Zaidan's four novels set during the 'Abbasid dynasty, have not been translated into English. The third novel, *The Caliph's Heirs—Brothers at War: The Fall of Baghdad,* in addition to the current one, was translated into English.

set in the context of the war of succession between al-Rashid's two sons, al-Amin and al-Ma'mun. *The Bride of Ferghana,* the last of Jurji Zaidan's novels set in the 'Abbasid period, takes place mainly in the non-Arab countries of Central Asia. The action centers on Ferghana, the capital of a province in eastern Uzbekistan, and cuts across the borders of Kyrgyzstan, Tajikistan, and Uzbekistan, all countries lying outside or at the frontiers of the Arab Empire.

3. How much fiction and how much history are there in Zaidan's historical novels?

The short answer is a lot of both. Listen to Jurji Zaidan describe in his own words the task of the historical novelist as he saw it in his introduction to the first edition of this novel:

"We have described the age of Harun al-Rashid in a grandiose way in all its splendor and pomp and its most important attributes. And even though some of the events may not have happened exactly as described herein, it is easy to imagine that they are plausible and could very well have happened. For the historical novelist it is not sufficient to relate events in a matter-of-fact way devoid of emotions. The events must be embellished with all kinds of details about the social mores and customs of the peoples so that the reader can imagine himself to have been present at those events and to have lived and interacted with the heroes of the novel; witnessed their processions, gatherings and other activities. Just like a painter who needs a year or two to paint a scene, the novelist needs time and space to depict events in detail—events that are described in history books in no more than a sentence or two.

"For example Ja'far al-Barmaki's death was recorded by historians in one or two lines. But the historical novelist cannot recount this event adequately without describing the customs and manners of the age, the type and color of clothes worn in those times, the furnishings that adorned their houses, the types of arms that were commonly used and so on and so forth so that he can fully represent how the executioner and the one who is executed looked and acted and their surroundings. And he must understand and describe the emotional state of those concerned— their facial expressions and the reactions of their bodies to fear, grief, depression and all the conflicting emotions of the one who died and the one who killed. All this in addition to describing the location of the event, whether in a room, street, garden or desert as well as the time when it all took place—noon, evening or at night. And all these possibilities have different features that need to be pictured and described in order to represent any event completely and adequately.

"This is how the historical novelist needs to look at history—representing the conditions in his own words and elaborating the historical event with his knowledge of the literature of the times, of the emotions, looks, demeanors and expressions; and he should apply his knowledge of social science to the conditions of the family in that period. And if the reader were to see how historical events are depicted in their totality rather than the details which may or may not have happened as we said above but are plausible, then he would realize that they represent the truth. Which is what we strived to do in all our series of historical novels."

This excerpt shows how Jurji Zaidan fictionalized historical events while remaining true to the actual events as they were known to contemporary historians of his time and as is shown by the numerous and serious historical sources listed at the beginning of his novels. Because his main purpose in writing historical novels was to educate the public and teach them history in an enjoyable manner, he sought to be true to history as it was then understood. In that, he differed from many Western historical novelists whose emphasis was more on entertainment than education. His desire to adhere strictly to historical events is illustrated by his response to a question in *Al-Hilal* from one of the readers of *The Caliph's Sister*, who asked him why there was such a dramatic ending not at all to the reader's liking. His response was that, unfortunately, he had no choice in the matter—he had to be true in the novel to the events of history. Having said that, it should also be noted that studies of Islamic history since Zaidan's time have shed new light and interpretations of many of the events depicted in Zaidan's novels and accepted as true at the time he was writing.

In conclusion it should be said that Zaidan's novels were highly successful. They were translated in some ten languages and remain popular to this day. They had a major influence on giving Arabs in particular and Muslims in general a common sense of identity and shared history, even when some of the events of that history as recounted in those novels was sometimes contentious or subsequently questioned.

4. What is the early history of the Arabic novel?

Like most new kinds of literature that appeared in the Arabic-speaking world during the nineteenth and into the twentieth century, the novel's development involved a combination of imported examples translated into Arabic from Western literature and revived and adapted examples of types of narrative from the premodern heritage. Among the first European works to be translated into Arabic were Alexandre Dumas's famous novel *The Count of Monte Cristo*, which served as a model and precedent for the appearance of a number of serialized works, including, for example, those of Salim al-Bustani published in his family's journal, *Al-Jinan*. Alongside these translations of European works and imitations of them there were other narratives that revived earlier types and styles of Arabic writing, such as Ahmad Faris al-Shidyaq's *Al-Saq 'Ala al-Saq* (One Leg Over Another, 1855) and Muhammad al-Muwaylihi's *Hadith 'Isa ibn Hisham* ('Isa ibn Hisham's Tale, 1907). The novels that Zaidan wrote and published were a very important part of the developmental process through which the novel was accepted into Middle Eastern culture as a form of narrative that could express the hopes and aspirations of people in quest of national identity. In the first three decades of the twentieth century, these different strands were gradually fused together into a form of narrative writing that was to see its acceptance into Arabic culture crowned by the work of Naguib Mahfouz, the great Egyptian novelist and winner of the Nobel Prize in 1988.

5. What historical period does *The Caliph's Sister* cover?

The events of this novel occur during the reign of Harun al-Rashid from 170 to 193 AH (786 to 809 AD), and, more precisely, in the years just before 183 AH (803 AD) that saw the beginning of the fall of the Barmakids. The Islamic calendar begins with the emigration (*hijra*) of the Prophet Muhammad from Mecca to Medina in the year 622 AD. By the time al-Mansur became caliph at the beginning of the 'Abbasid caliphate in 132 AH (750 AD), the Islamic Empire stretched to Syria,

Iraq, and Egypt first, but then east toward India and west along the northern shores of Africa. The 'Abbasid caliphate covered over five centuries, from 132 to 656 AH (750 to 1258 AD), and the caliphs were all descended from 'Abbas, a member of the tribe of Quraysh of Mecca who was an uncle of the prophet Muhammad. The 'Abbasid family seized the caliphate following the overthrow of the Umayyad dynasty of caliphs. They established their capital in Baghdad and held the city until the Mongols sacked it and killed the last 'Abbasid caliph in Baghdad.

Harun al-Rashid (149 to 193 AH or 766 to 809 AD), or Aaron the Upright, was the fifth caliph (170 to 193 AH or 786 to 809 AD) of the 'Abbasid dynasty. He was the son of the third 'Abbasid caliph, al-Mahdi, and succeeded to the throne on the death of his brother al-Hadi. His reign marked a period of notable cultural development. Baghdad became one of the most flourishing cities of the period. Tribute was paid to the caliph by many rulers, and splendid edifices were erected in his honor at enormous cost. He is said to have exchanged gifts with Charlemagne. Harun was a generous patron of learning, poetry, and music, and his court was visited by the most eminent Muslims of the age. He was celebrated in countless songs and stories, and is perhaps best known to the Western world as the caliph whose court is described in the *Arabian Nights.*

Philosophy, medicine, mathematics, and other sciences flourished as the Islamic world appropriated and developed the knowledge and wisdom of earlier and surrounding cultures. Particularly important were the science and philosophy of the Hellenistic Near East, and the ninth and tenth centuries saw the translation into Arabic of several works by Aristotle, Plato, Euclid, and others. The work of translation was also encouraged during the reign of the caliph al-Ma'mun. Arabic-speaking Christians were especially active in the production of translations. Arabic numerals were adopted at this time by Islamic civilization and then later transmitted to the West.

Following Harun's death in 193 AH (809 AD) a civil war of succession occurred between his two sons, al-Amin and al-Ma'mun. The war between the brothers was an expression of the tensions that undermined the centralized authority of 'Abbasid Empire. Al-Amin's reign (193 to 197 AH, or 809 to 813 AD) was a short one, but al-Ma'mun's spanned some twenty years (197 to 218 AH, or 813 to 833 AD). Just like Harun al-Rashid's reign, it was a golden age in promoting knowledge and learning, especially in the sciences. By the end of the ninth century the 'Abbasids were unable to exercise real religious or political authority. The territories they controlled fell apart as independent states arose in regions previously under 'Abbasid rule. Although always honored to the end of the 'Abbasid caliphate as symbols of the unity of Islam, no claimant to the office achieved anything like the general recognition among Muslims that prevailed until the reign of Harun al-Rashid. When the 'Abbasid Empire started to decline, the eighth 'Abbasid caliph (al Mu'tasim) had to depend on Turks, Circassian, Tajiks, and other Central Asians mercenaries to man his armies to defend the eastern part of his empire, centered in Baghdad, while the western part broke away into autonomous states.

6. Why did Ja'far renege on his promise to Harun? And what motivations explain Harun's actions?

Zaidan's novel imagines answers to these questions that are woven into the narrative. There is scant historical evidence to either support or refute the details of his answers as they relate to the motivations and machinations of some of the historical characters or the details of the events that are depicted. But they are all plausible. In his own introduction to the first edition of the novel, he says this concerning the trade of the historical novelist concerning the events that are depicted: "they may or may not have happened but they *could* have happened." And indeed, many details of the events and their interpretation were proposed by medieval scholars and some modern observers.

How and why Ja'far reneged on his promise not to consummate his marriage to Harun's sister no one is certain. There was a great political advantage for Ja'far to unite himself with the daughter and sisters of the caliph. But did his mother, who was close to both her son and the caliph's sister, prod them in that direction? Or was their deep love sufficient to consummate their marriage, as Zaidan seems to imagine? No one knows for sure, and the novel does not speculate on what really happened.

The disgrace and fall of Ja'far has been the subject of intense speculation. Many explanations have been put forward for Harun's ungrateful behavior toward men to whom he owed so much—the whole Barmakid family had served the 'Abbasid for three generations with competence and devotion. But Harun never disclosed the reasons for their chastisement. Disloyalty, family honor, political and family intrigues, jealousy and, last but not least, reasons of state all undoubtedly provided part of the explanation.

There were many stories about Harun's resentment of Ja'far's wealth, extremely luxurious lifestyle, and ostentation. More decisive than his fits of jealousy and irritation was the chamberlain al-Fadl ibn al-Rabi''s hostility toward Ja'far. Both men detested each other and did everything they could to destroy each other. Opposition to Ja'far crystallized around al-Fadl. It did not help that Ja'far was said to have Shi'a sympathies among the Sunni 'Abbasids. Nor did Zubayda, Harun's favorite Hashemite wife, like Ja'far. He had been a tutor to al-Ma'mun, the son of a Persian slave girl, her son's rival. It was known that Harun admired al-Ma'mun's gifts and was thinking of promoting him over al-Amin in the order of succession. There is every reason to believe that Zubayda exercised her considerable influence against Ja'far in the last few weeks. She was shrewd, skillful, and willful.

Zaidan never explicitly speculates to what extent al-Rashid's reaction was politically or emotionally motivated. The narrative and dialogue suggest a combination of those factors. Ja'far appears to have been killed in a sudden fit of anger, and the appalling manner of his death lends credence to strong emotional underpinnings for his demise. He had been disloyal to Harun and had stained the family honor: his disobedience could not go unpunished. The same was true concerning the behavior of Harun's sister.

But as the narrative also makes clear, Harun was shrewd and feared for his power and influence—even worrying that the Barmakids might usurp the 'Abbasid caliphate. And there were equally strong indications that his actions were motivated by reasons of state. How else to explain the execution of Ja'far's two children who had 'Abbasid blood, the imprisonment of Ja'far's father, and the confiscation of the Barmakid family property and estates, followed by the removal of all the other Barmakids from any influence in the affairs of state?

Other questions to discuss concerning *The Caliph's Sister*

1. Many readers of the novel will know from their knowledge of history how the events recounted in the novel turn out, ending with the fall of the Barmakids. But the novel still manages to create suspense. How?

2. Like the novels of Charles Dickens, *The Caliph's Sister* originally appeared in separate episodes printed in a newspaper. How does Zaidan keep the action moving forward across episodes?

3. Zaidan's novels are based on the idea that a specific national group, the Arabs, have participated in something called Islamic civilization. Does this idea make sense? How does the novel support it? In what ways does it undermine it?

4. Many of the characters in *The Caliph's Sister* are identified as Persians or as members of minority religions. How does Zaidan treat these characters? What about characters who are *not* identified as belonging to a religious or ethnic group?

5. Like the press in many countries during Zaidan's time, the Arabic press helped readers create an image of themselves as citizens; as members of national, ethnic, or religious groups; and as men and women with specific gender roles. In what ways might *The Caliph's Sister* have helped shape these images for readers?

Other Resources

Bennison, Amira. *The Great Caliphs*. New Haven: Yale, 2010.

Crone, Patricia. *God's Rule: Government and Islam. Six Centuries of Medieval Islamic Political Thought*. New York: Columbia, 2005.

Thomas, Philipp. *Gurji Zaidan: His Life and Thought*. Wiesbaden, Germany: Steiner Verlag, 1979.

Philipp, Thomas. *Jurji Zaidan's Secular Analysis of History and Language as Foundations of Arab Nationalism*. (forthcoming).

Zaidan, Jurji, *The Autobiography of Jurji Zaidan*. Edited and translated by Thomas Philip. Washington, DC: Three Continents Press, 1990.

Zaidan, Jurji. *The Caliph's Heirs—Brothers at War: The Fall of Baghdad.* Translated by Michael Cooperson. This novel follows the current one and depicts the civil war between al-Rashid's sons. It is being published by The Zaidan Foundation as part of this series at the same time as *The Caliph's Sister.*

Made in the USA
Middletown, DE
08 August 2015